John & Betsy —

Enjoy!

Bob Cook

PATRIOT
& ASSASSIN

Also by Robert Cook

Cooch

PATRIOT & ASSASSIN

BY ROBERT COOK

(An Alejandro "Cooch" Cuchulain novel)

(The second in the Cooch series of national security thrillers)

ROYAL WULFF PUBLISHING

Copyright © 2012 by Robert E. Cook
All Rights Reserved.

ISBN: 0984315535
ISBN-13: 9780984315536

Print edition

Royal Wulff Publishing
Post Office Box 853
St. Helena, CA 94574

For my booboo

Acknowledgements:

I again needed help in structuring this Cooch novel, and got it from many. My sincere thanks to, among others, Art Allen, Bob Bressler, David Campbell, Gay Wind Campbell, Bruce Coleman, Pam Coleman, Bob Elders, Cyndi Elders, Judith Hamilton, Tor Kenward, Jim Krueger, Sally Krueger, Jim Loy, Rich Moore, Michael Proctor, Wil Shirey and Rex Swain.

Prologue

Three bearded young men slipped into the algebra classroom and leaned against the back wall. Arms folded, they glared silently at the instructor, Hamza, as he ended his class for the day. Hamza usually ended his lectures with a passage from the Holy Word, the Koran, and some thoughts about current events in Yemen. He was finishing his comments just as the men entered the room.

Hamza had a voice that was beginning to be heard by the young and impressionable. His practice of saying a few critical, and sometimes incendiary, words to students at the end of classes was becoming fashionable. There was a burgeoning view among university professionals at Sana'a University, the largest in Yemen, that the intellectual freedom fundamental to their profession gave them license to criticize anything they viewed as wrong or inappropriate. Other professors were beginning to make their opinions heard in the classrooms.

Hamza was a member of a small group of devout Shiites. They met to study the Koran and to plan for the eventual overthrow of the Sunni powers that ruled Yemen and for the installation of Sharia law as interpreted by devout Shiites. It was the return of the caliphate to ruling the Arab world that drove their imaginations. As late as the twelfth century, Islam had ruled the world from Mongolia to Spain and would do so again, and more, when the Sunni apostates were defeated.

As young men drifted from the classroom in the cramped mathematics building, their feet caused mushrooms of dust as they scuffed from the room. When one student saw the men at the back, he began to walk with purpose, speaking quietly to a man at his side. In a moment, all of the young men were scurrying to avoid the gaze of the strangers.

Their instructor of algebra, Hamza, nervously gathered his papers from the table in the front of the room, shoved them into a small cloth case, and turned to the door. Suddenly they were there. One flipped open a worn, black nylon case with a five-pointed, gold and black badge attached.

"You will come with us," he said.

The other two men grasped his arms and rushed him outside, where a dusty black Fiat sat idling, its rear door open at the curb. A fourth man sat behind the wheel, watching and waiting. Hamza began to struggle and yell to draw attention to his abduction.

"Call the police," he screamed. The first man spun and buried his fist in Hamza's stomach.

"We are the police," he snarled. Hamza was thrown into the backseat by the other two men and the car lurched from its place. A black hood was thrown over Hamza's head and tied. He finally drew a breath and then another.

A few minutes later, he was dragged from the car and rushed across a rough surface, inside a building. His hood was removed and he was thrust into a small room with a single chair bolted to the floor. Ragged, stained straps hung from its arms and legs. Hamza struggled. A wooden baton cracked across his shins. The blunt end of the baton was shoved into his solar plexus with a two-handed thrust. Hamza was again helpless as they strapped him into the chair. The policemen stood silently by the closed door and gazed at him. He stared defiantly back. One of them was pulling thick leather gloves over his hands.

The door opened and a smiling man walked in, light on his feet. "So, Hamza, my friend," he said. "I am Major Mohammed Vati." Vati was a thick, dapper man. He wore a black wool suit with a matching waistcoat, despite the heat. There was a yellow cravat with blurred, faint blue horizontal lines. "You have been making talk to our students. Tell me what you had to say. Tell me all about your seditious friends."

Hamza spat on the floor and snarled, "I will tell you nothing. You will answer to Allah for your apostasy."

The smiling man nodded at the man with the gloves and stepped back quickly. A gloved fist smashed into Hamza's nose and mouth, then again as flesh and blood sprayed around him. He spat a tooth to the floor.

"If you are not going to talk, Hamza, then you have no need for that traitorous mouth of yours to remain undamaged. You may nod your head when you have seen the errors of your ways and would like to speak. I suppose we should save your face from further damage until we have had a friendly conversation. We can have you cleaned up and out of here in a few minutes if you are reasonable. Would you like to speak now and be done with this unpleasantness?"

Hamza shook his head violently, and blood sprayed from his bleeding lips. A drop of Hamza's blood hit Vati's cravat. His face flushed as he stepped back.

"Well then, shall we get on with things, Hamza?" Major Vati took a white linen handkerchief from his back pocket and dabbed at the crimson stain. "You're making a mess." He walked to one of the men by the door and took the wooden baton from his hand. It was made of a thick wood and about thirty inches in length. There was a leather thong at one end, looped through a hole.

Vati walked to Hamza, still smiling as he slipped his hand through the leather loop. With a quick, wristy swing of the baton, Vati hitt Hamza on the outside of his left elbow. Another quick strike hit his right elbow. A dagger of white-hot pain shot into Hamza's brain. A casual baton strike to his left knee and then the right caused the pain to magnify, intensify.

"Those little pain points will be sore tomorrow. We'll work on them a bit more then. The next time they will hurt much more. If you fail to see reason, the low back is an attractive target. Are you ready to talk to me now, Hamza?"

The negative shake of Hamza's head was less vigorous, but firm.

"We won't break anything, Hamza, other than your nose, of course. Delivery of pain is hampered by broken bones. Pain is our ally when we ask urgent questions. We were hoping to visit with your friends today to convince them of the error of their ways, perhaps to frighten them. But there is more than one way to send that message to your seditious colleagues."

Hamza sprayed scarlet spittle through broken lips. "Allah will curse you."

"Will he? *Inshallah*. Perhaps the one cursed first is the one cursed worst, Hamza. Think about that.

"Feed him," Vati said. "We'll begin again in the morning. I have work to do. There is no hurry. Trash like this always talks." He walked through the small door and closed it.

•   •   •

Two days later Hamza rose slowly from the ground where he had been shoved from the small portal where he had first arrived. His weakened arms had failed to arrest the impact of his fall, and his face had bounced on the rough gravel in the courtyard. He struggled to his feet and limped away from the government building, a stain spreading on his pant leg. He had soiled himself while strapped in the chair. Hamza was carrying his small case with assignment papers still to be corrected and a little money. It had been thrown on him as he hit the gravel. His feet shuffled erratically as he struggled for balance, and the pain lancing across his low back kept him stooped. He pushed at a ragged tooth with his tongue and moved his head to allow light to reach through the lumpy mass around his eyes. At a bus stop across the dusty square, he finally slumped on a bench.

The bus marked A4 would take him to a stop near his home. The two days of questioning before he provided answers to their questions should have provided enough warning for his brother and his other friends in Allah to have fled or gone into hiding. The wisdom of Allah would prevail on its own schedule. His wife would treat his wounds. She was due soon with their second child, another boy, Allah willing. His first son was now five years old and beginning his study of the Koran as he memorized key passages. Before long Hamza would teach him other things and initiate him in the study of mathematics. Learning the word of Allah, memorizing it, was of paramount importance, but mathematics was also a study of beauty.

A battered orange and tan bus with its side windows open stopped beside the bench with a hiss of its brakes. Its door swung open. The burly driver came down to help Hamza ascend the three steps. He jerked his face away from the stench when Hamza collapsed into a seat near the front of the aging bus, just behind the driver's seat. The other passengers averted their faces; the square of the Secret Police was well known to a wary populace. One never knew when the Secret Police were watching. After a few minutes, the driver stopped the bus just a few blocks from Hamza's residence. He rose from his seat and helped Hamza to the door and down to the pavement. He held Hamza's hand and supported him for a moment.

"Good luck, my friend," he said, as he climbed back in the bus, wiped the cracked vinyl seat with a piece of old newspaper, swung the door closed, and drove off.

The narrow street that led to Hamza's small house was crowded with shops and cafes. As he struggled past, no one came to help him. The stench of cooking smoke hovered in the air.

At the end of the street, Hamza froze. His home was destroyed. The roof had partially collapsed. Tendrils of smoke curled from broken windows. He tried to run to it, but fell. Hamza struggled to his feet and made his urgent way more carefully. The front door was askew, nearly ripped from its hinges. On the floor a remnant corner of a burned rug was smoking at its fringe. Beside it lay the twisted body of Hamza's son. The larger form of his wife lay sprawled on the floor, her mouth a rictus, belly ripped open and a tiny fetus still connected to her by the burned cord. They were charred nearly beyond recognition. Major Vati's message to Hamza's seditious colleagues had been delivered.

Hamza slowly went to his knees, head back and mouth open. A keening screech rose in pitch and intensity. He was alone. The call for afternoon prayers sounded from the nearby mosque, and the timeless cadence of Allah's word slowly wormed its way around his voice, into his consciousness. Still on his knees, Hamza prostrated himself and prayed for revenge. Finally, he prayed for guidance.

PATRIOT
& ASSASSIN

Southwest Texas
Several years later

T he afternoon shadows from the pool house stretched up the gravel path toward the huge, log-framed ranch house. Alex Cuchulain walked beside his friend, Brooks Elliot, talking idly about the travails of the economy and the housing bust. Both men seemed fit, light on their feet and balanced. Their T-shirts were wrinkled and newly dry, with damp circles at the waist of their swim trunks. Behind them walked two women, their dates. One was the owner's daughter and their host, LuAnn Clemens. The second was Dr. Caitlin O'Connor. The hair on both was slicked back and still wet from the pool. Each carried a bath towel wrapped casually around her neck.

A sharp snap sounded just behind Alex. He turned his head just as a sharp pain hit the seat of his wet bathing suit, accompanied by another snap.

"Ow!" Alex yelled and turned to see LuAnn pulling her towel back, and Caitlin's towel snapped just past him as she pulled back on its base. They were grinning and giggling.

As LuAnn snaked her damp towel out again at Alex, he snatched the end from the air just before it unraveled and gave it a pull. She sprawled forward and fell on the sharp gravel. She let out a loud yelp.

As Alex opened his mouth to apologize he heard a footfall behind him and immediately felt a slamming force just under his rib cage that drove him into the air. *Eh?* He felt himself reacting to thousands of hours of training. This happened to be Form Twenty-Eight of the repetitive martial arts drills the CIA had designed to counteract the seventy-two most common forms of physical attack. For each of those there was a physical response that was drilled, nearly endlessly, into workers who were chosen for the violent work of the Agency. As his mind turned to identify what other dangers lurked, reflex drove his response. Alex threw his legs uphill, using his stomach muscles and twisting his body over the force, drove his assailant under him as they fell. The part that took the longest to master was next: the impact of Alex's fall must be broken, lessened somehow. His right arm was extended, slightly bent. As the impact of the man hitting the ground was first sensed, Alex drove his right elbow into the mass of the head and neck beneath him, accompanied by a loud exhalation, "Heeyaaa!"

The impact of that blow went through his assailant's face to the dirt below. Bone could be heard snapping as the force of impact from Alex's fall was countered. Judo used Newton's law of motion that for every action there was an equal and opposite reaction. The slowing of his fall allowed his feet to continue to swing over the base of the conflict, then tighten the arc to hit tight to their landing spot. His upper body twisted along in the earlier arc of the feet, the arms of his assailant no longer grasping him tightly. Alex came to his feet in a balanced crouch, looking for an adversary. The flesh on his face was tight and bunching around his eyes. His breath was whistling loudly through his nostrils. Brooks had spun, back to the scene, and was standing with his knees flexed, one foot in front of the other in a crouch, hands raised, looking for others. There were none.

"What the hell was that?" Caitlin yelled, looking at the large cowboy still on the ground, inert. She looked at Alex, crouched and lethal. She thought of a big cat, some kind of nasty cat. His thighs were quivering, his head was up with nostrils flared, but there was no new threat. His lips were drawn back, exposing his incisors. The whole scene was erotic in its ferality, Caitlin thought; she had always been thrilled by violence.

Easy, laddie. It's apparently over.

Jesus Annie, here I go again, Alex thought. He had just had a brief street fight with an amateur and here he was looking for someone to kill, to maim. As Brooks had once said, "Lose the Cooch look, if you can. It scares the civilians." Still, that reflexive, preemptive hostility and readiness built over so many years had done Alex more good than harm. He was alive.

Alex dropped to one knee to reach for the man's neck. He felt a strong pulse and noticed a shard of bone sticking from his jaw. A steady trickle of crimson flowed from the bone to the gravelly soil and was quickly absorbed.

"Darned if I know, Caitlin, but he appears to have hurt himself in the fall," Alex said with a frown.

As Brooks helped LuAnn to her feet, he brushed the gravel from her. With a pounding of feet, three cowboys rushed around the maintenance shed. They skidded to a stop, and saw their friend, Jeeter, lying motionless on the ground, then looked at LuAnn, unsure what was going on.

"What the heck?" one of them yelled to LuAnn.

"I tripped and skinned my knee," LuAnn said, pointing at her bloody kneecap. "Jeeter must have thought Alex here was acting up and tried to defend me. He missed the tackle, and there he is."

After some confusion the ranch hands started to figure out how to move Jeeter. When they first saw the jawbone protruding from

3

his face and blood dripping into the soil, there was some muttering among them and hostile glances at Cuchulain and Elliot, who stood with the women, watching. A ranch hand showed up with a canvas stretcher, and they began to move Jeeter to it.

LuAnn led her three guests toward the ranch house. On its porch, Virgil Clemens, her father, leaned against a tall wooden column with a wooden toothpick dancing at the right corner of his mouth. He watched them approach. As they got to the porch steps, she could see his upper lip twitching in what was Virgil's idea of a grin.

"Hell, LuAnn, you just got here and there's trouble already," he said. "I'd better buy everyone a drink before things get out of hand. Cocktails start now and dinner is in ninety minutes. That should give you time for a few drinks and a change of clothes. I expect my foreman will fill me in on the details of the excitement before then." Virgil waved his hand in the general direction of a wooden sideboard with wine and whiskey standing on it. There were pretzels and nuts in a big wooden bowl and a refrigerator beneath.

Alex and Caitlin each carried a glass of wine up the wide, wooden stairs and into their bedroom. Caitlin had a bowl of peanuts and popped a few into her mouth as she gazed at the room. She thought of it as upscale cowboy décor. The guest space was longer than wide, with bold Native American print cloth on the walls, and a random-width, planked oak floor with rugs scattered along it. The bath had a sliding paneled door and a floor tiled in alternate light and dark triangles. Beyond the dual sinks and mirrors, on the back wall of the bath, was a long, glass-enclosed shower. *Nice shower*, she thought. *Now that could be interesting.*

Caitlin turned to Alex with a frown as she walked to a desk and said, "Well, that was exciting. You could have killed that guy. That would have been a real vacation stopper for me."

"For all of us, actually," Alex said, shaking his head at her familiar self-absorption. "A two-inch miss would have put my elbow into his temple and lights out. I'm getting old and slow. I should have heard him coming."

"It was pretty exciting," Caitlin said. "It turned me on. I'd like to see it again, in slow motion, and watch your face. I don't think you ever told me your whole sordid story, and something has been bugging me a bit. When you bailed me out of that biker club nightmare in New York awhile back, your face got really weird looking, like you were someone else, some evil, snaky creature. Today it happened again or at least it started. Do you have any idea what I'm talking about?"

"I do," Alex said as he dropped into one of the leather-upholstered chairs. "Put your best credulity hat on; my story might strain it some. Believe it or not, there's an ancient Irishman named Dain who lives inside my head. It's something that drove the CIA psychiatrists crazy when they figured out that I didn't manifest symptoms of schizophrenia other than believing in Dain. When there is a lot of danger coming at me from something or other, this Dain personality comes out in me and as part of him showing up, my face changes. My respiration ramps way up and becomes loud breathing. Dain manages the fighting; I do the fighting. I'm an invited guest with an almost slow-motion view of the action because I've done all the moves so often that thought would slow me down. My father said he hosted Dain, as did his father before him. This visitor, this avatar, this fantasy perhaps, whatever he is, has allegedly been in my family for centuries. Today there wasn't enough time for him to take over completely and there was no real danger. I doubt if you'll see him again, since I'm mostly out of the danger business. Still, if my face starts to change like that and you hear wind whistling through my nose, get on the floor. Cover your head. It's going to be ugly."

"Yes indeed, I've seen your ugly. I didn't know the CIA had shrinks. Wow. Waste of money?"

"You'd have to ask my old boss, MacMillan," he said. "He likes you and may admit to something, a rarity for him. Sometimes he reminds me of Yoda; Mac's seen it all and remembers, and he thinks about it. But I don't think Mac is Yoda; his ears are too small. Anyway, I met with Barry the Shrink, the CIA resident psychiatrist at the CIA's Farm in Virginia, almost every day I was in town from the time I was seventeen until I left the CIA spec ops unit eight years later. All of our guys talked to him about the killing and the danger, but I was Barry's special project. I started so young that he was fascinated at the way I developed, the way I handled and rationalized the danger, the violence, the killing. He gave me drugs to mitigate the stress, but I wouldn't take them. He was glad, I think. His little project and observation would otherwise been masked by chemicals and an uncontrollable variable. Barry wanted to publish a paper, but Mac wouldn't let him. When Mac didn't want people to do something down there at the Farm, they didn't do it."

Caitlin gazed at him from over the rim of her glass, took another sip of wine, and said, "And how did you happen to become, and I quote from times past, 'the baddest motherfucker in the whole world?'"

Alex gazed at her for a few moments, then grinned like a teenager. Caitlin liked that grin; it often came out when things were about to be fun. One of their first dates several years before had been in New York.[1] Alex made a stop at the men's room as he and Caitlin were leaving a lower Manhattan biker bar named Choppers. Caitlin had been abducted at the front entrance. She was rushed to a biker club in lower Manhattan to be the evening's entertainment, followed by the ingestion of a few pills that would make her a bad

---

1   See www.robertcooknovels.com/footnotesPatriot for more historical event texture.

witness if the police made things tiresome. By the time Alex figured out where they had taken her and got there, he was late. In the club, where he was decidedly not welcome, Alex found himself faced by twenty or so bikers and their leader.

They had Caitlin. Her blouse had been ripped open and her breasts were exposed. She was being held in a chair by two large men. A small man near the door had a look of balance and athleticism that Alex recognized. A closer look revealed the edge of a tattoo on his left forearm. Its edge showed lines similar to the official Budweiser beer logo, which shows a similar image. It has the spread wings of an eagle at its top, over an old, vertical anchor; a flintlock pistol and a trident are crossed over the anchor. The tattoo was the logo of the Navy Seals. After a few quick words between them, the smaller man, named Dodd, said loudly to the others, "Listen up. I know about this guy. A lot of Seals think he is the baddest motherfucker in the whole world..." Dodd's comments were mostly ignored by the others. They watched Caitlin and waited.

Violence ensued, then Alex left with Caitlin; the gang leader was writhing on the floor holding his crotch. Two large men bled from their faces onto a wooden picnic table at the rear of the room, holding their mangled hands. Alex had the leader's gun and an eerie, serpentine cast to his face. The rest were quiet; the sound of wind whistling through his nose was loud.

Alex chuckled quietly.

"I had forgotten about Dodd saying that back in that biker club, but he probably believed it. I nurtured that image for awhile. My specialty was in explosives. I became the go-to guy at the CIA for combat explosives, so I often got assigned to accompany Seals and Delta Force on missions that needed complex demolition support. Once I showed I was good at blowing stuff up and an unhesitant killer, they nurtured me. In CIA spec ops, nurturing consisted of teaching me things that would keep me alive longer so I could keep on going out and killing people, and making sure I had any training I needed to make me a better boomer or more of a survivor. That's what I was, the CIA's boomer and a survivor. Mac was a friend of my father, so he sort of took me under his wing and mentored me."

"Well, boomer, I'm going to get out of these damp clothes and dress for dinner," Caitlin said. "I have some business ideas I want to flesh out before we go down there." She walked to the closet and picked out some clothes, then stepped into the bathroom.

Alex pulled on a pair of jeans and a dry T-shirt. He reached into his traveling bag and took out a black, pocket-novel-sized device and a small cloth bag. He sat with one leg thrown over the arm of a soft chair that was covered in a black and white steer hide. He brought up the day's *Financial Times* on his Kindle Fire and set it on his lap. He opened the cloth bag and brought out a device that had five vertical valve springs from an old truck held with narrow plates welded on them, top and bottom. A nylon cord loosely connected them. He put the bottom in his palm and casually squeezed one spring after the other, then again, as he read. The stuffed head of an eight-point elk glared down at him from the wall, seemingly irritated by the rhythmic squeaks from the springs.

Thirty minutes later Caitlin walked from the bath fully dressed, her short hair again damp. "All yours, cowboy," she said.

Caitlin dropped into a thick-legged log chair in front of the desk in their guest room, back straight, leaning forward and looking at her computer screen. Her cell phone was just beside it. Nearly immediately, the clicking of the keys on her laptop was a soft blur of sound. Alex took his clothes from the closet and walked into the bath.

Later, Caitlin finished her typing with a flourish and stood, then reached for her wine glass and scooped out a handful of peanuts from a ceramic bowl beside it.

"I guess we should go down to dinner soon," she said. "I wonder if this will be a big bore."

"I suppose it depends on how curious Virgil is," Alex said. "LuAnn is clever enough. Did you finish what you were working on?"

"Yeah, as much as I finish anything like this. I got one whole thought down and structured."

Alex tilted his head and drained his wine glass. "So, let's go see what we have, now that I've beaten up on one of Virgil's hands," he said. Caitlin wore gray cotton slacks and a light blue western shirt with an embroidered pattern on it, showing cute cattle at play. It occurred to Alex that the shirt was not really Caitlin, but maybe the store hadn't sold bullfight shirts.

They opened the stained oak door of their room and started down the wide stairs together. Brooks and LuAnn stood with Virgil to the left of the staircase, in the living room, talking. When they noticed Alex and Caitlin coming down the stairs, Virgil moved to them and waved them to a place at the dinner table, seating Caitlin and pointing out a seat to Alex.

As Brooks seated LuAnn, Virgil moved casually to the head of the table set for five with a white linen tablecloth set with fine china and Riedel crystal. A Latina servant stood by an iced, sweating wine bucket that held *blanc de blancs* bubbly white wine from Schramsberg.

Two bottles of California wine, a chardonnay from Tor Vineyards, and a cabernet sauvignon from Bressler Vineyards stood opened nearby. Water had been poured into pewter goblets in front of each place. LuAnn sat beside Caitlin and across from Alex and Brooks Elliot. The serving woman stepped forward and began to pour the chilled Schramsberg.

When all were served, Virgil lifted his champagne flute.

"LuAnn and I welcome you to our home," he said. "I apologize for the excitement down by the pool this afternoon. That's not the way Texans like to greet guests. I'll be hearing from my foreman before morning and will let you know tomorrow about our hand, Jeeter, who got himself hurt.

"Now, let's see," Virgil said with a smile. "We have us a Rhodes Scholar Seal, Brooks; a MacArthur winner Cal Tech physicist, Caitlin; my darling daughter, LuAnn, the editor of the *Michigan Law Review* from a few years back whom a Dallas newspaper editor once described as a bitch pit bull; and an Arab sheikh who's built like an NFL linebacker. Now, if that don't make for a good dinner talk, I don't know what will. LuAnn tells me y'all are up to some interesting things in the Middle East. I'd like to hear a little about that. LuAnn also tells me that she's learning Arabic, studying Sharia law, and working with Brooks on papering deals for your company there. I guess the part I haven't figured out is where the physicist fits in."

Caitlin sat back in her chair and was silent for several moments, gazing into space. "I've always wanted to do something big, to be important in *my* eyes. This is it. I'm helping to change the face of the world."

"Hell, most people just want to get rich," Virgil said. "How's that changing the world part working for you? Where do you fit in?"

"I joined the effort late, just a few years ago," Caitlin said. "Alex and Brooks believe the Middle East is ripe for a major positive change in thinking, a rebirth of the masses to a new and better life. They came to me a few years back for some serious help. They used a bunch of models from the eighteenth and nineteenth centuries in

10

the West to convince me that our effort is likely to be effective if we help it along. I'm convinced. I'm helping, full time.

"I'm the information technology guru," she said. "We're off to a good start. It's challenging. The problem that Alex handed me was twofold. First, I had to find a way to communicate effectively between, about, and among all the interested players. Those are mostly our team, US intelligence types, and Arabic speakers, as it turns out. Second, I had to manage and analyze the boatloads of information that we gather. The buzz word for great heaps of information like ours is 'big data.'"

Alex interrupted. "The communications part required some way to help train and educate masses of Muslims, while still keeping an eye on them. Mass education is fundamental to any Muslim rebirth. I had no clue how to scale that kind of an effort. We certainly couldn't afford to hire enough teachers to handle even fifteen thousand students, the way we do now."

"We have already videoed courses from more than a hundred gifted teachers, the best we can find on everything from arithmetic to advanced calculus," Caitlin said. "We've found sources for a lot more, like Accounting 101 through 404. Up to high school, everything is in both English and Arabic"

Virgil frowned. "I thought we were talking about what you do for the team."

Caitlin gazed at Virgil for a long moment. She sat still at her place, a neutral, distant expression on her face.

Oh, shit! Alex thought with a glance at Brooks, who had one eyebrow high on his forehead and a grin pulling at the right corner of his mouth. *One doesn't diss Caitlin about education and her thinking, even if you don't know you're dissing her.*

Alex could sense LuAnn paying more attention to the discussion, as she leaned forward a little.

"Indeed we are," Caitlin said. "I'm terribly sorry. I thought you were keeping up with the nuance. I shall be more direct and simple for you."

Virgil's head snapped up as she stood and faced the entire table. *Damn,* he thought, *I think I've just been disciplined by the teacher.*

"The communications device that was our first challenge must be capable. Beyond the obvious of being a smartphone and a hand-held computer, it must be secure. Things became more interesting when the five of us thought through the various needs we had beyond what a modern smartphone can provide."

"Five? There are five of you?" Virgil said.

"Yes, so far," she said flatly. "But we digress."

Caitlin lifted her cell phone from the small wooden table and held it in front of her. Her shoulders squared a few millimeters, or at least gave that impression. She dropped her chin slightly and fixed her faded blue eyes directly on Virgil. It was a look that Alex and Brooks called "School Marm," which had seen much use at universities and conferences around the world. Caitlin used it on them when something had to be explained for a second time.

"This is a smartphone that we call a Kphone. We built it. It is an essential part of a larger data system that I named Emilie, after a heroine of mine, Emilie du Chatelet, who happened to be Voltaire's mistress. She also was a math savant who gained widespread fame by rewriting and modernizing Newton's definitive work on math, *Principia Mathematica,* that he developed before he discovered the calculus. She would have fit into CalTech in a number of ways. She played by her own rules and got away with it.

"The Kphone acts as our user interface to technology support. It is roughly a hundred times faster than the smartest cell phone on the planet. It has vastly more memory. Anything you can do with a top PC or Mac, you can do with this. It is the primary link, via

Emilie, to Kufdani Industries. Cooling the damn phone, with all its circuits, was interesting..."

"Caitlin," Brooks said sharply. "That's classified. DARPA owns that patent, not you. They paid Axial good money for it."

"Oh, yeah," Caitlin said. "I forgot. I've been thinking more about that cooling problem lately."

Virgil had recovered from the impact of the change of behavior in Caitlin. *The rest of her talk could be fun,* he thought. *I'm at least learning something from a CalTech PhD.* Virgil wondered if he had been the slightest bit discourteous earlier. He may not have asked that same question of a Nobel Prize winner in a discussion. If it even was a question.

"Anyway, those are the basics of the Kphone," Caitlin said with a shrug as she set it back on the small table. "Emilie, the information management software, is more complex. There are two necessary but not sufficient components for Emilie, beyond the obvious."

Alex and Brooks were looking at each other and shaking their heads. Caitlin was on a roll. The whole problem of cooling that many circuits in a Kphone-sized space had boggled calculation until one day Caitlin had it figured out. Luann was absorbed. Virgil mused and listened.

"Alex, Brooks, Jerome, MacMillan, and I, the five team members I mentioned earlier, sat down a few years ago for a few weeks. We figured out what we needed and wanted in IT to support Alex's company, Kufdani Industries. Then I went off to build it with an eye to including my company's software as its core, since I had spent fifteen years or more on it. It quickly became apparent that a useful intelligence gathering and conclusion system could be easily embedded in its development. The user interface is the Kphone discussed earlier. The underlying data-handling system is based on the software product of my company, Axial Systems. That system is heuristic. That is, it learns from itself as it runs everything. I find that a big time-saver."

"Whoa, Dr. O'Connor," Virgil said as he stood. "I'm going to need a nature break. Let's get back together here in ten minutes or so."

When they returned, Caitlin was still standing erect with her hands in front of her waist. She had that distant, neutral smile on her face.

As they sat and just before the tenth minute passed, Caitlin picked up her champagne glass and took a sip, then a drink from her water glass and said, "Back to the discussion of Emilie. First, we must reliably detect and verify the identity of every user, then use that identity to both provide encrypted systems access for individuals and to correlate user-specific data we gather. After some time, every user has a distinct personality to Emilie so we know where each one is in training, the job he is supposed to do, how well he is doing it, and the relative value of the information he provides as part of the daily job. There is a thumbprint reader to verify identity biometrically; it has some cute features. We call that complex personality profile a reputation, and the software module that administers all of that is a reputation server. It is more useful than is obvious to have a daily record of the activities and performance of persons of interest."

"Do you mean persons of interest as the police describe them?" LuAnn asked. "Someone suspected of something?"

"I don't know of police terms," Caitlin said. "We specifically discuss employees of Kufdani Industries in this example, as an initial descriptor. As we expand the user universe, use of a reputation server becomes more interesting and useful."

Caitlin had now fixed her professorial gaze on LuAnn. "But that is again a digression.

"Second, Emilie collects, correlates, and analyzes a stream of information coming from the ground up across the Muslim world, from required daily reports of the situation in the environment of each Kufdani Industries office, from each employee. Newspapers from several hundred different nations are scanned into the system each day. The United States provides input data from various satellites, embassies, and so on. From this data and a lot more, Emilie draws conclusions to some degree of likelihood about what is happening somewhere or is likely to happen at some place. It's a matter mostly of experiential probabilities and inferences that get more accurate, real time, as more information flows into it. It works pretty well. It also turns out to be an intelligence dream come true for Americans in dealing with the Middle East."

There was a long silence, then Virgil said, "Wow."

"Yeah," Alex said. "It's pretty spectacular."

"It does indeed have promise," Caitlin said. "I like this job."

"Jesus," Virgil said. "This is spooky. It seems like an enabler on steroids for Orwell's *Nineteen Eighty-Four*. On the business side, though, I can see that if the scheme works, operating costs for Alex's company must be low. It's all electronic, or mostly all." He looked at Elliot.

Brooks laughed. "It works," he said. "The operating profits are enormous, plus the US government pays Caitlin's company a lot of money for access to Emilie. Kufdani owns a lot of Caitlin's company and gets dividends. We use Emilie without charge. Kufdani has some other rights because of Alex's role in helping design it, for paying for the early work to prove the concept and for using Kufdani folks as guinea pigs for the e-learning technology. I find and acquire products or technologies that will provide a competitive barrier to entry in the markets we serve.

"I try to find creative ways to keep vendors from getting too greedy and lately, LuAnn writes them down," Brooks said. "We assumed that gross margins would be great if this worked, and they are, but profits are a tool, not our real goal. As Caitlin mentioned, the real goal is to transform the Middle East to a more productive, thoughtful society."

Brooks picked up his water glass, took a long drink, and said, "I've studied the way our developed world got relatively more creative, rich, and fair. So has Alex. When the Muslim masses learn to read well and to think critically, their lives will get enormously better. They'll want a real job and a better life because they will seem within reach. Women will have fewer children, and have them later. Education is the first big step. We're on it and winning. Vocational training is next. We're working hard on that now.

"There is quite a bit of evidence that younger Muslims want a different society than the religious fundamentalists are selling and have been trying to deliver. The whole Arab Spring movement is, in part, a reflection of that dissatisfaction. We're in a good place at a good time to help move that ball down the field."

"Uh-huh. Big field, long game, I imagine," Virgil said. "OK, Alex, tell me about you being a sheikh and all. Make it simple. This is a bit much for dinner talk."

"Long story short," Alex said with a smile as the main meal was served. "I inherited Kufdani Industries from my maternal grandfather. His only expressed desire was that I attempt to make the Muslim world a better place to live; he wanted a rebirth of Islam. That's what I want. I speak quite a few dialects of Arabic, decent Farsi, and a few dialects of Spanish, so I'm mostly accepted as a local where they speak those languages. Right now there are about eight thousand Kufdani employees in twenty-six countries across the Middle East. Before Kufdani I studied business and ran a tech hedge fund for several years in New York and now have a person running that firm. I had some tools to work with, but my grandfather bequeathing Kufdani to me was where it all got going. I assumed that I could find or grow good operating executives. I knew what I wanted to do as chief executive."

"Let's eat this food before it gets cold," Virgil said. "I'll listen to the rest of this later. My head is spinning. It used to be that all you did with a damn phone was talk to it."

"You haven't heard the last of that phone, their Kphone," LuAnn said with a smile. "The story gets better. Emilie is the one teaching me Arabic language and Sharia law."

Southwest Texas
Dawn, the Clemens' ranch

Cuchulain walked from the ranch house with the ochre light of dawn casting long shadows across the rough grass toward the main corral. He wore a faded pair of Wrangler jeans and a blue cotton button-down shirt. His still-wet hair was slicked back, black and shining, with a few threads of silver showing on the sides. A middle-aged man was sitting on the top rail of the corral, smoking a cigarette, one foot hooked under the second rail. His wide-brimmed hat was pushed back on his head and a steel-gray brush cut showed beneath it. A large rectangular silver belt buckle on his jeans caught an early ray of sun. There was lettering of some sort on it.

"Howdy," he said, and jumped down from the rail. He stuck his hand out. "I'm the foreman around here."

"Hello," Alex said as he reached with his hand to greet him. "How is the cowboy who fell yesterday? Jeeter?"

Cuchulain's hand was suddenly squeezed hard, and Alex instinctively returned the pressure. He could feel thick calluses against his as the pressure increased. The man was strong. The pressure leveled, then dropped as the foreman gazed into Alex's eyes; then he nodded almost imperceptibly and let go. He jumped nimbly back up on the rail.

"Well, his jaw hinge is shattered and the jaw's broken in one place," the foreman said, as he settled himself. "But I reckon he'll live." He flicked his cigarette to the dirt. "How do you pronounce that last name of yours?"

"Coo-HULL-an," Alex said. "Why?"

He studied Cuchulain. "They ever call you Cooch?"

Alex shrugged. "Seems likely with a name like mine."

"I was in the marine corps for twenty-some years. Word gets around. You that Cooch? The one who worked for the spooks?"

Alex sighed. "I'd rather not make a fuss about it. That was a long time ago. I'm a businessman now."

"I figgered. I've broken hands with less pressure than that. My name's Proctor Mikey. They call me Mikey. Took me awhile to figger you out. Then I remembered that your buddy Elliot was a Seal; the boys was all excited about that. They thought maybe they'd have a fight in his honor."

"It's not too late," Alex said.

Mikey dug a small sack from his shirt pocket, unfolded a paper from a small orange packet, and began to roll another cigarette. "I never got to meet your daddy. Never met a man with the Medal of Honor. Wished I had."

Alex looked at the dawning sky for a long moment and said, "He was a good man."

"The boys sort of gave up on the fight in Elliot's honor. They figure you fucked up the ranch's honor when Jeeter got hurt going after you. Jeeter's jaw's wired shut, but he wrote a note at the infirmary. It just said, 'Protectin LuAnn.' They're planning to work on you some. We call it 'riding for the brand,'" Mikey said quietly. "They like that LuAnn girl."

"Hell, I like her too. It was an accident, or at least not what it seemed," Alex said as he sighed and looked away. "Well, does recovering honor for the brand include guns and knives? If not, Elliot and I will deal with it. But you'd better call around and get some more folks for your side. If that guy who jumped me was one of the bad guys, you don't have nearly enough folks to make it fun."

Mikey snorted a double laugh and then coughed violently. He hawked a wad of phlegm and spat it on the dirt.

"I reckon the boss would be highly pissed if he had a bunch of hands in the hospital or the hoosegow," he said. "Anyhow, they're fixin' to have you ride a horse that will do the job for them. You ride much?"

"Only a little," Alex said. "I've ridden more camels than horses."

"We got us a big horse named Cottonmouth. Good name. He's meaner than a blind fucking snake. They got him in mind for you, for a bumpy little ride across the prairie. And Cottonmouth's a biter."

"Hell, the fight's sounding better all the time. Any advice?"

Mikey sat for awhile, pondering. "My claim to fame around here is that I was national high school rodeo champ a thousand years ago," he said, and pointed to his belt buckle. "I know horses."

"And?" Alex said.

"Two things," Mikey said. "First, if you punch a horse really hard just between his ears, high up, and you can punch right, he'll go to his knees. Maybe a trained guy like you would kill him, but he'll behave if you don't. Second, and sneakier, but you may be able to pull it off if the rumors about your hands are true, and I just seen some evidence that they might be: you just whisper a bit in Cottonmouth's ear while they are holding him and run your hand up just between his ears and press hard. The place is called the poll; it's where nerves cross under a horse's skull plates. The plates don't quite meet there and there's a little dip, so there's room to push a strong finger down in. Horses don't like pain; it makes them behave."

"Good to know, I guess," Alex said. "I don't suppose you could show me how to do that on a horse."

Mikey smiled. "I reckon I could, both of us being marines and all. It's the least I can do to stop a massacree on my ranch." He eased himself from the rail, stripped the paper from the remaining tobacco, and dropped it into the dirt. He ground it with his heel and walked toward the stables with Alex beside him.

Mikey stopped just as they reached a stable and turned. "I need to ask you something, but it's really none of my biddness," he said.

"Sure." Alex shrugged and smiled. "Asking is free."

"Do you have any contacts left? Where you can give someone a heads-up to see if something's funny?"

"Funny, how?" Alex said. "Who would want to know?"

Mikey studied Alex. "There was a different crowd of Mexicans came to town about three, four days ago. Not like most of the coyotes that bring illegals across. They're a bunch of bad asses, plus a guy who dresses funny and speaks bad Spanish. The locals are scared to death of them."

"Yeah?" Alex said.

"Yeah. We get a pretty steady stream of illegals coming through this part of Texas. We're on a good smuggling route from Mexico. It's been going on for quite awhile, but it's really none of our biddness, so we stay out of it. The immigration game changed with this crowd that just came in. One of my ranch hands, Gomez, is a former marine. He did his Iraq time, twice. He was in town when those guys came into the cantina. Gomez thinks that a funny-looking guy was speaking Arabic to one guy who translates to Spanish. The bad guys were pissed when they did it in public, but still treated them like royalty.

"So, if they're bad asses, they're too expensive to be moving illegals. What are they moving?" Mikey said. "It don't smell right, and my nose works pretty good for smelling trouble. Gomez took a picture of the guy with his cell phone. Quality's shitty, but it's a picture."

"Did he now? Well done," Alex said with a tight smile. He dug out his wallet and found a slightly wrinkled business card to hand to Mikey. "Ask him to e-mail me a copy of that photo soon. It could be anything or nothing. Still, it's a change in behavior for them, isn't it?"

"Yup," Mikey said. "And it might be worth looking into, or not. You know anyone to alert? Word was that you were doing spook work for awhile and were good at it. I thought there might be a loose connection or two you could tweak. Immigration is one thing, but they don't need those guys for that. What worries me is what they are planning to bring across the border."

"I'll make a call," Alex said. "Maybe someone will take a look. Are you available to talk a little more and maybe Gomez too? I might want to go to town to night after dark and get a beer with Gomez. Check things out."

Mikey glanced up sharply and said, "Hell, we're marines. You know that."

"Yeah, sorry. I've been a civilian too long. Once a marine, always a marine. *Semper fi.*"

Mikey snorted, and said with a grin, "Fuckin-ay-tweedie-grunt."

• • •

Breakfast was Texas big: eggs, blueberry pancakes, three kinds of toast, jalapeño cheese grits, home-fried potatoes, two kinds of fresh squeezed juice, and meat galore. When they finally pushed back from the table, Virgil said they should get ready for the day's trail ride and meet at ten at the corral. On the stairs to their room, Alex quietly asked Caitlin to turn Emilie's intelligence assessment loose on any West Texas/Arab connection and explained his plans.

LuAnn hurried to catch her father as the guests walked to their rooms.

"Daddy," she said. "I need to talk to you, now!"

"Sure, honey," he said. "Come on into my office and set a spell. Hell, I always have time for you. Since your mother passed, there ain't no one else that matters."

"Look, Daddy," LuAnn said. "That thing by the pool where Jeeter got hurt was an accident and it was my fault. The hands are acting like our honor was violated, and I'm afraid Alex is in trouble with them somehow."

"Honey, don't you worry too much about that, but I'm glad to see that New Yawk hasn't screwed up your powers of observation," Virgil said. "I talked to Mikey a little while ago, and he said that it's under control, mostly. If it gets out of hand, I'll have him stop it."

LuAnn shifted in her chair, looked out the window for a moment at the dry rolling hills, then said, "I really don't like this, and I don't know Alex well yet. His date is a barracuda with a foul mouth and an IQ in the stratosphere. If she gets to thinking this is about her somehow, things could get ugly. I like her, but she's scary smart, tough, and it's all about her. If she had a lobotomy, she'd make a good lawyer. But I think what they are doing is exciting. I think I want in."

Clemens chuckled and stood up. "Best-looking barracuda I've ever seen. Well, let's just see how it works out. Mikey thinks that your friend Alex is safe enough. As far as the rest of it goes, if you're in, I'm in, at least sort of. Let's just see how things play out."

A little later, Alex sat in a wooden rocking chair on the broad veranda, uncomfortably wearing a brand new Stetson cowboy hat

Caitlin had bought for him. He was nursing a white ceramic mug of coffee in one hand and had his Kphone in the other, reading messages. Caitlin came through the thick double door. She was dressed in skin-tight jeans, a plaid cotton shirt, and a white Stetson. Her high-heeled cowboy boots were hand-tooled black leather, with math symbols carved on them in white. She wiggled her behind and trilled, "Ta-da!"

Alex jumped up, spilling hot coffee on his hand.

"Wow! You look fabulous! The horses and cowboys will be in love."

She plopped into the chair beside his and waved her hand lightly.

"On your cantina speculation, I should get two good runs from Emilie by the time we get back from lunch. We'll soon see if there is increased bad guy activity in West Texas. As for my cowgirl outfit, I didn't put it on for them, asshole, I put it on for you. Now that you're back in lust, just as I demand, I'll get all dusty and nasty on the ride to lunch. Later, I might let you lick the sweat off, since I haven't seen you socially for a few months."

Alex grinned that grin. "With bated breath I await," he said. He took a sip of his cooling coffee. "Can you imagine lunch out on the prairie?"

"I must have gained three pounds at breakfast," Caitlin said. "I'll bet there will be Rolls Royce pickups bringing a caviar and champagne lunch. But hey, I'm on vacation. I can swim twenty miles again next week."

Alex chuckled. "We gotta get there first. Let's go see our chosen chariots, or steeds, maybe. The others should be down there soon."

As they stood, Brooks and LuAnn walked out the front door, followed by Virgil Clemens. All walked toward the corral, talking idly about breakfast, where four saddled horses waited, one with two ranch hands holding its bridle. Another very large saddled horse was standing by Mikey, looking at him as a favored Labrador retriever might.

Mikey walked over to the group and began to assign horses. Each guest moved to the assigned mount. LuAnn was beside Virgil while her horse stood waiting, patiently. Alex was last.

"Young feller," Mikey said to Alex, "the boys picked this horse out special for you. They thought he'd be good transportation."

"Daddy! Cottonmouth?" LuAnn whispered. "Stop it!"

"I'll stop it later, if it gets nasty," Clemens said quietly. "Right now, it's just fun. Let's see if Mikey is as good as I think he is."

Alex walked to his horse and stood in front of the left stirrup, just behind his nose. They looked at each other. The horse started to turn his head, and his lips curled from flat, yellow teeth. Alex blocked Cottonmouth's head from turning with his left forearm and stepped forward, sliding his right hand up and over his thick neck to his ears, then between them, probing. There was indeed a tiny gap between his skull plates. Alex slid a forefinger just above that gap and dug a little. Cottonmouth settled back, unsure. Alex leaned to whisper in his ear. "Look, horse, one of us is liable to get hurt here. I'd rather it was you." He pushed down with his forefinger between the skull plates. Cottonmouth shifted a bit and Alex pushed harder. The horse became still and Alex eased the pressure slightly.

The cowboys holding the horse looked puzzled and at each other quizzically. This was not the Cottonmouth they knew. One of them said to Alex, "Why don't you just stick your foot in this here stirrup and mount up, cowboy. Other folks are waiting for you."

Alex stuck his left foot in the stirrup and swung up and over the horse. He felt the horse's muscles bunching, ready to explode. He pushed much harder on Cottonmouth's poll. The horse stilled immediately and Alex felt him beginning to weaken at the fore knees. He eased back on the finger pressure. Cottonmouth turned his head, eyes rolled back, awaiting instruction.

Mikey swung on his horse and snuck a wink at Alex.

"Let's move out now, folks," he said.

Alex moved the reins against Cottonmouth's neck, then gave him a little kick. The horse moved obediently to the rear of the line. Alex took his hand from the top of Cottonmouth's head after one reminder squeeze.

The horses moved at a brisk walk away from the corrals with the mid-morning sun casting a yellow glow on the field. The light put in sharp contrast the mechanical nodding of steel oil well donkeys, rhythmically pumping money from the ground.

One of the cowboys who had been holding Cottonmouth's bridle said to the other, "He's a daggone tenderfoot. How did he get onto Cottonmouth and just ride away like he was on a rental pony?"

The second man, older, said, "Beats me. It was spooky. He whispered in Cottonmouth's ear and that was the end of the horse acting up. I never seen the like."

"I'd sure like to know what the heck he said to that horse," the younger man muttered.

Old Executive Office Building
Washington, DC

Mac MacMillan, the deputy assistant national security advisor of the United States, pushed his chair back from his computer and put his heels up on an old mouse pad that occupied the left front corner of his desk. Beneath the heel marks and stains of black Kiwi polish was a rubberized maroon surface with the fading symbol of the United States Marine Corps. Mac stared at the fading GI-green ceiling of his tiny office, beside the White House, in the Old Executive Office Building, considering the situation.

For quite a few years, MacMillan had led the CIA's special operations unit. It was often deployed around the world in roles of violence too small or visible for Seals, Rangers, or Delta Force, or as a specialty force attached to those more traditional of the country's special operations warriors. Mac filled his current obscure role within the national security apparatus of the United States, until recently serving the president as a resource to solve problems that were otherwise difficult to solve, at least legally. Mac had been the leader of what was essentially a tiny private, deniable army consisting of Alex "Cooch" Cuchulain, Brooks F.T. Elliot IV, Jerome

Masterson, and the occasional "volunteer" for this or that mission-related chore, such as bugging an office. The little army was backed up, very selectively, by the entire force of the Department of Defense. Mac had known Cuchulain since Alex was sixteen years old, and had employed him for eight years after that in a CIA special ops role, in the organization that Mac had run for many years. Mac and Alex had spent many evenings after dinner at the Farm, talking and drinking vintage port. They became good friends as Alex matured. Their relationship survived Alex's moves to college and then to a career.

Alex's e-mail from Texas a few hours ago had attached a poor quality photo of a plump, middle-aged man with an unkempt beard. The text was interesting. It said:

Mac-

Attached is a bad photo of a guy holed up in a cantina in Texas. He seems to be waiting for something, I'm told. Also attached is the story I heard of who he is and the circumstances. Please see if anyone at the Company knows him. Emilie will allow forwarding and printing of the attachments and Caitlin has her on point for Texas bad guy news. I plan to pay a quiet visit to the cantina tonight to see for myself.

I'll make a dinner appointment with Abdul from the Arab League. We need a better handle on what is going on with the bad guys over there. He should be able to confirm or deny my instincts of what's going on among the radical Muslims and the monarchies' response to them. I'll let you know what I learn.

Cuchulain

Mac had put new encryption on the photo attachment, then sent it on to the CIA photo mavens to search for an identity. The information about an apparent hookup between the Latino druggies and Al-Qaeda was troubling, but not surprising to him. The US national security team had been worried for years about Latino druggies and Arab terrorists teaming up against the US. They had motivation, since the rewards for success in such a liaison were good for both, and the cash costs low. For drug dealers the terrorists could provide access to distribution channels in Africa, the Middle East, and Europe in markets for cocaine that was largely untapped. For terrorists, the drug dealers could provide physical access to the United States for both goods and people, usually through Mexico. The druggies brought cash. The terrorists brought ambitious goals. This intersection of capabilities and ideas had become a dangerous place. Mac typed a short message to the Marine Corps liaison to the White House and sent it. He picked up the phone, punched a few keys, and said, "Shirley, it's Mac. I need to see the general again—soon." He listened as she rustled papers and tapped on her computer, then said, "In ninety minutes: sixteen thirty for thirty." He heard her disconnect; they understood each other. Shortly, his secure printer started up as his Marine Corps request was satisfied. He picked up a legal pad and began to organize his thoughts.

• • •

Shirley glanced up at the wall clock as Mac entered the reception office of his boss, the National Security Advisor, General Patrick Kelly, USMC (Ret). She recognized him with a brief nod. He was five minutes early, as usual. MacMillan was a big man with short, steel-gray hair parted on the left, grey eyes, and a scar running from the corner of his left eye to the base of his earlobe.

He wore a once-expensive suit and a white cotton shirt with a worn silk tie. He had been a serving marine during the early part of his government service and maintained that relationship during his years running the CIA's special operations unit.

At 1635 the office door opened. A tall, haggard man in a wrinkled white shirt and red tie, striped in blue and white, waved him in. They shook hands casually, then General Kelly took off his jacket and threw it over a chair. He sat on another chair and pulled one leg up and pushed out of one black, well-shined loafer, then the other. Mac sank into a leather-upholstered armchair that was in front of a glass-topped, magazine-covered table.

"Don't give me bad news, Mac. It hasn't been a good day," Kelly said with a groan and a faint grin as he put his stockinged feet up on the table.

"What days are all good?" Mac said. "I bring mixed blessings. I got a heads-up from Alex Cuchulain, the guy we've been talking about and the leader of the budding Muslim society fixers we've been discussing. He's on a getaway in West Texas with Elliot. He ran into a retired marine NCO there who thinks the rag heads are up to something in Mexico and on their way here. Alex has good instincts and we've been waiting for something like this."

"Rag heads in Mexico, heading our way," Kelly said. "I don't like that even a little bit. Any clue what the hell they are doing there?"

"Nary a one, but there is a group of top-end Mexican druggie troops, plus a couple of other players who may be Arab, hanging out in a cantina in West Texas near the border. They seem to be waiting for someone. Who they are waiting for is the issue. We've been hearing rumors for months about some kind of hookup between the two. The latest ones have been from Emilie, O'Connor's intelligence system, which newly puts it at a sixty-eight percent probability. She tends to be more reliable than most."

"Dr. Caitlin O'Connor," Kelly said, with a grin and a slow shake of his head. "A true piece of work and I say that not having met her. It wouldn't matter much if she is homely; you can fall in love with a mind that makes your life so much more effective. I can't imagine spending much time with someone that smart, but I'd like to try sometime. The mining of that much raw data to synthesize conclusions that are mostly correct is simply spectacular. The signal spooks at NSA are bat shit to get their paws directly on it, but they complain she plays with them when she explains it. The drone monkeys over at your old shop in Langley are going to town with Emilie's conclusions; they don't care how she got there. We've killed three of Al-Qaeda's top ten in the past two months. It isn't that hard, once you know where they are."

"Yeah, we should get Caitlin and Cuchulain together with you," Mac said. "You already know Elliot. I'll work on it. She's not all that homely. The story of the building of Emilie is a fun tale. That same information system is running Kufdani Industries. The team is expanding now.

"Anyway," Mac said, as he held out copies of the Marine Corps service records of Proctor Mikey and Hector Gomez that had been sent to his secure printer a few minutes after he made the request, "these former marines seem like solid citizens. There's no reason for them to cry wolf and some reason to believe they know trouble when they see it. They've seen a lot of Arabs, between the two of them. Cuchulain said he might go take a look at them tonight."

A wolfish grin crossed Kelly's face as he waved away the need to review the files. "Maybe we'll get lucky," he said. "I'd sure like to nip this evil partnership in the bud by overreacting. We're going to have to look into this right now. I'll alert the air force to make sure they have a drone around there and fueled. Probably can't arm it and fly it too near Mexico without really pissing off State. You let me know about any ID from the photo down there that got sent."

"OK. I thought maybe we should put a Delta Force team on alert. Tell them to use Northern Mexico and Southwest Texas for an ops-planning terrain view."

"Yeah, good idea. Give them a heads-up on the quiet. I'll talk to Spec Ops. I think he's across the river in the five-sided puzzle palace this week."

As Mac rose and turned for the door, Kelly said, "I'm going to talk to the man about meeting with you, like you've been bugging me to do. I must be fucking crazy. If you see my head rolling on the White House lawn, you'll know he was skeptical."

Mac looked over his shoulder and grinned. "Hey, maybe I'll get your job and a pay raise. No downside for me. If you get fired, can I have your pretty gold Rolex? I'll give you fifty dollah for it."

"Yeah, you're a great ass-kisser and should have this job," Kelly said with a snort. "The president thinks you're a really nice fellow for a serial killer and a rule breaker." He reached down and pulled on his shoes. "Let's get with it. There are eight hours left in the day."

"I have an ICOIN meeting in the morning at Langley," Mac said. "I'll let them know we may have more excitement coming in our lives."

Headquarters, the Central Intelligence Agency Langley, Virginia

The conference room in the first sub-level of the main CIA building was the meeting site for the mostly weekly face-to-face get-together of the Interagency Intelligence Coordination Committee on Impending Salient Events. It was known to its members as ICOIN, the Intelligence Committee on Impending Nightmares, at least partially because none of its members could think of an acceptable acronym for its official title. Each member was charged with ensuring cooperation between the various agencies by heatedly discouraging turf fights and other "bureaucratic parochial protective measures." Their mandate was to ensure that actionable intelligence was shared within the intelligence community. Decisions made without access to every relevant piece of data had been proven to be dangerous and shortsighted. Trusting politicians with the same top-secret data had also proven to be stupid unless public disclosure in some form was likely to be helpful.

ICOIN membership consisted of the top career officer or his appropriate deputy of the Central Intelligence Agency, the J2 (Intelligence) of the Joint Chiefs of Staff (JCS) of the Department of Defense, the Defense Intelligence Agency, the National Security

Agency, the National Reconnaissance Office, the Department of Homeland Security, and the White House. Political appointees were not welcome, but a second in command could be sent to meetings in unusual circumstances. The exception, and sometimes a difficult one, to the top career officer rule was for the White House, since everyone there was viewed as a politician and thus with suspicion. Caution was the watchword. MacMillan was the designee from the White House and ran the meetings, despite his meaningless title and apparently low career status. No one thought of him as a politician. He was a veteran of the CIA, having twice served as the acting Deputy Director for Operations and once as the acting Deputy for Intelligence. He had declined offers to discuss permanent positions at those levels. At the CIA, operations meant action, and intelligence meant information; Mac was an acceptable hybrid. He was well connected with DOD's special operations management and had worked with many of them. He was a combination of frustratingly vicious bureaucratic infighter and creative consensus builder. The common consensus about Mac was that he would freely give up credit for any effort jointly made that was successful and accept full blame for any shared failures. That had a comforting resonance for many of the ICOIN attendees.

A recurring concern of the group was the progress of the Islamic Republic of Iran in building a nuclear weapon and the efforts of the Israelis to hinder that progress, violently if necessary and secretly if possible. Assistance with violence was not unheard of, if secrecy seemed achievable. Unauthorized disclosure was ravenously consumed by the press, then disgorged in some form likely to enrage the liberal voter and thus the president. Lately, the successors to the Stuxnet virus and several assassinations of key Iranian scientists had been hot topics, colored by thoughts about how to protect key US scientists from the same fate. There had been a few apparently random killings of important US government scientists and their families recently, but there was no evidence of foreign involvement.

Mac's description of the impending visitors from the Muslim world arriving through Mexico evoked some interest, and notes were made to get the reports from subordinates or to find a way to watch inevitable surveillance of the trip unfold. CIA and JCS were nodding, showing their prior knowledge as the story was told. Information was solicited from all in support of the upcoming mission.

Southwest Yemen
East of Aden

Hamza, now the chief operations planner for Yemen-based Al-Qaeda in the Arabian Peninsula, was savoring some imminent fruits of his long efforts in the service of Allah with his aide, Bazir. The afternoon sun warmed him and softened the ache of his shriveled leg.

He had made a long journey for Allah since his tragedy in Sana'a. The trip from Sana'a to Kabul was frightening. Men locked him in a windowless room in the mountains of Pakistan for two days without food. He prayed often. Then two men came to talk to him, day after day. One was old and plump, with a full gray beard. The other was middle aged, dark, and lean, with the flat emotionless gaze of a panther. They talked to Hamza about the Koran; they talked about the Great Satan. Finally, they talked about learning new skills. Hamza was accepted among them.

Hamza was posted to Iraq from his long-time position in Afghanistan after the second invasion of Iraq's sovereignty by the Great Satan. He was twice promoted there, even though he was Yemeni. His devotion impressed many. A senior acquaintance there offered him an important role in training and selecting targets for the martyrs, the suicide bombers. Hamza leapt at the opportunity. Under his leadership and guidance, casualties among the enemy went up fivefold. Fatalities, a key metric for the infidel press, had tripled.

As one of his first operational planning victories, Hamza found a new source of plastic explosive to replace the aging Semtex that they bought for exorbitant prices. A faithful Shiite in Serbia worked in an explosives factory there. He was able to arrange for Hamza to purchase endless supplies at good prices, albeit with cash in advance and no receipt. The new explosive had twice the force as did the same weight of Semtex, yet it detonated far more reliably.

Hamza also created a new program, Allah's Flowers. Young Muslim women were volunteered by their parents, in return for modest compensation and Allah's favor in the afterlife, to bring glory to both her and her family and for the devout maiden to achieve martyrdom. At first Hamza was disturbed and offended that many of the young women, even faithful servants of Allah, proved notoriously headstrong when presented with their opportunities. It was a complication for his schedule. Hamza bought some of the crop of the faithful from a jihadist recently arrived from Afghanistan. He soon provided a steady diet of the opium to the young girls. They quickly became compliant and eventually willing participants in training for their martyrdom as carriers of the explosive wrath of Allah. Hamza had decided that their daily ration of the medicine of martyrdom would not be provided unless each was an enthusiastic trainee. The planning of attacks proved to take patience and intelligence. In several early incidents, the martyrdom of the devotee produced few tangible results. The apparently robotic movement of certain young women with a strong appetite for Allah's medicine alerted the targets that all was not well; two were shot by the infidels without having the opportunity to detonate their wrath of Allah. In the face of criticism from his superiors, Hamza had a new trigger designed to allow detonation by a cell phone signal rather than by a thumb switch triggered by the martyr. The routine dosage of medicine was reduced. Subsequent mission explosions were at the immediate will of Hamza until the technique was perfected.

Until the leadership and wisdom of Hamza became apparent, most bombs were similar in size and impact. There were few ways to kill more broadly until the generous supply of new explosive caused Hamza to consider other means for delivery of explosive to a target. To Hamza's credit, the pickup truck often replaced the young women as the means to deliver optimum destruction to the enemy. A truck could carry enormous quantities of explosive and still require a martyr of only modest training and a tiny amount of opium to smooth his path. The enemy built barriers to prevent the trucks from reaching their targets, so the young women first walked to the barriers when a truck was expected and destroyed those who manned those barriers. The confusion among the enemy was extensive and the planning brilliance of Hamza became legend.

Hamza's work on detonation techniques proved a bonanza of opportunity for a scientific planner with the skills Hamza had developed. What the infidel called improvised explosive devices, IEDs, were enhanced such that detonation triggers no longer required pressure from a foot stepping on them for the loss of only a leg or a single life or a truck rolling over a pressure switch to lose only a wheel and a driver. The IEDs could be made as large as required and buried for days until an acceptable target came near, when they would be detonated from a distance by a cell phone message, a garage door opener, or whatever signal the enemy had not yet discovered. Buried with the explosive were scraps of metal and glass that had been soaked in latrines for a few hours to enhance the chances of infection in the infidel wounded.

Late in his service in Iraq, Hamza had occasion to be with a mortar crew preparing to shell the primary base of the Americans, called the Green Zone. The crew was nervous about retaliation expected from the Americans. Hamza was present to calm their fears and to instill the grace of Allah into their perspective. After a few rounds were fired from the mortar, Hamza would leave them to their work and find a safer spot that allowed observation and encouragement. Any credit from a successful shelling would be shared by Hamza. Casualties from retaliation were unfortunate but of no real concern; Allah would care for the faithful who joined him. Mortars were plentiful.

The first shell was dropped into the mortar tube and went successfully on its way to the target. Hamza stood, gathered his water bottle and small pack, and departed after a word to the gunners. A second shell was dropped quickly into the tube and fired as Hamza walked behind the hull of a destroyed truck. Suddenly the area just in front of the mortar lit up with a sharp, nearly deafening crack. Hot shrapnel drove down upon the three gunners, shredding them.

The computer-directed counter fire by the Americans was getting faster and more accurate. When the radar on the artillery counter-battery detected an incoming round, an alarm sounded to alert the friendly troops to "incoming." The counter-battery system quickly computed the back azimuth of the projectile in flight and fed aiming instructions directly into the loaded 105mm howitzer that was an integral part of the system. The grid coordinates of the target were checked by the counter-battery computer on a digitized map database to ensure that no crowded market, hospital, or school, among other sites, was targeted. The 105mm artillery shot that responded to the mortar attack was ordinarily fired within thirty seconds of detection of the incoming round, a huge improvement from the two-minute response of just a few weeks earlier. A second 105mm round was usually fired within sixty seconds of the first.

Hamza was on his belly on the ground behind the destroyed truck, hands covering his head, when the second 105mm round exploded a few yards nearer to him than the first. A hot spear entered his left leg at the knee. His left shoulder seemed on fire as blood soaked his garment. After a few minutes of patience to ensure that no more artillery was forthcoming, several men ran to Hamza and dragged him to safety behind a wall. His injured knee bumped against the rough street as they pulled him, and he cursed the infidel invaders through the agony of it.

Hamza's new lack of mobility combined with his impressive record caused him to be rewarded with the role of chief planner for Al-Qaeda in the Arabian Peninsula. He had returned to his native Yemen, where he had a small stone house as personal office and quarters not far from his staff and their trainees. The distant port of Aden shimmered in the South Yemen heat, the ragged image stretching and closing again randomly in the sultry breeze. The terraced fields below were mostly deserted. The slight breeze and a lazy ceiling fan cooled the large room. Distant popping of AK-47 fire, punctuated by the occasional small explosion as Hamza's men practiced, was soothing and added to the peace of the moment.

Afternoon prayers had allowed Hamza to renew his pledge to Allah, in his service, and to feel waves of contentment flow through his person once again. Hamza sat on a collection of large pillows and smoked from an ornate water pipe loaded with Turkish tobacco mixed with a small amount of Allah's medicine. A pot of mint tea, half empty, sat beside him; he had a small cup in his hand. He was soon to savor his largest victory over the infidels and distract them from their godless wars with Islam. Final arrangements had been made with his brother and Hamza's nephew in Dallas.

Bazir was sitting silently across the room. The worn butt of a Makarov pistol was visible in his waistband.

"How many of the devils do you think we will kill, Hamza?" he asked.

"Tens of thousands on the first day, and over several growing seasons, perhaps even millions," Hamza said. "It will be a glorious time for Islam."

"May it be millions," Bazir said. "We are blessed to be a part of it and you will be doubly blessed for planning every step of it."

"Indeed we are blessed. But at first we will kill few, perhaps only fifty thousand. Far fewer than we have lost to them. In the passage of time, the number may become many millions. Our hidden triumph may dwarf what we will soon deploy at their decadent sporting event. The government of the Great Satan will have no time to watch our activities. They will be caring for their own dead and dying. The Jews will use oxen to till their fields and serve the soldiers of Allah who will soon attack the Zionists from every direction."

Bazir's face flushed and he asked excitedly, "You are confident that the Russian weapon claim is accurate, and will cause infidel deaths for weeks? It would be a glory to distract them so."

"Indeed the Russian claims for their weapons are accurate and the impact is likely to be one of years, not weeks," Hamza said. He poured the last of the tea into his cup and held a puff from the pipe in his lungs. "Our best scientists have verified their research. The weapons have been developed and tested over many years. And, Allah be praised, we have access to several more nearby."

"We should find a guest to interrogate," Bazir said. "You are at your most creative in the midst of an interrogation. It is strange not to have a prisoner or two for you. You have a gift. I delight in watching the prisoners try to cope after you complete an interrogation session."

"A gift from Allah," Hamza said as he stroked his beard. "It may indeed be time to deal with a few of our enemies here at home. That will likely yield a prisoner to discuss their methods and ways. I shall consider it. I may be too distracted while awaiting news from the land of the Great Satan, but the thought of a few months with a new guest is indeed pleasant to savor. After our success becomes public, I undoubtedly will be chosen for a far more senior job, now that the Sheikh has been martyred in Pakistan.

"Perhaps we should remind Yemenis of our presence and of the penalty for defying us while I am still here," Hamza said. "There is a limitless supply of young and eager jihadists. Just this morning I was told that we have nearly finished training fifty young warriors, eager for martyrdom, to go to the cities of infidel influence; London, Paris, Rome, Amsterdam, Berlin. But something local would be good practice, to check once again for ways to improve our delivery of death. We could use a girl who has proven unsuitable for travel."

"Thanks to your planning, we have found a way to put a pleasant image on a big bomb, and make it look safe just because it is carried by a young girl," Bazir said. "Once we began training them, your brilliance in planning has allowed us to build their ability to carry large weights for short distances. And they seem to like the exercise. A promotion for you would be a glory, and overdue."

Hamza nodded contentedly and took a final sip of his tea. He leaned back on his pillow and reflected on the years of his essential role in the service of Allah, busily gathering information, discouraging slackers, and punishing infidels while he made plans to return Islam's caliphate to world rule.

Hamza was blessed with the opportunity to supplement his planning efforts with a role as a lead interrogator. His gift had been recognized and "high value" persons were often sent to him. He liked to get to know his guests; it was his holy mission to get the information he wanted and needed, and to tease everything from their unwilling psyches. It was with the infidels that Hamza felt a particular connection. The apostate Sunnis were also a pleasing subject.

After enough pain, enough time, enough despair, all subjects talk; there is little talk and much arrogant defiance at first, and then a torrent of sound as the pain is administered slowly, thoughtfully. An interrogator's gift is to tease truth from a thicket of pain-driven lies.

Hamza liked to watch their eyes while he interrogated. He savored the fading of hope from them and at just the right moment, for their eyes to tell him which pain sounds were the music of truth within the cacophony. He viewed himself as a musician or, better perhaps, a composer. Allah had blessed him with many skills and the opportunity to use them in His service.

When word came to him that a new guest was prepared, he would close his eyes for a moment and calm himself in anticipation. His gift could not be hurried.

His lieutenant would help him to his feet; the shrapnel-withered leg needed a moment to adjust to his weight. Support was added by his long, gnarled cane, made many years before from a branch of a tree long ago planted on a small hill overlooking the sacred square, just outside the holy city of Mecca,

Hamza would descend the worn stone stairs slowly, with his halting motion a discordant hitch in the cadence of movement, as the withered limb swung out and sought a place on the step beside the good leg. It then would reach for the next step. Halfway down the stairs, usually in the afternoon after prayers, his nostrils would begin to twitch and he would stop to savor an essence. The first scent of fear and pain would drift to his nostrils. His genitals would stir against his trousers. Sometimes the trigger was the faint, rancid essence of vomit, the handmaiden of fear. Often he was aroused by the copper-metallic scent of fresh blood. At times he could discern the blossoming of tiny molecules of feces in his nose, floating on the air sucked from the underground through the rusted grates to the sun-baked hillside above.

As he descended, the scent blossomed to a mingled stench. When there was more than one guest, the screams of one could be heard by another. Some were merely mourning missing parts thought to have been essential, extracted from them slowly. Others were contemplating the pain that dominated them just then. Each guest provided to him a palette of opportunity that allowed him to quiver and even pulse a bit in his groin, as he anticipated the exquisite opportunity to be once again in the service of Allah.

Pain could be crude, and Hamza personally disdained its brute use. Better that Bazir or others beat the prisoners and remove fingernails or teeth. All the better to prepare and serve a subtle platter of pain, a plateau that the subject, the apostate, thought could not be exceeded. They must believe things can't get worse. Then Hamza, in the glory of Islam and the service of Allah, slowly, gently, would prove that their nearly frozen minds could not yet plumb the depths of what pain, what degradation, what ineffable despair and humiliation could be teased into their consciousness. Each discrete plateau of increased pain was its own little glory. Elegance was the key to a release from Hamza's arousal, an arousal provided by Allah in reward for his piety and as a guiding path for extracting truth. A tiny piece of coarse steel wool, wielded with a firm, circular motion just beneath the glans of a circumcised penis, likely a Jewish penis because they own everyone not in the service of Allah, would produce many minutes of agony.

Pain could be managed like a string quartet, with motion and pressure, albeit with sound always a little off-key and an octave too high. *Fortissimo*, as the musicians said. Often, a bit of probing with a needle was useful for punctuation. Desist, let the infidel fall into a near trance from the pain relief, and then begin the interrogation. Often, they are anxious to talk or to do anything else to mitigate the pain or to cause it to stop. There is a moment when loss of vision, loss of sexual equipment, loss of nearly anything greatly valued in the past becomes secondary to anything but the mitigation of pain, however slight. It is an exquisite moment for a skilled interrogator. The sounds of confession could be discerned amidst agony's cacophony and truth from mere reaction to pain, given the interrogator had the blessing of Allah and the skills of Hamza.

Arlington, Texas

Hussein, the son of Hamza's brother who had fled Sana'a long ago as Hamza suffered the attention of the Yemeni Secret Police, worked for an airline in his new home, Texas. Hussein had finished his shift at Dallas/Fort Worth International Airport, where he was supervisor of a cleaning team for American Airlines. He and his charges cleaned airplanes flown back to Dallas after a day or three of carrying passengers from hither to yon. The detritus of air travel was disgusting in its completeness. They cleaned dried vomit, baby waste, paper, even used condoms. There was disturbing hilarity in the voices of his infidel coworkers as they speculated on needing a condom on an airplane and the contortions required to make effective use of it. Despite Hussein's college associate's degree in sociology and no matter how hard Hussein and his team worked, it never seemed quite enough for his boss. Hussein was twenty-six years old and had not had a promotion for nearly five years. It was no doubt because he was an intelligent and devoted Muslim among stupid and godless infidels. It could also be, perhaps, because of his open and vocal disdain for his female supervisor, who called him "Hoss" instead of Hussein. She sat on her fat behind at a desk doing paperwork all day as she sneaked frequent peeks on her computer at *Oprah* and other tawdry daytime shows.

At day's end, Hussein drove his truck south, toward the Interstate 30 freeway just northwest of Dallas. It was crowded with the afternoon rush of cars, trucks, SUVs, and buses, as Hussein approached it. The ratio of trucks and SUVs to passenger cars on the freeway was higher than would be found in most Eastern cities in the US, perhaps because of the pervasive influence of what was called the "cowboy" mentality in Texas. Texans tended to view themselves as superior to the citizenry of the rest of the country, in general and as outdoor specialists requiring special transportation; it was frustrating to many that they had yet to be proven wrong. Hussein's truck was an unusual one, appearing from the outside to be an aging Ford F350 three-ton truck with dual rear wheels and a white plastic cap covering its bed. The engine was expertly maintained by Hussein. He checked the electronics daily to avoid lighting problems that might attract police scrutiny. Inside the truck, precisely in the center of its bed, was a pair of round steel plates, one with a hole in the middle and clamps jutting within the hole. The plates were held by a number of new truck shock absorbers bolted around their perimeter. A stainless steel storage box was mounted across the front of the bed, secured with a heavy padlock. The roof of the cap had a long, wide panel that had been sawn out of the fiberglass, then clamped back roughly in the same place. It rattled as Hussein drove the truck just over the speed limit, west to his home in Aledo and to his wife and four children. Another child was about to join his son and three daughters.

Hussein merged to the ramp, west on Interstate 30. In a few minutes, he approached the enormous, domed mass of Cowboys Stadium, just to his south. Hussein slowed and gazed at it for a long time. He loved American football. He was in awe of Cowboys

Stadium. It was new and had seats for eighty thousand people, with room for twenty thousand more to stand. Its cost was said to have been more than one billion dollars. There was a domed roof that opened and closed. Near the top of the structure, rooms as big as a house were decorated for the rich and powerful to watch sporting events in decadent comfort. Or so he had read.

The home team, the Cowboys, was to play the New York team, the Giants. It promised to be an exciting game. The last time they had played, there were more than one hundred thousand people inside, watching and working. Cowboys Stadium was perfect.

In a rented storage unit garage not far from where Hussein drove were several items that together comprised a gift for Cowboy Stadium and its infidel inhabitants. He had a steel tube painted green with a locking mechanism on its closed bottom and adjustable steel legs in front that folded out to keep the open end of the tube pointed skyward once attached to the base plate in his truck. He had a GPS to record the location where he would choose to park his truck for least notice. Grid coordinates from Google Maps would pinpoint the Cowboys helmet logo painted at the middle of the fifty-yard line in the stadium. There was an electronic sighting mechanism. Hussein knew how to connect the dots.

Planning was not difficult for Hussein since he was quite bright. He had been to training in Afghanistan several years before, but was forbidden by his father's brother to return lest Hussein's importance be discovered by his infidel government. Since then, he had been sent computer disks by mail with videos that instructed him in the best use of the mortar. Written responses to questions were required by return mail to ensure that both his devotion and understanding were acceptable, if unsupervised. Hussein invariably scored well on the examinations. There were four mortar rounds in his storage unit; three were yellow and seemed new. The fourth was old and painted gray. The mortar rounds were to be aimed and fired at Cowboys Stadium during the football game between the Cowboys and the New York Giants and were set to burst twenty meters above the Cowboys logo. The halftime delay, midway into the contest, was the ideal time to fire since television coverage would be most intense then and the field would be crowded. Shrapnel would be hot, driven rain on the people within. Their response would be panic. Many would be trampled in their cowardly rush to the exits, Allah be praised.

Hussein had done extensive research to find the best firing spots for his mortar, and for personal egress. The best spots had easy exits to the freeway system. Hussein was confident that his skills, once demonstrated, would be required on a regular basis. It was thus important that he not be captured and interrogated. His father's brother was a noted warrior and planner in Yemen; he had planned the attack on Cowboys Stadium. Hussein had received a recent message that his mortar rounds would soon be supplemented with six new, more reliable and potent ones. He was to fire the new rounds first, then drive away to a second site and turn his lovely mortar's attention to the enormous parking lot surrounding Cowboys Stadium. Google knew its location too. Parking lots would be crowded with dead and dying as emergency units attempted to deal with Hussein's handiwork. Those still living would be in a panic. He would set his TiVo to record the event and watch its glorious execution later, perhaps twice or more. It was possible, even likely, that there would television coverage from helicopters or even the garishly painted blimp with the white dog on its nose.

Hussein's new orders had been specific. He was to drive to a specific shop in Plano, a city he knew well, just up the freeway, on each of three days to meet the deliverer of the new ammunition and several boxes containing a secret substance. The time for each meeting was in the early evening when most were at home following the evening meal. There was a password and response to be given, just as shown in the spy movies. If the man did not arrive with the merchandise by the end of the third day, Hussein was to proceed with the attack as the previous plan specified. If the man arrived, Hussein was to use the new rounds as specified in the stadium and subsequent parking lot attack, then drive north and west toward Denver to evade any police that may find a way to identify him. He was to disperse a pinch of a secret substance from a hand held high in the air anytime there was a breeze coming from the west. Hussein swelled with pride each time he thought of being chosen to disperse a secret agent on behalf of Allah.

Allahu Akbar.

West Texas

It was late afternoon when the riding party came ambling back to the Clemens ranch, horses close and their riders talking casually. Cottonmouth, with Alex aboard, seemed happy and placid while he walked beside LuAnn and her mount. As they entered the yard and turned to the corral, ranch hands came forward to take the horses and help the riders down from their perches. As Alex dismounted and turned to Caitlin, one of the hands, a young man, reached for Cottonmouth's bridle. In a flash, Cottonmouth spun his head and knocked the man to the ground and then bared his teeth, reaching for him. Alex yelled, "Hey!" and Cottonmouth stopped as he felt Alex's hand on the top of his head, pressing hard, then faced back to the front, again apparently placid. Alex stuck out his hand and helped the ranch hand to his feet, then brushed a little red dust from his shirt.

"Sorry about that, young fellow," he said. "He's sensitive. I whisper nice things to him. He likes that." Two older hands stood, jaws agape at the horse's change in behavior, then shook their heads. Just across the yard, Mikey relaxed on his horse with one leg thrown over the saddle horn, grinning and rolling a smoke.

Virgil leaned against a log pillar at the main house, in the shade, watching the four chatting casually, making their way to the house. When Alex and Caitlin came abreast of him, Virgil said, "Alex, could I have a word with you in private?"

"Sure thing, Virgil," Alex said. "Caitlin, I'll catch up with you at the bar in a minute." Caitlin nodded over her shoulder as she walked inside.

Virgil stepped inside the house and said quietly, "I heard from Mikey that he told you about those nasty critters in the village. If there's anything I can add to the picture to make a believer out of you, let me know. I'd like to make them go away."

Alex smiled and said, "I e-mailed the photo that your man, Gomez, took in the cantina to a friend in DC this morning, along with a heads-up. I imagine someone is already looking into it. I may drop by there after dinner for a look."

"Is this likely to be something where you or Elliot gets involved?" Virgil said. "Mikey said you were in that business for awhile. Elliot for sure was in the violence business."

"We're out of that business," Alex said. "If there is something to be done, the pros will do it. Brooks and I are old and tired. We'd just get in the way, but if I hear that something went down, I'll let you know."

"Good. I'd rather not have any trouble here, but if it's coming, I'd like to be ready."

"I don't think it will come to that," Alex said. "You're too far from the border. Still, I'll keep my ears open. I'm heading back to DC tomorrow for a few days."

"Thanks. Brooks and LuAnn are headed back to New York. Caitlin's going with you, I think."

"At least for a day or two," Alex said. "Right now, I think it's time for me to have a glass of wine."

"Caitlin may be getting impatient," Virgil said with a chuckle. "She's not one that I'd keep waiting. Good information technology managers are hard to find."

Caitlin handed Alex a glass of red wine as he reached the bar. She picked up a small bowl of peanuts and walked toward the stairs. He was a step behind.

Alex dropped his hat on the bed, then sank into one of the chairs. He put his glass on the side table. Caitlin pulled off her boots and dropped them to the floor. She plopped into his lap, kissed him lightly at first, and then with more attention. Her left hand tangled in his sweaty hair, as her tongue probed his. She began unbuttoning her shirt with her right hand.

"You seem to have something kinky in mind, my dear," Alex murmured. "May I be of service?"

Caitlin pulled one arm from her shirt and then leaned back against Alex's grip. As she arched, one breast brushed Alex's lips and the shirt slid from her other arm to the floor.

"Unfinished business," she said. "Do you want to lick the sweat off me now, or should I jump in the shower for a minute first?"

Alex chuckled. "Tough decision. Shower, I guess. Shall I join you?"

"Charmed, I'm sure," Caitlin said, as she rolled from his lap to her feet. She unbuttoned her jeans and worked them down over her hips, then stepped out of them. She threw the jeans in a pile in the corner, kicked her shirt in that direction, peeled off one sock and threw it on the pile, and then the other, hopping from left foot to right. She bent over and looked at him through her legs and stuck out her tongue. She walked toward the bathroom, shaking her bare behind at him.

Alex pulled off his boots, stood, and undressed. He folded his things and put them beside a large wooden dresser. Then he picked up her shirt from the floor, then the pile of her clothes, folded them and put them beside his. He put both pair of boots next to them.

A Bose speaker set up was on the dresser with Alex's iPod beside it. He turned it on and thumbed through a few albums from iTunes until he found what he wanted. He hit Play and stuck the base of the iPod into the player. The soft sound of a tenor saxophone playing a tune named "Mosaic" floated from it.

As Alex stepped into the shower, Caitlin handed him a large bar of soft wet soap. She was covered from neck to toes with thick suds. There was a large bath towel in the corner of the glass-enclosed shower, by a triangular seat built into the corner.

Alex began to lather his arms and chest. When he finished with his feet, Caitlin stepped closer, and said, "I'll do this part here."

Alex was having trouble focusing. "You're taking first dibs?"

"Uh-huh, I wouldn't want you to be distracted during your delicate forthcoming endeavor," she whispered in his ear as she led him back under the water cascading from a shower head that seemed the size of a manhole cover, then stood on her tip toes and ran her tongue around the inside of his ear.

"Sit right there," Caitlin said and pointed at the triangular seat by the now-sopping towel.

Alex sank to the seat. Caitlin moved the showerhead to point the flow at Alex's stomach for a final rinse, then away. She moved the bath towel to a spot between his feet, doubled it over, and knelt on it.

"What do you think, big guy? Like the view?" Caitlin said with a wide grin, her startling, faded blue eyes locked on his. She leaned forward and reached for him, maintaining eye contact. Her elbows were on his upper thighs. Her chin was on her left hand.

"It's both erotic and stunning—a first," Alex groaned. "You are truly a witch, aren't you?"

Later, they lay on the bed, sated, while Caitlin played idly with his hair.

"I'm liable to chip a tooth with all that jaw clenching," she said. "That was a good ride, cowboy. Who would have guessed you could demonstrate such verve and subtlety while accompanying old John Klemmer playing his tenor sax?"

"I do a good Bob James too. He has a great duet with Earl Klugh. If you have to chip a tooth, how better than accompanied by good jazz, my sweet?" He turned his head and kissed her inner thigh, then slid down and rolled from the bed.

"I guess we'd better get dressed," Alex said. "That should last us both for a little while. The short time that refreshes."

"Uh-huh. I think I'll keep you around for awhile," she said.

She walked nude to a small table with a mirror and began to comb her hair. "Last night was interesting," she said. "Are you going to hit Virgil up for some help in our project tonight, or let it go for awhile?"

"We need to let Virgil absorb the idea, and give LuAnn time to talk to him. She gets it. We should wait until we see how well Brooks does with his father on the Elliot Scholar idea too," Alex said. "Clothe your magnificent body and we'll see what's next. It might help if you allowed that post-coital glow to fade a bit."

"Uh-huh. Well, the good news is that's it's not post coital, just post orgasmic," she said. "That's what I like about you."

"Well, there's that," Alex said. "The relationship is certainly different, but I like it. It's enough for now."

"For now?" Caitlin said. "You aren't getting serious about me?"

"It's crossed my mind. I'm around you often, but we date seldom. I like you a lot. Is that a problem?"

"I like you too, but serious? That would be a problem," Caitlin said. "That would be a bad thing. I don't need or want anything serious. I like working with you, but I don't want any part of a serious relationship, with you or anyone else."

"So what are we doing here?" Alex asked. "I guess I don't have anything figured out, beyond the obvious."

"Okay, here's the way it is," said Caitlin. "I have zero interest in being married, and far less in having any kids. I'm fully committed to myself. There's no room for anyone else. A lover is a plaything, used to scratch an itch. Still, you're the best thing I've found in awhile, all things considered."

"And what things would those be, that you considered about me?"

"First, you're handy for sex because we work together. Second, you don't bore me, which is easily done."

"I'm glad you don't get bored so far. I'm certainly not bored. I guess the control thing is okay, as long as you don't get to tying me up."

"I like the sex with you better than I have for a long time with anyone."

"As an 'after' statement, that's a good recommendation," Alex said, "even just after I get told that I'm not marriage material. I can't quite recall anyone commenting quite that directly about it. Tell me more."

"You want me to stroke your ego a little, huh?" Catlin said. "Well, it ain't the size of your whatchamacallit. That could be a big negative, at least in a more traditional sexual relationship than we've had so far, except maybe to provide shade at a private picnic. The sex is good for me. I imagine the sex is good with me, the way I prefer to do it. That seems to be what guys like best, if they can watch. I like it that you don't try to get control. You leave it all up to me. I simply can't abide the thought of you having my legs up, knees against my chest, your weight pinning me down while you have your way, as they say. You've never tried to be on top—in control. I like that."

"Well, you do have a well-developed skill that's unusual in a woman as good-looking as you."

"Yeah," Caitlin said, with a grin. "I know all the tiny spots. I work at it."

"I can't imagine anyone better. You are truly in control. Instinct?"

"Nah, DVDs and investigative morphology," she said. "I bought some instructional DVDs on Amazon, 'Fellatio for Dummies' kinds of things, and watched them two or three times each and took notes. Then I did a bunch of fieldwork on one of my colleagues at Caltech who was older and had been married twice."

"He didn't mind you being in control?"

"He learned," she said. "Once he put his hand on the back of my head and grabbed my hair as he neared the explosive end of a practice session."

"Did he? That would be a bad thing for a control person to suffer," Alex said. "Did you counsel him about that?"

"Nope. I bit him—hard."

"Yikes!"

"Yeah, he let go of my hair and my head and went limp as soggy vermicelli, in the course of about fifteen microseconds. I was ready to punch him in the balls a time or two. I had a very good angle. But he didn't act up; he just rolled away, curled up, and groaned for awhile. Maybe they were whimpers, but no happy ending."

"I'm still not going to let you tie me up, even if you promise not to bite."

"So, you get a decent-looking woman who wants to be with you socially and sexually from time to time," Caitlin said, "and will work at making sex work for both of us. I've worked at being good at the stuff that gives me control. I'm kinkier than you, given that you're not all that kinky except that maybe you're a homicidal maniac. I'll try to make sure you have a good time. And I won't tie you up. Does all that work for you?"

"Is this an exclusive arrangement?"

"God, no! I'll see others when I choose. If I see someone else, I'll try not to embarrass you. Just don't bring some ugly malady home. I'll be careful too. You see whomever you choose. Look at it from my point of view, which is, of course, pretty much the only point of view that matters to me. You're smart enough, usually, you give great head, and you have enough to work with that I can be unusually creative. I'm devoted to the big idea of rebirth of the Muslim world and working my capable ass off at it. I'm usually horny. You are a handy confluence of the needs I have."

"On that mixed note, let's get dressed and go get a drink before dinner," Alex said. "It works for me, I guess." It occurred to him that it was increasingly unlikely he'd find a wife if he maintained his current course with Caitlin. Worse, no kids. Alex began to consider life with Caitlin in another ten years. She made no promises of continuity and apparently had no interest in a relationship that was closer than the one they had. On the other hand, Alex loved being around her professionally. The product of Caitlin's intellect had become essential to their efforts. Her work was indeed a major accelerant for their combined path of profits and societal rebirth, one funding the other over time. At his urging, Caitlin brought Emilie each month to a point that it could run at current levels and capability "if she got hit by a bus," as she put it; she hated doing it, but did it and carefully backed it up. She had yet to ignore a solid, logical argument about important or even mundane things that could be done only by her. She was supremely and frustratingly logical. She neither denied her egocentricity nor argued for it. It just was and she was not going to change it. It was a part of how she viewed her world. How Alex viewed his personal world was of only mild interest to her and then only as it affected her. She neither denied that nor apologized for it.

. . .

At the other end of the house, LuAnn's suite was large, with two desks, a large sitting area, and a bath complex with two sinks, tub, shower, and steam. She and Brooks finished at their desks, then sat in two of the chairs in the sitting area in front of a big window.

"You're not looking for trouble with your little trip to town with Alex later, are you?" she asked.

"I'm not. Alex just wants a look at the guy that Gomez saw. I'll tag along and wait for him outside."

"If there's trouble, though, you don't want to miss it," LuAnn said with a little snort. "Right?"

Brooks smiled. "Call it an addiction," he said.

"Anyway, good news about Jeeter," LuAnn said. "I'm glad Alex wasn't hurt."

Brooks picked up his water, looked at her, and smiled faintly. "Yeah, me too."

"What?" LuAnn said. "It's not funny. Jeeter is a big guy. He wins most of his fights."

"I'm glad Jeeter is still alive," Brooks said. "An inch higher with the elbow and his head would have been caved in. No need for an ambulance."

"Well, I'm glad too, but it was Jeeter who attacked Alex," she said. "Alex could have been hurt."

"That's why I was smiling. There was close to a zero chance that Alex could have been hurt," Elliot said with a chuckle. "I had never seen that move Alex used. It's fabulous, but I can't imagine how many times he had to practice it to get the move that smooth."

"You're telling me Alex wasn't surprised? That he practiced for Jeeter doing this, or someone else?"

"Oh, he was surprised by Jeeter, but the way he took the hit drove his reaction. The move was too smooth and too reflexive to be a casual response. He had practiced being tackled, at least hundreds of times. Maybe a lot more. Alex is enormously strong, but he moves like a Pakistani squash pro. He's smooth, quick, and huge."

"You aren't telling me he's better than your top Seal?"

"He's a killer, not really just a fighter. He could have been a top wrestler, I'm told, but he's always looking for the chance to kill the opponent, not pin him to the mat. That's what they taught him for eight years, from age seventeen. He taught our top Seal instructors his brand of things when they came to the Farm."

"Jesus."

"Yeah."

"You met him at Oxford?"

"No, I met him several years before that."

"You're closing up on me again," LuAnn said. "Are you going to talk to me? I've been rather open with you about my life because I like you. That's part of the reason I'm learning Arabic and Sharia law. Here you are meeting my father. If Alex, the charming monster, is going to be in my life, and I like him, mind you, I need to know about him. It's mostly because I seem to need to get to know more about you. I know almost nothing personal about you other than the observation that you know your way around a woman's body, God bless whoever she is or was. But this relationship will end soon if I don't think I know who you are and you don't want to tell me."

Brooks leaned back in the chair and put his hands behind his head. After a long pause, he said, "I've been looking for a chance to tell you all of this for awhile. The time hasn't yet been right. There a lot to tell, in a lot of different genres."

"And when was this little mea culpa to start?"

"LuAnn, we'll start whenever you're ready. I've been waiting."

"You are so full of shit, Elliot," she erupted. Two big hoots of laughter later, she said, "But I just love your mind. That's why I put up with this shit from you. You can create a positive listening environment when you get stuck with the truth as a bad reply. I think you went to the Oxford school of sales for smart people."

Elliot sat with his hands still behind his head, gazing at her with full attention. He had raised his right eyebrow. "You got a two-fer. You got a very clever person to be around, who is fun to work closely with. I got one of those too."

LuAnn had her chin on her hand, leaning on the arm of the chair. She had a faint, almost whimsical smile on her face. Her face was a little sunburned, which made her hazel eyes seem to glow.

"So here it is," LuAnn said. "I'm getting interested in you. That's dangerous for me, and a first. What you didn't choose to say was that the information about your group was a tad sensitive to discuss in depth with any old stranger. I was being vetted and now I've passed. There is no real line drawn between Kufdani Industries and you five. It's all one game. I want to know about it."

Elliot grinned. "Another two-fer. Good for you. You got Kufdani under your immediate disclosure covers too."

"Thanks," LuAnn said, "I thought it was cool. I'm merely trying to catch up to you."

She stood and walked to the long bar and pick up a bag of peanuts. She ripped the top corner off as she walked back to her chair.

"As I said, I'm getting interested in you, no surprise since you're here at my home. It's time to freeze things in place or let them continue to develop. I like where things are going too. But tonight will be interesting."

Brooks had come forward on his seat. "Pass, fail?"

"Yeah, pretty much pass, fail on our relationship," LuAnn said. "I can't take the chance of getting hurt that badly if I let it run. I've done what I can do."

"You'll tell me?"

LuAnn smiled that same smile. "You don't think you'll know?"

Brooks again put his hands behind his head, leaned back in his chair, and began to talk.[2]

"I met Alex early one morning a little north of Beirut near a seaside village named Halat. I was lying in the dirt at the edge of the beach, shot and bleeding heavily, unable to do my job as the escape shooter on a Seal mission. The escape shooter is the one that covers friendly guys as they run away from a target and back to the boats; I was good at it. Alex was there as the demolitions man; he's good at that. I could see him in my night scope with the four corners of his vest lit up in infrared the way we did to identify the good guys in a shooting crowd. He was running faster than I would have guessed, given his size. Then I got hit. Suddenly Alex was beside me, mopping up the bad guys giving chase, using my M14 and picking fresh magazines from my bloody vest. When the last Seal went by, Alex picked me up in a fireman's carry and threw me over his shoulder. He ran about a hundred and twenty-five yards at a sprint, passing other runners along the way; I was told I weighed one ninety-six with my gear. He tossed me into a RIB, a rigid inflatable boat, and a corpsman started treating my wounds. I would have bled out in another two minutes, I was told later. I heard the story from the sub

---

2   For detail and context, see: www.robertcooknovels.com/footnotesPatriot

surgeon while he hung a blood transfusion bag on my arm. I looked Alex up on the sub on the way out to say thanks. We've been friends ever since. Better friends since we were at Oxford, when we spent quite a bit of time together."

"Enough about Alex. I get it," she said. "I'm interested in you. Tell me something that helped make you who you are. Tell me a Brooks Elliot story, how you were formed, O Rhodes Scholar, Princetonian, investment banker, Seal. The interplay among those must make for some good stories. Probably some good insight for me too."

Brooks sat thinking. If there was a formative time, it had probably been when he was about fourteen.

"My mother died the summer I was fourteen," Elliot said. "I needed a place to live, other than the family houses in Connecticut and DC. So I went to boarding school at Stafford, in Connecticut. All-boys school, good faculty. I didn't have a good record for getting along with poor teachers. My father was a big time senator, even then. The senator was dealing with his grief and I was struggling with mine. I went to prep school. My father went to work in DC. I was maybe five foot four and a hundred and twenty pounds.

"The groundskeeper from home drove me to Stafford for first-year orientation. I heard a speech, I got a class schedule, got assigned a room and a roommate, a really geeky kid. The geek was obscenely fat and passed a lot of gas. His name was Reginald Ketcher Edgeworth. He said to call him Edgie. I was not happy.

"That evening we walked together to the dining hall for dinner and I figured out on the way that Edgie was a pretty good guy, just really shy and really smart. Halfway through dinner the two of us start to get a ton of crap from six or eight of the older boys who were returning to Stafford rather than just entering. They started making fun of Edgie, calling him Tubbo, Fatman, Lardass, names like that.

Then one guy reached in and pinched him on the stomach, then another. There was a lot of noise, and Edgie started to cry. A guy pinched me on the stomach, and I slapped the hand away, hard. The biggest guy in the crowd grabbed me out of my chair by my shirt-front and shook me. He said, 'Apologize to my friend here for slapping him or I'm going to slap you.' I saw that he had whiskers—that he shaved, for crying out loud. He had to be seventeen. Big arms. I was scared to death, but still shook my head no."

LuAnn leaned forward. "Not an august beginning," she said.

"No," Brooks said. "It seemed a too shameful capitulation of some sort. I'm still not good about giving in or quitting."

"A useful trait, sometimes."

"Useful if you want to be a Seal, for sure."

"I assume things got worse, quickly," LuAnn said.

Brooks had a sudden recall of getting hit for the first time. "Boom, I was on the floor with the big guy on me, kneeling on my arms, punching me in the face, right in the middle of the dining hall.

"'All right boys, enough of that,' yelled the dining proctor, one of the staff, who ran over and dragged the guy off me. I got up. My nose was bleeding a little. I walked back to my place at the table. Edgie was still crying and wouldn't look at me, for fear they'd start on him again. Everyone sat down.

"'What's your name, pussy?' the big guy—it turned out his name was Shelby—asked me. The entire table was watching.

"'Elliot,' I said.

"'Well, I don't like you, Pussy Elliot, and I don't like Lardass either. When we walk out of here, I'm going to kick the living shit out of you and then him. You are going to cry.'

"I had no idea what to do. I had never been in a fight. I was terrified. Neither Edgie nor I ate much after that and we got up quickly to head for the door before the others finished eating. The others scraped back their chairs and were right behind us. Edgie was through the door first and started running back to the room. I was tripped and went down. I tried to bounce up quickly when I got slammed to the ground and rolled over. It was Shelby again, who tried to get his knees on my arms, but I was bucking to get him off me, panicked. So he just sat on me and punched me in the face with both hands until he got tired, then got his knees on my arms and punched me some more. When Shelby finally got up, I had a bloodier nose and two eyes that would swell and turn purple and green. Two teeth were loose and I had a screaming headache.

"'Come on, guys,' Shelby said. 'Let's get back to the dorm and let this piece of shit lie here. He'll get up after a bit.' They walked off laughing and talking excitedly. 'He'll say he's sorry tomorrow and again next week.'

"I got up after I was sure they were gone and limped back to my room. The door was locked. 'C'mon, Edgie, it's just me, Elliot. I'm alone,' I said. There was scraping as something was moved away from the door and then the click of the latch.

"Edgie was there, eyes streaked red and bulging like a cow's, but no longer crying. 'Jesus Annie, Elliot, you're a mess. I'm sorry I ran.' He started to cry again.

"'Yeah, well, I tried to run and didn't make it,' I said. 'Help me get cleaned up, Edgie. I can't see too well and tomorrow is our first day of school.'

"The next few days were ones of getting books, meeting teachers, and doing admin chores. I didn't run into Shelby, although I saw him across the quadrangle from time to time. I was afraid of him and the swelling in my eyes hadn't gone down yet. My face was sore. I didn't want to see Shelby or any of the others.

"Later that week, I was walking to an American history class when I saw Shelby coming directly down the path across the quadrangle at me with two of his friends. Shelby's face lit up when he saw me. He turned his head to laugh and say something to a boy walking beside him. The American history book was heavy. I thought about dropping it so I could run better, but the two boys with Shelby spread out to either side of the path, cutting me off if I wanted to make history class. As Shelby swaggered close to me, I grabbed the bottom of that history tome with both hands and swung it like a baseball bat into Shelby's face. My follow-through was good and Shelby dropped onto his back, his face bloody. I dropped the book and jumped into the air with my feet tucked under me and landed with both knees on Shelby's stomach to the fine whoosh of breath exploding from his throat. I punched him in the face twice. I felt someone grab my left arm, pulling me to my feet. I came up fast, and out of instinct turned into my new assailant and drove a knee into his lower stomach. I got a grip on his shoulders, then pulled my knee back and drove it into his chest as he folded over. The third knee was into his face. I turned for the third boy in the group, but he was running, yelling. I picked up my bloody history book and turned to jog to my history class. My hands were starting to shake wildly. Shelby had come to his knees and was trying to catch his breath. He got a soccer kick to the face and went down again, moaning. I turned and kicked the second man in the stomach, then jogged off to class. For some reason, I was more scared than before the encounter.

"That afternoon, Mr. Brooks F.T. Elliot the Fourth was summoned to the office of the headmaster.

"'You are a coward and a ruffian, Mr. Elliot,' Headmaster Hansen said. 'There are witnesses to your brutal, unprovoked attack on two fine young men at Stafford. They were to be your mentors and your friends, Mr. Elliot, not your punching bags or objects of your dirty fighting. Have you no honor?'

"'Look at my face, Mr. Hansen,' I said. 'The three of them attacked me just the way you say I attacked them, and they did it first.'"

"'We at Stafford know those fine young men and their generous parents, Mr. Elliot,' Hansen said. 'We know little about you other than you are apparently not the sort of young gentleman we seek at Stafford. At worst these matters should be disputed with organized fisticuffs; boxing is a gentleman's sport. Socrates was a noted wrestler, but there is no mention of him kicking or kneeing his opponents. I am aware, however, of your personal situation and your terrible loss. I understand this new situation may have colored your emotions and your judgment of appropriate behavior. You may remain at Stafford, on probation. But a single additional example of ruffian behavior will result in your immediate dismissal from Stafford. That is all, Mr. Elliot.'

"'Yes, sir,' I said. 'Thank you, sir.' I walked through the door in a hurry.

"I couldn't imagine my father's reaction if I got tossed out of Stafford, but he would be disappointed. I feared his disapproval and disappointment, but most of all, the senator didn't like surprises. I had found I could get away with a lot if I didn't surprise my father with what I said or did. So I called my father when I got to my room.

"When I finished with the telling, there was a long silence. Finally Pop said, 'I haven't known you to tell whopper lies, so I'll buy your telling of the story. The issue at hand is what you should do next, how you should live your Stafford life.'

"I immediately promised not to get into anymore fights.

"There was a sigh and a pause on the phone. 'Bad promise, I'm afraid, Junior,' the senator said. 'If people know you won't fight, they'll be comfortable baiting you. Sooner or later, you'll react, and out of Stafford you go. That wouldn't be the end of the world. We can find another school, but I imagine you can stay at Stafford and like it, if you choose. The worst of the first year hazing is probably over.'

"'Then what should I do, Pop?' I said.

"'The boys who attacked you are bullies. Bullies have mostly predictable behavior. I think you should find a way to raise their fear.'

"'Fine, Pop, but I don't know how to do that.'

"'When you see the leader, ask him for a quiet word alone. Then tell him that this time was not so bad, but if there is a next time, it will be worse, far worse. Use your imagination when you tell him what you'll do to him next time. He'll toe the line, I imagine. But don't hesitate if he comes after you again. Tear into him with everything you have before he is set; always do it before he is set. Feet, fists, knees, teeth, all of it. We'll find another school.'

"A few days later, outside the auditorium, I encountered Shelby and asked for a word in private. When we were alone, Shelby said, 'I don't like you. What do you want?'

"I leaned to Shelby's ear and said, 'Shelby, you sucker punched me, twice. That pisses me off. The reason you're not in a wheelchair for the rest of your life, or blind, is that I'd like to stay here at Stafford. I tried not to hurt you. If you fuck with me again or one of your stooges does, I'm going to hurt you bad, real bad. Your football days will be over. Your father can buy you a dog to guide you around in your wheelchair. Got it?'

"Shelby wouldn't look at me, but murmured, 'Got it.'"

Brooks smiled at LuAnn and said, "And the rest of my time at Stafford was very pleasant. I studied, swam on the team and no one bothered me. In fact, everyone was quite pleasant."

LuAnn laughed. "Yeah, I can see that. Who wants to be blind or crippled before they even get to college. Would you have done it?"

"I don't know, but neither did Shelby."

"And you were happy?" LuAnn said.

"Actually, I was miserable," Elliot said. "I went through three years with everyone wary of me, maybe even afraid. I didn't have any friends other than Edgie. I swam and studied. Being a swimmer yields a lot of time to think. Sometimes I woke up in the middle of the night and cried while I listened to Edgie snore and fart. Worse, he ruffled his covers a lot. Alex is the first real friend I ever had."

LuAnn sat for a few long moments, then said, "Would Alex have hurt them badly on the second opportunity if it arose?"

"I didn't know him at fourteen, but I'd guess not."

"But now he would, I gather," she said. "He's changed? He seems civilized. What happened to change him?"

"The evolving definition of civility, I suppose. I think Alex might have been happier with a horse and a lance."

"Well, between the two of you, I imagine you'll be safe enough down at the cantina."

• • •

Two hours later Mikey grinned as Alex and Elliot walked down the path from the ranch house to Mikey's office and quarters beside the bunk house. "You're a bit scruffy now, aren't you, Mr. Cuchulain?" Alex was in a dark T-shirt with a bandana tied around his hair. Elliot was quiet beside him, with a dark shirt, dark pants, and dark-leather hiking boots.

Alex said, *"Si, Chico."*

"You speak a little Spanish, do you?"

"Yeah, I do," Alex said. "It's a secret. All this shit is secret. I was never in the cantina with Gomez."

73

"What do you want to wear?"

"I'll wear my boots and my jeans. I'll need an old open-necked shirt, an old worn hat, and a crucifix maybe, to give me luck."

"Can do. One of Jeeter's shirts will fit you; he doesn't need them right now. The rest is easy. Listen, Gomez isn't sure you can pass as a Latino. He's nervous about it."

Alex laughed. "Going into a cantina full of bad guys makes one nervous. Let's get my clothes together, then Gomez and I will talk. You sit by. If he's still nervous about me, maybe I go in alone."

Mickey shrugged. "Gomez is a solid guy. It should be fine. It's not like we have a sand table to plan this mission. It's a sneak and peek."

"It is, indeed. And that's all it is. If trouble starts, I'll start it."

• • •

Later that evening, just after full darkness fell, Alex and Hector Gomez walked into a small cantina several miles closer to the Mexican border than the Clemens ranch. A quick, casual glance showed two small groups in the room, separated by a number of empty, cheap, wooden tables with flimsy chairs at them. On one side of the room were six men, most dressed in casual clothing. Two of them, with scruffy beards, were seated in the center of the group, dressed a little differently, with coffee mugs in front of them. Two others, who were younger and lean, drank beer from bottles. A very large man sat beside an older Mexican, who seemed by his body language to be in charge.

Alex and Gomez found a table at the edge of the other group, made up of a few locals. As they sat, Gomez studied Alex. If he hadn't seen him as part of the Clemens riding party, Gomez would have guessed he was a dangerous Mexican, someone to avoid. His Spanish was fluent and now colloquial, with a vague Mexican accent. Alex had done something to darken his face a little and the scars on his face stood out in white. There were many tiny scars on his forehead and the old furrow of a knife scar slid down his left cheek through thick wrinkles around his eye. The wrinkles were beside both eyes and seemed to bunch up in a hood beside them. He wore an old blue denim shirt, tight across the chest, with the sleeves rolled to the elbow and three buttons open at the neck to reveal a thick thatch of black chest hair with an ornate crucifix on a gold chain hanging amidst it. His forearms were huge and tracked with distended veins. Alex had large, lumpy, battered hands.

Gomez could hear Alex breathing fairly heavily through his nose. *This is so fucking exciting! Alex said call him Cooch before we left. His Spanish started as pure, upscale Castilian. He listened to me, then asked questions, then listened carefully again. After twenty minutes or so, Cooch said, "I think this language is close enough." He started talking in an accent that sounded like he was Mexican, from somewhere. For Mexicans that spend a lot of time out of the country, their accents get blurred. Cooch nailed the accent. Who the hell is this guy? Mikey seems to think he walks on water.*

A man brought two beers to them, and then spoke to Gomez.

"So, Hector," he said. "Welcome back. Who's your big friend? It's always nice to see a new face."

"A distant cousin from Baja California, Pedro," Gomez said. "We were childhood playmates. This is Alejandro. He's on his way east and stopped in for the evening. We decided to have a beer."

Pedro stuck out his hand, and Alex took it, standing. He loomed.

"*Hola*," Alex said, as he glanced across the room. Everyone in the room was looking at him, the newcomer. Across the room, the older Mexican studied him carefully.

75

Alex sat down as the bartender walked away and said to Hector, "These are bad guys. I know one of them, so we got what we came for. Let's finish our beer and get out of here."

Gomez nodded and tilted his bottle to his lips. He took two big gulps and put it down.

Alex tilted his bottle and took a sip, watching the leader in his peripheral vision. After a few moments, the older man turned and leaned to the large man beside him. He spoke a few words.

The man set his bottle on the floor and stood. He was wide, with no discernible waist. His hair was dirty, pulled back and held with a rubber band. He hitched his pants and began to approach their table, rolling a little as he walked. There was a confident grin on his face.

When he reached the table, Alex stood up from his chair.

"I am Gordo," he said, belly bumped Alex back into his chair, and smiled. Gordo had a gold rim around one of his front teeth and there was an incisor missing on the left. Alex reached to Gordo's elbow to catch himself as he was bumped, and again came to his feet, his index finger digging hard into the little elbow hollow where the funny bone is.

"Ngggh!" Gordo grunted. The surprise of the sharp electric pain immobilized him for a moment.

Alex turned the big man to his left after another deep squeeze into the elbow and brought his left hand to grasp Gordo's neck. His fingers reached under each ear to the point where the soft mastoid bones are most exposed. He squeezed hard with his thumb on one side and two fingers on the other side of the neck and felt the bones there yield slightly to his grip. The man was still, quivering from the pain.

"*Senor*," Cooch said to the older Mexican. "Your colleague is impolite. Is there a reason we should be adversaries?"

"Why are you here?" the man asked. He watched curiously as his messenger stood silent. It was out of character for Gordo to be passive.

"I am here to have a beer with my cousin before continuing my journey to the east. I have no reason other than that to be here. Have we met?"

"We have not, but you don't fit in here."

"We don't, it seems. We're happy to leave. A noisy altercation might draw the attention of the gringo police. I cannot afford that."

There was a long silence. "Neither, I suppose, can I afford that. But there are just two of you. We could easily kill you and hide your bodies. We plan to be here only a few more days."

"There are six of you and five of us," Alex said. "There may be no one left to dig the graves. And there is no profit in it for you or for me. You will be the first to die; your colleague beside me will be the second. I will likely be the third. It may be better if we just leave now."

"I think you are lying to me, *senor*. I see but two of you. The man of mine beside you appears to be useless as an enforcer. So kill him now as a gesture that you are not from the police, then convince me there are more of you. Do you need a knife? Your time is short."

• • •

On the drive to the cantina from the Clemens' ranch, Brooks had been in the passenger seat beside Proctor Mikey. Alex and Hector Gomez sat in the back seat of Mikey's Crew Cab F250 Ford pickup truck. It was the off-road model, painted a deep red, with big tires and four-wheel drive.

"Nice truck!" Alex had said.

77

Mikey smiled. "I call her BART, my big-ass red truck. I spend my money on trucks and rifles. I sell a little venison and some boar that I shoot. Since my old lady dumped me ten years ago, life's been pretty good."

"OK, let's keep life good," Brooks had said. "Here's the way we do these things, and this is all classified, so no bragging rights back at the ranch. Cooch and Hector will find a table that we can see, that is not in our line of fire, but in our vision. We'll zero in on the leader, if he is obvious. Cooch will look directly at him when he is standing.

"If it is going to get nasty, Cooch will point at something, like the edge of the bar or a vertical timber. There will be a knife sticking out of it. Shoot the knife at the center of the blade. If he points again, shoot a bottle. If he points at someone, shoot him dead. Then work from right to left and shoot anyone who produces a gun. One shot each. I'll put the two guys in the corner down and work left to right. At first, I'll avoid killing anyone who looks like an Arab, because we might want to talk to them. Hector, do *not* stand up after you sit down. If you have to shoot, drop and shoot from a kneeling position."

Mikey had grinned. "Fucking Seals," he said. "You don't leave much to chance."

"It sounds like you've been there, Mikey," Brooks had said. "With bad guys we try to leave nothing to chance, but we still manage to get a few buddies killed, from time to time. I'd like to avoid that here."

"Yeah," Mikey had said. "I don't disagree. It's just nice to work with the A team."

Cooch and Hector had been dropped short of the cantina, to walk the last fifty yards. Mikey had planned a spot to stop and Gomez had made a rough sketch of the interior of the cantina. The F250 moved quietly past the cantina, then switched off its lights and turned left onto a dirt road that curved back toward the way they had come.

Mikey had night-vision goggles pulled down. In a short time, the cantina was visible from the driver's window and Mikey had turned the truck with its hood away from the open window. The two men got out and lowered the tailgate, then crawled up on the bed of the pickup. Two thick mattress pads were laid out with several small sandbags of dull black nylon stacked at their sides.

Mikey opened a long box mounted against the side wall and picked up a bolt action Remington Model 700 rifle chambered in .308, with a Swarovski Z6*i* three to eighteen power scope mounted. He had a Leupold range finder dangling from his neck. He reached again and handed Brooks an old M14 semi-automatic rifle that showed signs of loving, professional care. It had a tactical scope mounted. Next came two loaded magazines for it. Mikey had reached again and came out with a small handful of cartridges. He opened the .308's bolt and began to push them, one at a time, into the ammunition well of his rifle.

"It's eighty-seven meters to Cooch. Your M14 is zeroed at one hundred yards with 140 grain Nosler bullets. What are we looking at here?" Mikey said a few moments later, as he looked through his range finder.

Elliot looked through his tactical scope, and said, "We can't see into one corner of the room. I'm going to go twenty-five yards west and find a new spot with a better view. In the meantime, shoot where the man points. Nice M14, by the way. I love this rifle."

Mikey reached again into the box, brought out two Motorola two-way radios, set the channels, and handed one to Brooks. Brooks dropped it into his shirt pocket and slid to the ground from the extended gate of the truck. He pulled his night-vision goggles down over his eyes. They were not the Generation Four goggles the Seals used, but Generation Two was good enough to see his way on a partially moonlit night.

• • •

Cooch reached with his right hand to Gordo's chin and released his left to hold the palm along his jaw line. Just as Gordo started to move, Cooch gave a hard, twisting snap with his right hand as he held the neckline from yielding with his left. There was a sound like a dry branch cracking. As the man crumpled to the floor, Cooch dropped his right hand behind his neck and in one motion threw a knife from a scabbard that hung there. It stuck, quivering, in a vertical wooden roof support beside the Mexican boss.

"I don't need a knife to kill him," Cooch said. "He's dead. There are now five of you. I could have made it four, but thought I would use the knife as a demonstration of your risk. As I said, I would rather not have noisy trouble."

"Do you have more than one knife, *senor*, or is that danger gone with your showmanship? What now? I've seen no evidence that there are more of you than I see."

Cooch pointed at the knife. It disappeared with a loud *spang;* the sound of a nearby shot followed closely through the open window.

"Now you have evidence," Cooch said. "May we now leave in peace?"

"You have murdered one of my men."

Cooch sighed loudly. "He was killed only at your request, *senor*. He wasn't much. I imagine he'd have died soon anyway if you are in the violence business. But I suspect violence is just a byproduct of something else you do."

"You know of the violence business?"

"We are *in* the violence business, *senor*. All we do is to sell violence and its enabling tools. It's usually a good business, but this evening is about to be bad for business. We aren't getting paid."

"You may leave, but I will remember you. I hope to kill you slowly someday."

"And I you, *senor*," Cooch said. He pointed at the bar. A bottle broke. He reached in his pocket, pulled a roll of bills from it, and dropped several on the table, then turned his back and walked to the door with Hector close behind, a 9mm Sig Sauer Model 229 pistol dangling from Hector's shaking hand and a huge grin on his face.

• • •

When Mac got out of bed the next morning, there was a note from Alex in his Kphone e-mail:

> Mac—
> I checked the cantina guy out last night—bad guy. I forget his name, but he was on the kill-on-sight list in Iraq five or six years ago. He's a little chubbier now. There are three Mexicans on guard and two Arabs. The civilians sit separate.
> Cuchulain

Early the following morning, Alex again relaxed with a mug of coffee in an unused rocking chair on the Clemens' porch. He had packed his things and picked up after Caitlin. She was back on her computer. Her packing would get done in the last forty-five seconds before they had to get in a car for the airport, everything stuffed randomly into three large bags.

He keyed his Kphone and waited.

"Alejandro Mohammed Cuchulain, as I live and breathe," a warm voice said after a few moments, in classical Arabic. "I thought you and Elliot would be off dogging horses or whatever one does at Texas ranches when traveling with overpaid and overachieving women. Good time had by all, I assume?"

Alex laughed. "Abdul, my friend. It's nice to hear your voice. No horse dogging, no cow dogging. You'll be disappointed to know there was not even sheep dogging. We all gained ten pounds. Eating, that's mostly what you do in West Texas. Good times were had by all. I'm heading for DC today. I plan to be hungry for real food."

"Well then," Abdul said. "Eating is something I do well. All sheep jokes can wait. Since I'm not going to cook and you can't cook here without your tools, let's have someone else cook for us. Any ideas?"

"I'll call Tagine. I won't tell Freddy that I'm bringing a Saudi, so I can get a decent table for us."

"I'll have you know the Arab League practically buys that place each month, we keep it so busy. But since you are about to undertake what civilized Arabs think of as the vast inconvenience of talking to a native Moroccan and understanding his dreadful accent, I shall bring an acceptable wine."

"Moroccan is the only true Arabic," Alex said, as he fluidly slipped into the least standard of all the Arabic dialects. "The rest of you are just jealous. Still, wine will be welcome."

Abdul Al-Fraih was the chief economist for the Arab League. Many years before at Oxford University, where he was a final year PhD candidate in economics, Abdul had given a lecture at the College of Oriental Studies, where Alex was a graduate student in Islamic history and philosophy. The lecture was to address the evolving economic dynamics of Islam, so Alex invited Brooks, who was at Oxford as a Rhodes Scholar, to join him. Elliot was a serious student of economics and its history in the seventeenth and eighteenth centuries, particularly among the Scottish thinkers. Their confluence of interests had caused the three of them to click that evening after the lecture, during consumption of a few pints at a local pub. A deep friendship evolved over a period of a few months. Many subsequent evenings were spent back then at Abdul's tiny house, just outside Oxford. Those meetings were still topics of intense discussion, where ideas and observations discussed were then argued, and argued again. Traditionally, Alex had cooked Moroccan-style foods in one of several *tagines* he owned, sent to him from Tangier. Brooks and Abdul did the cleanup. Some facet of the Muslim world was usually the topic.

Northwest Washington, DC

T hat evening Alex surrendered his rental car to a valet after dropping his bags at the Hay Adams Hotel.

The restaurant, Tagine, was a moderately well-kept secret, except among Arabs, in the Northwest quadrant of Washington, DC. It was near MacArthur Boulevard on a shady side street beyond Georgetown University. Its namesake, *tagine*, the uniquely Moroccan terra-cotta pot with the open-topped conical lid, was used for braising food. It was also used as a brazier-top or stove-top oven. The conical top traps heat and steam and the design causes it to circulate, much like a convection oven. There was more heat on its bottom than its top, so meat was put in first atop the prepared liquid for direct heat, then vegetables layered on top to cook in the flavorful circulating steam from the stock on the bottom. A *tagine* became evident on every table, on a small, raised, wrought-iron stand, as food was served. The color of a *tagine* often discloses its origin by the color of the clay that is used to form and fire it. Red *tagines* are made near Marrakesh, while those of a golden hue are from northern Morocco.

Tagine sat behind a wall of greenery. It was small, with both an indoor and outdoor seating area. Its exterior was filigreed in the Moroccan style and the door ornate, painted a deep gold. The noise of an engaged eating crowd floated over the wall.

Alex opened the gate and walked toward the door. From the side, by a table near an outdoor fireplace, a man in a white chef's jacket came running. His face was bearded and flushed, and a toothy smile flashed amidst a face of sweat-shined creases.

"Kufdani," he yelled in Moroccan-inflected Arabic. "I am so happy to see you." He grabbed Alex's hand and pumped it. "Come sit near me until Dr. Al-Fraih arrives. I am dying to hear someone speak our language properly. There are barbarians all around us."

He pulled Alex to a small table near the fire. "Tea, bring tea," he shouted to one of the servers. An ornate pot with matching cups showed up in seconds, filled with strong mint tea. Someone had just lost his tea order for a few moments. "Make Freddy happy" was Freddy's motto. Those who understood, lasted.

Alex was pulled to a chair. Moroccan Arabic is a difficult and distinctive dialect. Its rapid, staccato use is a matter of pride among the Moroccan masses and in the markets. Classical Arabic is the *lingua franca* among the various Middle Eastern countries and regions, used almost exclusively among intellectuals and politicians. Freddy was an ethnic Bedouin from near Tangier, and had several relatives working for Kufdani Industries. Tagine was the most common meeting place of Abdul and Alex. That was a matter of pride to Freddy.

"Dr. Al-Fraih called. He'll be a few minutes late. Saudis, you know."

Alex smiled. Ethnic bigotry was no stranger to the Muslim world. To any world, he supposed.

"I had a meal not long ago at Aziza, Mourad's place, in San Francisco," Alex said. "It was a berbere-cured chicken liver mousse, served as an appetizer. He used a little pink salt with it in the curing. It was sublime."

"I have his cookbook," Freddie said. "You put me onto it, I think, but no matter. Mourad is a culinary genius. I haven't made that dish yet, though. I shall, and soon. I must get back out West. I have a few thoughts for Mourad that will help his business. He's young and would benefit from my culinary wisdom."

"He skipped one of the milk soaks after the overnight cure with the berbere, and just did two soaks," Alex said. "Unbelievable. It was light and fluffy, with a pink cast like a *foie gras* preparation. He got a Michelin star for his fusion of Moroccan and California cuisine."

"And here you are, talking food again," a voice boomed in classical Arabic from the gate. Alex and Freddy both jumped to their feet and greeted him.

"Tea, more tea," Freddy yelled at no one in particular. It arrived quickly.

Later, Alex and Abdul were seated at a very private corner table in the back of the room. "I saw Brooks a few weeks ago," Abdul said. "We talk often, as you know. He's excited about progress in your endeavor. So am I."

"I'm certainly excited," Alex said. "The work within Emilie on education is stunning, simply stunning. We're doing both basic and trade education for about five cents per day, per student. Testing shows performance results in the eightieth percentile range compared to traditional teacher-led programs. In the US, school systems are spending, per student, anywhere from five thousand to thirteen thousand dollars a year. By definition the schools together perform at the fiftieth percentile. Twenty-five dollars or so up to seventy dollars, they spend, per day per student. They fudge their performance numbers. We don't."

"As our friend Brooks has said, 'There's a long running pony there,'" Abdul said. "We certainly need one."

A server arrived at the table with a small plate of *rghaif,* a crepe-like pastry stuffed with marinated red onion, goat cheese, and chopped dates. Freddy didn't like to be told what to serve his special friends. There were two *rghaif,* cut into thirds.

Both men reached for a piece and took a bite. "I remember from a hundred years ago that you used to make these in England and serve them hot with honey and melted fontina cheese," Abdul said, chewing.

"These are better," Alex said, as he raised his hand to Freddy, who was watching anxiously for a sign of approval. Freddy had once had Alex's *rghaif* in Tangier and declared it superior. "I haven't had *rghaif* for months, but that time in Oxford does indeed seem like a hundred years ago."

"I saw you handed a wine bag to Freddie when you came in," Alex said. "A good find?"

"I'll let you decide," Abdul said, grinning. "You have a great red wine palate, especially among us Arabs who don't drink unless forced by the infidels. A deputy ambassador was transferred back to Saudi Arabia from here recently. He had thirteen hundred bottles that he said were too much trouble to ship, plus he claimed he had no room in his wine cellar in Riyadh. He sent it over along with the electric portable cellar where he was storing it."

A nod from Abdul brought Freddy hurrying across the room with a decanter in his one hand and an unopened bottle in the other. He plucked a corkscrew from his back pocket and opened the bottle. He sniffed the cork, then wiped the bottle's opening with a clean napkin and turned the bottle to Alex to approve the label and the wine.

"Oh. My. God," Alex said. "I've died and gone to heaven. A forty-seven Cheval Blanc?"

"A whole damned case. Can you believe it?" Abdul said, nearly giggling. "This is the first bottle of it that's been opened."

"I think Robert Parker, the wine critic from up the road in Baltimore, gave it a max score and said something like, 'it poured more like a port than a Bordeaux.'" Alex swirled the wine in the base of the tall Riedel glass, then tilted it and buried his substantial nose into its top. His mouth was slightly open as he took a deep breath through his nostrils. He lifted the glass to his lips, took a small sip, and held it in his mouth. He looked like he was chewing, then swallowed. "I believe 'unctuous' was the adjective he used for its texture. How appropriate."

"Freddie, I think you'll have to check this," Alex said. "And pour a little nip for Dr. Al-Fraih too, before you decant it." After a taste, the three of them began to chatter about the wine, the way some grown men do. Freddy soon hurried away to see to his preparations.

The main course came with a beet and whipped avocado salad and lamb shoulder braised in stock with saffron butter and cumin salt. There were carrots, turnips, and onions layered above the lamb shoulder in the *tajine*. The 1947 Cheval Blanc was poured. There was little conversation until the dish was devoured and half of the Cheval Blanc had been consumed.

"What's new with the Arab League and the Middle East, Abdul?" Alex said. "Lots of riots and unrest, it seems. Has the Arab Spring sprung?"

"Indeed, it has at least started to spring," Abdul said. "The monarchies are worried, perhaps because jihad is losing its attraction for the young. The rewards of becoming a martyr are being questioned, just as anger at the rulers is growing. Yemen is particularly troubling. Most of the south of Yemen is under Al-Qaeda control. They are starting to consolidate their power there and they will make trouble. The appetite of the Great Satan for foreign wars may be fading as well. A dangerous combination for my clients who rely on America. A trillion here, a trillion there. After a bit the costs become noticeable."

"Indeed they do," Alex said. "That's one of the things that I hope to point out, albeit indirectly. "Kufdani's Yemen office is in Aden, at the southwest corner of it," Alex said. "We've had a few threats about our schooling and the jobs we've asked women to do. I'll need to figure out how we secure our people there. I'd hate to close that office, and I don't want anyone hurt."

"How are you coming with extracting big money from the president?" Abdul said.

"I might get in to see him soon, Mac says. Are you having any success selling the Arab League on the idea of funding mass public education?"

"I've talked to most of the countries where there is a guy that I trust. The Arab League will react positively to introduction of any affordable technology that will make the populace more malleable, no surprise. We have a committee looking at Kufdani's educational results over five years with its employees. I chair that committee. I anticipate a very positive report, if expensive for my clients to support."

Washington, DC
The White House

General Kelly had done as promised and asked President Roberts to see MacMillan "on an opportunity to transform the Middle East." Roberts had reacted with scorn.

"I'm not quite sure where you got your idea that I wanted to meet with your trained killer, General Kelly," he said. "Why should I, given that I will probably never buy your assertion that MacMillan is a closet intellectual?"

"MacMillan is our main contact with Emilie. He put us on to the system and he is close with its author. We need continued goodwill there badly, Mr. President."

"That's a very good reason, General Kelly. Since this Emilie system made my job easier, my popularity greater, and everyone is terrified of losing her, I'll do the meeting. Thirty minutes for Colonel MacMillan," Roberts said, standing, "and this better not be a waste of my time."

. . .

Later that afternoon, Mac sat rigid, back straight in his chair in front of the desk made of planks from the hull of *Old Ironsides*. The president sat back in his chair, quiet.

"I've decided that I don't like you and I don't like your ways," Roberts said. "I think they lead to fascism if successful."

"Yes, sir."

"You are a man of violence, Colonel MacMillan, and you seem prepared to be called a fascist. That is unsavory at best."

"I'm neither prepared to be called a fascist nor am I one, Mr. President. I'd take umbrage at that assertion, if made. I think my efforts have proven to be an influence in the opposite direction. We enabled national security, upon request from time to time—sometimes violently in situations we hoped would remain secret. But you know all of that. The team that built Emilie has asked me to intercede for them with you. They'd like an audience with you, to propose to you a fix for the Middle East, or the beginnings of one."

"OK, I'll take one of those. Can you deliver it on Thursday afternoon?"

MacMillan was silent, gazing at the president.

"OK, MacMillan, enough of this small talk. Tell me what is on the table for me to look at. Take five or ten minutes. Sum it up, give me some evidence that you are right, point me to evidence that a solution will lead affordably to the desired result, and when."

"In summary, use of Emilie's intelligence sub-system, which is fundamental to both scope and cost control, has already enabled dramatic results. We've spent substantial amounts of money on intelligence functions that were used to accelerate results. If much more money is spent by the US, the team believes it would be an accelerant for social change across the Middle East. That's what they are after. Money."

"Hell, MacMillan," Roberts said. "That's what everyone is after. How much?"

"As much as possible is the easy answer, sir," Mac said. "I'll try to put together a paper on the options."

"I'm starting to be interested," Roberts said. "That's scary. Do you even have a college education? Do the others?"

"Yes, sir," Mac said, "we all have graduate degrees. Some degrees are more notable than others."

"Even so, don't bother with the paper, Colonel," Roberts said. "Instead arrange an appointment for me with the leader of this little band soon. I'd like to get this off my table. If there is to be a paper asking for money, let him do it. The Emilie system has been good for my ratings."

Capitol Hill

Two generations of Elliot men sat in the office of the elder, Brooks F.T. Elliot III. It was a lavish space provided by the US taxpayer for the senior senator from Connecticut, who had long been the chairman of the Senate Armed Services Committee. There was a huge oak desk, stained dark and covered with papers and folders. Just behind, against the wall, stood an upright American flag and the state flag of Connecticut, each held aloft by an ornate bronze holder featuring an eagle of Colonial vintage. An exquisite hand-carved, white birch model of an F35 fighter was on a shelf to the left. White birches are a favorite in Connecticut for all sorts of crafts. The local touch was the hallmark of a well-known lobbyist. At the north end of the office, a tall cabinet stood open behind a sitting area with four maroon, leather-covered chairs and a coffee table with ornate, hand-carved wooden legs. It held a full bar and sink. On shelves to the left of the bar stood bottles of scotch, rum, bourbon, and any other spirit likely to be needed to conduct the Senate's business. Beneath the whiskey supply was a small bar refrigerator containing soda, beer, and soft drinks with four bottles of unopened white wine laid down in its door shelves.

To the right of the bar was a selection of crystal glassware on top, and on the bottom was space for twenty-five bottles of wine, mostly red, to be stored on their sides in custom teak slots. The end of the day was often marked by a quiet drink or two.

Elliot the younger was drinking a Walter Hansel North Slope Pinot Noir from a Riedel glass; the elder had Number 209 vodka on the rocks in a Waterford glass on the table in front of him, half full.

"You were right about Virgil Clemmons, Pop. LuAnn's dad turned out to be a great host. A good time was had by all, almost. One cowboy jumped Alex, with predictable results."

"I don't suppose Cuchulain killed him."

"He lived, but by only an inch or two. Got his jaw broken by Alex's elbow. It was the nicest counter to a tackle that I've seen."

"Other than by his size, in the old days I'd never have guessed Alex was lethal," Senior said. "You wouldn't be around if he wasn't, so I'm happy."

"I'll drink to that," Junior said, and they touched glasses. "May we all benefit from his current compulsion. Mine too, come to think of it."

"Transforming popular attitudes in the Middle East over several decades is so outlandish an endeavor that it might make a difference," Senior said. "It's certainly worth a try. Maybe if it starts working, you can use it as fodder when you run for my seat."

"First things first, Pop. Let's get the Elliot name tied to creating an incrementally better life over there. I think the Elliot Scholar idea will do a lot for that, over time."

"Time is the problem. I'm making a little progress on the funding, son, but the horizon is too long for a politician. My colleagues want something that will get them votes tomorrow, not in ten or fifteen years."

"We may need to hone the pitch a bit. Simplify it."

"Give me the new story to tell," Senior said. "I need something to use as a cudgel."

"Good word, cudgel. I wish I had one; you do. I'll give it one quick pass, then we'll work on it together."

"I'd like that. I don't see enough of you, son."

"We're going to do two things. First we're going to get the Elliot Scholars legislation going. Second, we're going to start the ball rolling on the US building a university in Morocco to train skilled Muslim workers. The Elliot scholars come first as a means to start to staff the subsequent university. There will be quite a few of them by the time a university gets built.

"OK, the basics," the son said. "Elliot Scholars, who are required to be graduates of US colleges, will be two thirds foreign-born Muslims, one third US citizens. Each scholar chosen will get a two-year free ride for teaching or public service in the Middle East, plus funded graduate study after that if they do it over there. The United States will pay two thirds, the host country one third. Five hundred students a year. Fluency in Arabic is a plus. I'll be the chair of the selection committee. You will be the scholarship sponsor to show Middle Eastern countries that we know more than how to kill them with US Armed Forces. It's your legacy. It's some giveback to society after all of those years you spent running the Armed Services Committee."

Junior continued. "Next, we have to pitch the idea that, just as the Peace Corps gave the US a good image, the Elliot scholars will take the next step by providing mostly Muslims as our ambassadors. We will educate Muslims well enough that they will have an immediate but small impact wherever they go to do their two years. They will be among the best thinkers wherever they go, because we will select them to be superior. Islamic terrorists are disproportionally college educated, but with little religious training and often mediocre academic records. Osama bin Laden was a mediocre engineer, for example. Over time the Elliot Scholars will become more influential wherever they work and live and are likely to have good feelings about the US that will rub off on their colleagues. They can find a ready ear among the college-educated Muslim. It would be harder if it had been peasants that led the global terrorist movement."

The older man shifted in his chair and drank a bit of his vodka.

"I suppose that's right," he said. "But there are so many illiterates over there, I can't see that sending a few hundred smart kids to help out is going to make a difference. There are basic problems of food, water, and the skills to earn those things that aren't going to go away. Unless you mind, I may use the legacy image. It has a nice ring."

The younger hung his head and laughed softly, then looked up and said, "You don't have political instincts, Pop, you have political reflexes. It didn't take you any thought to get permission to use an idea you liked; it didn't really interrupt the flow of the conversation. You just unconsciously slipped it in. You're indeed a political animal and I should learn, just in case I ever decide to run for this Senate job."

Senior smiled faintly.

"OK," Junior said. "There is a clear and well-documented model for us to use. The problem of endemic poverty went away in Europe and Great Britain from the seventeenth to the nineteenth century in circumstances enormously similar to the ones we see in the Middle East today. Our bet is that can accelerate that process for mitigating poverty. You and I have talked about this. The more Muslims learn and the more they think for themselves and for their self-interest, the easier they are to deal with, not because we trick them but because they become more like us. The education of women is a key driver of population growth, so Muslim growth will slow as women participate in the workplace. Muslims will become more thoughtful. They will start to worry about losing what they have rather than hoping to punish those who have more."

"Education of the underclass is stupidly expensive, and we've shown here that it doesn't really work," Senior said. "I can't imagine that the five of you are going to do much better."

"Right now I don't want to get into another argument with you about where the fault for our predicament lies, but suffice it to say that we have failed to teach five generations of inner-city poor to read and write. As an accelerant to that tragic blaze of infamy, we broke up the nuclear family structure of the poor with stupidly designed social welfare legislation. To assure that anything that could be broken would be broken, we allowed union hacks representing the teachers to line their own nests while ignoring the problems their members were hired to fix. Education is expensive and unsuccessful because you and your esteemed colleagues traded our future for immediate votes. It's the worst form of power politics and you were there; you failed to even slow it. That nauseates me."

The older man flushed and started to say something, twice. Then he said, "We've had words about this for many years. I can't recall you being chary with your opinions nor of sharing your judgments, but you weren't there. You were mostly right, but it's done now and I don't know anyone who knows how to fix it. There is an ever-shrinking core of fundamental liberal thinkers in the Senate, and we increasingly lack the political currency to make changes or resist new entitlements. We neither have a unified voice, nor the votes to change things even if a considered solution were at hand. I have finally accepted that entitlements are on a ratchet; they only go up."

"Bullshit! We broke the model. We failed those kids. Now we can see the price, but are still kicking that financial can down the road so that the next generation gets to pay the bill for fixing things, even though they can't even read an invoice.

"There is a proven better way to educate children," Junior continued. "The model for educating the poor is changing in Morocco and wherever Kufdani Industries is located across the Middle East. We need master teachers, but we can't afford them in every classroom. So Kufdani has recordings of master teachers on a video screen in front of each kid at a direct cost of about five cents per day. Vocational training for Kufdani employees is at similar costs. There are videos of master teachers on every topic from word formation to Sharia law. From arithmetic to calculus to physics; Caitlin did the calculus and the physics courses and of course she designed the whole training environment. I was amazed she could dial her mind down to teach at that level, but she did a fabulous job. At each Kufdani location, a person acts as monitor, usually a moderately well-trained woman who answers basic questions that students may have. Backing up the monitor is an Internet help desk that has an enormous file of frequently asked questions and answers, plus it dynamically chooses a particular responder for a particular student's questions when a human interface is needed. Fast kids get sophisticated support; slower ones get fundamental support. There are no failing students; there are only systems that fail to support them adequately. Students learn at their own pace. I was amazed at the rate of change in which particular student was tested as strongest. It turns out that slow learners may just start slow, but often have better long-term retention than the fast learners, and with that retention a better understanding of the next topic taught. Caitlin told me she had long expected that, but getting it firmly into confirming statistics was a big deal for her learning to teach via video. She's working up to providing pre-kindergarten teaching since there is evidence that an early academic head start with fun stuff, and without a lot of pressure, really improves kids' performance in K through six education."

"Caitlin," the elder Elliot said softly, leaning back in his chair and hoping to get his son quieted a bit. "I do love that girl and her mind. I was crushed when you two broke it off in college. I had visions of grandchildren doing linear algebra in their cribs and me basking in their achievements."

"I had similar unrealistic visions," Junior said. "Caitlin broke it off when it became clear I wanted a traditional marriage with kids and all; she broke it off quickly. Caitlin said she could never love anyone enough to do that. She said she was much too selfish to give in to an emotion like love with its shared sacrifices. I owe her for making that clear before we did something stupid, like getting married."

"Well, she probably wouldn't have become the world superstar she is if she had been having kids and teaching somewhere."

"True enough," Junior said. "We're still friends, good friends. Alex has been tolerating her well. They seem to get along."

"OK. Got it," Senior said. "Bring them by sometime for dinner. I like them both and they're not the type to know Capitol Hill well. Dinner is where good laws and good politics are formulated."

"How could I not know that, the most fundamental emotional element of Bagdad on the Potomac," Brooks said with a chuckle. "It won't be this week. Alex is going to meet with the president tomorrow morning."

"Good for Alex! He's making the big university pitch, I assume. God knows we've talked enough about this. Let me know if I can do anything with the president for you."

"Yeah, Pop. The president is just your kind of guy. He'd love to go out of his way for you."

"That bastard is a closet communist," the elder Elliot snarled. "He's trying to give the country back to the Indians with his tax the rich and spend more on the poor visions. I suspect I won't get a dinner invitation from him, let alone a favor."

The younger eased back into his chair, then said, "Caitlin is in Fort Meade, at NSA, doing Emilie meetings. I'm going to pick her up tomorrow and head for the Bay. I had *Old Fashioned* moved down from Long Island. Alex, Mac, Jerome, and General Kelly are going to meet us there for a quick sail and dinner. General Kelly is proving to be thoughtful. Now let's get back to the topic at hand, getting the Elliot Scholar program funded and the ball rolling for hearings on the university."

Senior nodded. "Tell what you have that matters."

"The team will make sure the president allows the Eliot Scholar program if you get it into passed legislation, but you don't get to be cute. No controversial riders. Just do the basic politics. It'll get signed."

"You're pretty confident, but I always said you'd make a good politician. You have the basic tools required."

Junior snorted and said, "Yeah, I'm very smart, very rich, amoral, and I hold a grudge forever. I have sponsorship, and Emilie is huge leverage."

"Yup, Emilie is a gold-plated terrorist-killing machine and thus great leverage. Them's the basics and revenge is indeed a dish best served cold. Let me know when you want my seat. It will take some politicking."

Elliot the younger gazed at his father for a bit, and then said, "That discussion is not on the table right now. First I want to feel noble and satisfied about this whole effort, I shit you not. You should resist the urge to combine priorities on this one, Pop. This is a big deal for me. I've spent a lot of time since I was at Oxford trying to figure this one out—many years. If I lose the Elliot Scholars program because you get greedy on deal points, I'll be forever disappointed. Forever angry."

"I don't want to lose a son over this, so fine. I understand. Let's get Alice in here and let her figure out how we play this little game of yours."

"Is she still here this late? Let's do it, Pop. I feel like Alice was my intellectual nanny. She should have been the House Parliamentarian. The only person other than Alice who knows more about the guts of rules-based Congressional politics is Charley Johnson, and he had the job for forty years."

"Yeah. One hell of a pitcher too, earlier. Wrote a book that I bought about that political stuff. Alice bought one and actually read it. I think Alice had an unrequited thing for him. But some folks over in the House wanted certain other things more than they wanted Alice to replace Charley. I'm pleased."

"You should be. Cost you much?"

"Nah. A little goodwill and a small favor maybe." Senior reached to a button hidden beneath the arm of his chair.

There was a quiet knock on the door before it opened. A sturdy, buxom woman in her mid-fifties hurried in. Alice wore a rumpled black suit with a white cotton blouse that had a coffee stain just over her heart, in the shape of a kidney. Two pencils stuck out of her hair just above one arm of her rimless glasses. No makeup.

"Hi, Alice," Elliot the younger said. "You're a welcome sight."

"That's because I have big boobs and you lust for me, Junior," Alice said primly.

"That was twenty years ago," he said. "Now I love you for your mind."

"That's OK. The boobs are sagging a bit, but my mind's still good. Now, what are we to do about this Elliot Scholar business? Talk to me; educate this fine mind of mine on how we are supposed to sell the craven Congress on an idea that has no near-term votes. And skip the altruism shit; that won't buy much in this gutter."

Elliot the younger pulled a stack of papers from the leather case beside him and dropped them on the coffee table. "Let's the three of us brainstorm this a bit. The facts are in the papers. The votes are in our power play. No quarter."

"No quarter? What's this, the fucking Alamo? Jesus Christ, Junior," Alice said. "You sound like you're talking about your father going zipper down, balls out over this. Me too."

"Yep. Everything you have. A career or two may fall. The country can't lose this one. Neither can I."

"There is no possible way for you to hide the conflict you have in this," Senior said. "I'll get butchered on the conflict too. Any chance you would have of a senatorial career is zero."

"Alice?"

"I don't know about that, but I'd pay to watch you handle the questions. You're no virgin."

"Think about it," Junior said. "I have been rehearsing this gig for eleven years. Eleven years of building evidence of efficacy in mass education, because that's the key. I have it right in my head. Part of the plan is that I'll be attacked in the press. Me – Navy Seal, Rhodes Scholar, son of a big-time senator. I'll play Charlie Rose like a fiddle. He doesn't have time to catch up to my thinking and he loves a good story. We need to get the good news out. It's working."

Alice had always admired how hard Junior held his opinions, once he formed them. She looked at Senior. "Well, is it a go?" she said. "Hardball?"

"It's a go. Hardball. No quarter," Senior said as his face tightened. "There aren't too many who want to make an enemy of me when they instead can claim some credit for spending. They just have to have a little confidence that I'm serious. Go for it. We'll deal with the fallout later."

The younger raised an eyebrow at Alice. She winked at him, turned, looked at Senior and said, "There you go, Junior. Hot damn! A couple of careers are likely going to fall, or your pappy is. This is going to be fun. And no one who shouldn't get in the way is going to get in the way and survive the first confrontation."

"You might want to read *The Prince* again, Alice," Brooks said with a sly grin.

"Machiavelli's Management Manual? I read it at the beach, I read it at night or on a cold weekend by the fire. I savor it with Cabernet when something I have worked on for a long time comes to fruition without my fingerprints on it. He gets a grateful nod when someone I wanted to injure gets injured with no clear line back to me. Niccolo suggests that career destruction planned should be terminal for the destructee. And you must watch your backside. Lots of fun."

Brooks sat quiet for a few moments. His eyes nearly teared. "There are times when you remind me of Metternich. Others come to mind, like Rasputin. Occasionally, you are ruthless like MacMillan. You are simply marvelous. I love to watch you think. You are so cool."

"Fuckin-ay," Alice said. "I like it that you watch. Now beat it. This is not one that can be flung. It must be carefully planned to decide which of the dirtbags is likely to make trouble. There will be more vulnerable dirtbags, at least in the House. They can feel threatened and make a sweetheart deal, like rolling on another of the dirtbags that costs us nothing and helps the body count. Then there are the slimebags in the other chamber. They differ from dirtbags in that slime is smooth and has enough age-glitter to hide in plain sight."

"Alice," said Senior with a throaty and rising voice. "Don't go there."

She ignored him. "But the difficult part of deciding whom to suborn is that there are many who are not subornable. They are quiet, strong people who are simply public servants. They would take enormous offense if you squeezed them. It's about a third, maybe a fourth of the population of each elected chamber, the dirt-bag chamber and the slimebag chamber. There's the challenge."

"I grok it," Junior said with a grin. "Spectacular. I'm going to go away and figure a new model to describe you. Metternich was an amateur. Disraeli maybe. Whomever you resemble, you perform with little notice."

"The cognoscenti notice," Alice said, grinning. "One should ask no more. It's not that hard to figure out. It's putting the pieces together that gets tricky."

"It always is, Alice. You've been a wonderful influence on me. Go get 'em."

"Get out of here."

"Yes'm."

The younger winked at his father as he walked to the door and out. It swung slowly shut behind him and reset its electronics.

Annapolis, Maryland
The Edgewater Yacht Club

The forty-eight-foot, Taiwan-built custom sailing yacht, *Old Fashioned*, was tied up on the downwind side of a long wooden dock on the South River, just north of Annapolis, Maryland. She was a quiet display of wealth. Teak rails and fittings were paired with polished brass hardware. A bristle of antennae was set on the cabin roof and main mast. Past the bow in the shallower waters near the shore, there were fuel pumps and a provisioning store elevated on wooden pilings. Just across was a long, low building surrounded by boats out of water on trailers or wooden racks, and power hoists for pulling boats from the water for repair or storage.

Two men, one young and one middle aged, were pushing fat-sided wheelbarrows loaded with provisions down the bumpy, slatted wooden dock. They stopped at the bottom of a gangway jutting down from the deck of *Old Fashioned*. On the deck stood a square sort of man. He looked to be in his mid-fifties, wearing a white polo shirt without a logo and khaki shorts. He was holding an iced drink of something dark.

"Bring those things up here, gents," he said. "I'll show you where they go."

"Shit," the younger man said quietly to the other. "We're going to bust our asses for half an hour putting this crap away and leave without a fucking tip. Fatso there is probably half in the bag. He couldn't load this stuff his own self if he tried."

The older man turned slightly away from the rail and said, "Riley, I've been meaning to talk to you again about your fat mouth. I do this for a living. I suck up. I make nice. It's a pretty good living. Your mouth is getting in the way of that, again."

"OK, OK, I'll be nice, Cal. Jeez!"

"Remember the first time we had a discussion about your mouth?" Cal said. "You thought you could whip me. Joke. You got your ass kicked pretty good, because of your shitty judgment. Well, Fatso there could kick my ass without dropping his drink."

"So?" Then Riley looked startled. "You think?"

"I know," Cal said. "Now pick up some shit and get moving, or I'll sic him on you. We're wasting time."

Riley grabbed two duffle bags and ran up the gangway toward the deck, slinging one over his shoulder. He realized suddenly that the heavier bag weighed a lot more than he thought. He was leaning toward the side of the gangway, dragged by the heavier bag. There was only a flimsy canvas cloth acting as a screen, and to hold it only a rail of aluminum tubing to keep Riley and the duffle bags from plunging into the scummy, diesel-filmed water.

The bags were stripped from his shoulders by Cal just before he hit the canvas. Riley ducked low to hold himself to the edge of the rail, then felt his balance go. Cal moved quickly up the ramp with the bags, dragging one a bit.

Pulled onto the far bank of the anchorage was an old skiff with a big Mercury outboard motor hanging from its fading, wooden transom plate. Worn oars were in their locks, set across the faded rails. A large, bearded man named Jimmy-Lee Butruss was sitting on a chair tilted back on the deck, wearing a Cabella's baseball cap. He was watching the rich folks and working on his third beer of the afternoon. Butruss wore dirty Levis with dark stains on the upper legs where he wiped his crab-slimed hands. There was a bone-handled knife strapped in a leather sheath on his belt. His T-shirt was of faded camouflage with "Buster's Clams" stenciled across the chest and the outline of a soft-pack of cigarettes visible, rolled up in the sleeve. A spinning rod was lying on the deck beside a rusty bait box.

Jimmy-Lee was watching idly as Riley fell into the water, then sat up to get a better angle for watching the first notable event of the day. Paddling beside the dock soon came Riley, cursing and spitting diesel-fouled water. *I believe I'll have Riley over for a beer when he gets dried off. He'll know something about that pretty sailboat out there with all its pricey electronics and he won't be happy about getting wet. There might be a dollar in that mix somewhere.*

Some movement caught Jimmy-Lee's eye, up on the shore behind the store. He looked into the parking lot and saw a man and a woman walking down the path to the dock. The guy was a pussy, rich-fuck asshole. Little guy, maybe five-ten and skinny, in shape from tennis maybe. He was all slicked and pressed up with his pretty little shined boat shoes and ironed shorts with a crease in them. The broad, on the other hand, got better looking with every step, a tight ass in madras shorts and a cotton polo shirt stretched tight across her chest.

Maybe I'll let Riley have two beers. I'd dearly like to get me some of that. A woman like that shouldn't go through life without a real man, and I like the way those rich bitches fight.

Washington, DC

General Patrick Kelly sat poking with a silver fork at a ham and Swiss omelet in the dining room of the Hay Adams Hotel, just across Lafayette Park from the White House. Sitting opposite from him, Alex sipped on a cup of espresso and considered his impending morning visit with the president of the United States. Kelly had given Alex an update on his conversations with the president and those had by Mac, both designed to get Alex a chance to present his ideas for building long-term peace in the Middle East.

"I think President Roberts is intrigued by the prospect of being involved in a fundamental change in the attitude of the Muslim world," Kelly said. "He fancies his intellect. But it's not the kind of thing that he'll put in his Saturday radio addresses to the American public. His chief of staff hates the idea of you meeting alone with Roberts and will backstab you at any opportunity. With any luck the asshole will punch you and you can retaliate, once. The CIA and the National Reconnaissance Office, as well as Mac and I, have bent the president's ear about the evolving efficacy of Emilie as an intelligence system. So I'd say you have a small chance of being effective in your meeting with him this morning, if only because he is motivated to keep the intel from Emilie flowing and improving. Every time we pop an Al-Qaeda leader, his ratings go up a few points. Still, he won't like you."

"Any insight or advice you'd care to offer?" Alex said. "I have no idea how to play him or this game."

Kelly sat quiet for a moment, pondering how to structure his answer, then said, "The president thinks you were Mac's thug, and that Mac was the CIA's thug for a long time. You shouldn't expect admiration for what you've done, nor a positive mindset. I'd guess he won't be prepared for you to be articulate and thoughtful, nor for how well things have gone so far in changing fundamental Muslim attitudes. That's probably your best path; engage him intellectually in the problem of changing the views of the Muslim world. He's a curious guy."

"How much does he know about me and what we are doing?" Alex said.

"He knows you worked for the CIA and Mac for eight years, that you were a tech investor in New York and got fairly rich. He knows you inherited Kufdani Industries and that Emilie was built by O'Connor on your nickel until the Intel started to work, when Uncle Sam was willing to pitch in money for more access."

"That's enough, I guess," Alex said. "I certainly know more about Islam and Muslims than he does. I can play it from there."

"You have thirty minutes on the president's schedule, but I saw he had cleared the next thirty minutes, just in case," Kelly said. "I'll meet you back here afterward and drive you to Annapolis. We'll get picked up there, at the dock at the Naval Academy."

"I guess it's time for me to dress appropriately, and then go beard the liberal in his den," Alex said as he stood.

"Yeah," Kelly said. "Good luck with it. Don't let him bait you. Make sure that he knows that Emilie is still working for us."

. . .

Ten minutes later, Alex walked across Lafayette Park in his best charcoal suit striped faintly in green, white shirt with French cuffs, and green silk tie. After clearing White House security, he sat on a chair outside the Oval office, waiting his turn and a bit nervous. It was not every day one had a chance to meet with the president of the United States. Within five minutes, the door to the Oval Office opened and the president stood there in a white shirt and solid red tie pulled down a little from the neck, sleeves rolled to the elbow. Alex stood and introduced himself to the president, then followed him inside.

"Am I to address you as Mr. Cuchulain?" the president asked from across his desk. "Or should I call you Sheikh Kufdani?"

"Cuchulain is fine, Mr. President," he said. Alex was strangely pleased by the president's pronunciation as coo-HULL-an, provided no doubt by Mac. His father would have liked that the president knew that.

"I'm comforted," Roberts said. "Since you apparently haven't gone entirely native, give me some background and an overview of what you have in mind to ask me to do for you. I am motivated by the results your intelligence system has enabled. We don't have a lot of time."

"As background, the Muslim world is at a place in time that should allow us to provide a positive influence there," Alex said. "There is wide illiteracy, unhappiness, and a pervasive, flawed interpretation of Islam that attempts to control Muslim lives and thoughts. Women are deeply oppressed in many countries. In all, the call to jihad and violence has apparently run much of its course for lack of results. We can assist and speed its demise. Muslims are sick of killing in the name of Allah and starving with their families just after.

"Education is the magic bullet that will do the most to transform the Middle East. So, Mr. President, we have what many would consider an outrageous proposal. We want you to lead an effort to bring modernity to Islam. We can show them a better way. Our team has the education ball rolling. The next step is to build a university in Morocco for young Muslims. The United States should lead the way to doing that."

"That is indeed an outrageous proposal, Mr. Cuchulain," Roberts said. "And you waste my time by bringing it up. You underestimate its difficulty and exaggerate the importance of education."

"There is enormous evidence that gains in public education generate lower religious fanaticism," Cuchulain said. "Without that fanaticism we would have far fewer enemies blowing themselves up in our face and killing our innocent soldiers. An attribute of the Emilie system is that it is proven she can manage public education well, from age three to adulthood. We have trained nearly one hundred thousand people so far, at a cost of about five cents per day, per student. We're getting better at it. Training and education is done online. There are no classroom teachers, only monitors. It will scale."

"You're a well-trained assassin," the president said. "If you were also truly a patriot, Mr. Cuchulain, you would bring such technology to the United States right now to solve our problems and then, much later, to the rest of the world. We are the world's leader."

"I was born in this country, Mr. President. I went to public schools in this country. I served in the Marine Corps for eight years. I am indeed a patriot and I am, or was, an assassin. Neither of those labels requires me to be stupid or unrealistic. If what we are doing in education in the Middle East becomes sufficiently successful over a few years, there will be a grass roots movement to bring it here. The teachers' unions may not be able to stop it at that point, but today they could and would. That said, the entire resources of Emilie for public education are available if you choose to present them for use in fixing the ongoing tragedy of America's failure to educate the poor. Convincing the unions of Emilie's efficacy I'll leave in your capable hands."

Alex leaned forward to fix his gaze on President Roberts.

"Five years of verifiable, incrementally better and more accurate results from the time we enabled Emilie for mass education has turned most of us into believers," Alex said. "It works, and the way to make it better is apparent."

"Suppose it is? Do you have any idea what planning a scheme like yours would entail? We'd need the reliable cooperation of the Arab world, Morocco in particular. We'd need the support of Congress, which has not been readily available to me, even for the basics as I see them."

"Mr. President, we do have a sense of the difficulty and have been lining up support in the event you decide you would like to start this process."First," Alex raised an index finger, "we have decent relationships among the Arabs and have some indication that the Arab League would support an effort such as ours. The rising of the Arab Spring has alerted Arab leaders that their people are ready for something better. The leaders would like to keep their jobs, and their heads. They will be reliable in their support, if unobtrusive."

Alex raised a finger beside the first. "Second, the Congress is authorizing trillions of dollars for two wars that are costing tens of thousands of American lives. We are confident that an effort to bring the American way of life to the Muslim world can be initiated in Congress. Those costs must be mitigated somehow."

"And just how would you go about that?" Roberts said. "I've had a notable lack of success and I live in the White House. You're an Arab sheikh."

"One of our team members is Brooks F.T. Elliot the Fourth. He thinks he can convince his father to lead an effort of the type I describe."

"Huh, the Seal Rhodes Scholar," Roberts said. "I'm starting to be intrigued with this idea, despite myself. How long have you been working on this little project, Mr. Cuchulain?"

Alex smiled. "A very long time, Mr. President. Many years. Figuring out what to do was not too hard. Getting it started has been a multi-year challenge. We now have it well started and the concepts proved and tested."

"I assume you know how long it will take to get approval to build a university and then to build it."

"At least five and maybe ten years is our guess, Mr. President."

"So why are you here now?" Roberts said. "What is it you want right now?"

"First, we'd like your support on the objective of better educating the Muslim world. If something arises from Congress as a first step, we'd like your support. We'd like you to start down this path, to have people you trust evaluate our claims."

Roberts smiled to himself. This kind of promise was easy, unenforceable, and unverifiable. "Of course, Mr. Cuchulain," he said. "I want the wars and their costs to stop as badly as anyone. Is there something else?"

"Yes, sir, there is," Alex said. "Over time and incrementally, Mr. President, we want quiet favoritism for my firm, Kufdani Industries, from the US government in foreign aid and in contracts from you that are let in our patch. If you are going to create a university and a hospital in the Middle East, we want to build them and we want a say in where and how they will be built, including selection of all subcontractors. If there is to be food aid, we want to administer its distribution and procurement. Basically, we want to be the key nongovernment partner and general contractor for the distribution and administration of US foreign aid in the Middle East. In return we will continue to provide access to Emilie's information and enhance it aggressively. We'll do a good job of making your aid dollar effective. The fact that Kufdani controls a broad and diverse community of subcontractors would enormously increase the amount of data that comes into Emilie, and consequently enhance the value and accuracy of the intelligence she generates. Those same loyalty-generating health-care and educational services provided to Kufdani will be provided to the subcontractors and their families; we will thus probably gain their loyalty and enhance our effectiveness. Over time other companies will mimic our social behavior and begin to provide more services to their people, as a cost of competing with Kufdani that can't be ignored. That's a win I hope to live to see."

"Uh-huh," Roberts said skeptically. "State would have a shit fit if we tried to control foreign aid to the Middle East from the White House, and the whole control scenario you propose lends itself to graft and corruption, of which there is fully enough in the Muslim world. You are a long way from convincing me, Mr. Cuchulain."

"We have been getting financial support from the intelligence community for quite some time, Mr. President. Emilie is thought by the director of Central Intelligence, among others, to be a great value for the money spent, as you know. Intelligence support specific to the Middle East would be the first place we would ask for expanded dollars. On the broader aid front, even if the requested change in attitude started now, it would take several years to begin to have the impact with State that you describe. We are capable and have staff and expertise in place in many Middle East countries and provide security services for them. We can't stop graft and corruption, but I assure you that we can reduce their impact and influence a bias toward basic human equity. All I'm asking, for the moment, is that the black budget support we get now be given your blessing and allowed to grow and that Morocco be given a bit of favored status for big aid projects like hospitals and universities that will allow us to curry favor with the masses. We have proven we can seduce the masses with a promise of a better life and the demonstration of a beginning to that enhanced life. Without that seduction there can be no growth."

"How could you possibly have much influence in controlling graft and corruption?" Roberts said. "The Middle East is the most corrupt cesspool in the world. Anyone there who threatens religious power or growth of wealth risks being killed quickly."

Alex smiled coldly. "I'm rich, capable, and I don't disdain violence, Mr. President. I control a large and pervasive Muslim enterprise. If I have the favor of the Great Satan as well, those who threaten me or Kufdani do so at their peril."

The president gazed at Cuchulain for a long moment, then said, "I hate that Great Satan shit."

"We have the same goals, Mr. President," Alex said. "We want the Muslim community to join the ranks of emerging nations, to want more for their children and themselves than they have today because they see a path to that end."

"Don't lecture me, Mr. Cuchulain. You are a killer and perhaps not much more. Still, you make a convincing philosophical case for a path to change that I've not heard before. But I don't know that either the knowledge base or the genetic underpinnings are in the Muslim world to bring them out of their torpor. Do you have facile rationalization for that observation, Mr. Cuchulain?"

Cuchulain smiled and said, "I don't need even clumsy rationalization, Mr. President, I have fact. I don't need St. Thomas Aquinas to give me a verbal crutch. I have undisputed history to cite and I'm a reasonably competent Islamic scholar. In about nine hundred AD,

Arab forces sacked Rome. Back then the Dark Ages went on from four hundred AD to about one thousand AD. During that period most Europeans were still slobbering over raw meat in isolated villages, while Islam was the cultural and intellectual epicenter of the Western world. We brought the manufacture and use of paper to the West. We brought first Arabic numerals, then algebra. At the peak of Islam, China was its only intellectual rival."

"That was then, this is now," the president said.

Alex nodded. "Indeed, Mr. President, but the question, your issue, was one of Muslim genetic preparedness for a productive life in today's society. We seem likely to have adequate genetic underpinnings to support a more productive and thoughtful society."

"Indeed that was the issue I raised," Roberts said. "You are again facile."

"Truth and facts enable facility, Mr. President."

Roberts sighed and leaned back in his high leather chair. He gazed at Alex for a long few moments, pensive.

"I have twenty-two minutes remaining, Mr. Cuchulain. You're a somewhat different person than I expected and you're said to be an Islamist of sorts. Are you up to answering a few questions that are a bit tangential?"

"I'll do my best, Mr. President."

"You're a Sunni. Would you have us destroy the Shiite power in Iran and their allegedly budding nuclear prowess? That seems a hot topic these days."

"I've heard that issue discussed for many years among the smartest people I've met and known," Alex said. "Each premise for argument seems flawed, which makes the stunningly clever logic supporting each premise merely academic. The one answer I heard that made the most sense to me is that achieving peace in the world is a matter analogous perhaps to a movement decision in three-dimensional micro-chess where we are in mid-game after thirty years of play. Right now Iran is holding some pieces that perhaps can be taken at great cost. The value of taking those pieces is controversial even in the short term, but the long-term value and implications of such a move as destroying Iran's ability to go nuclear are vastly more complicated to evaluate. If we destroy the known nuclear capabilities of Iran, what of their use of any unknown capabilities that we failed to detect? What will the Chinese and Russians do, in their own interest of course, if we attack Iran? What of the impact on the world economy of the closing of the Straits of Hormuz for several weeks or months? The list of moves and countermoves seems nearly endless. Realistically considering moves and countermoves in two dimensions is difficult; in three dimensions a rational and comprehensive evaluation is nearly impossible. It is certainly not merely a matter of conflict between Shiites and Sunni, nor of the independent interests of Israel.

"To answer your question directly, I have no informed opinion as to whether the United States should or should not attack Iran, nor do I expect to have one soon."

The president gazed at Cuchulain for a few moments. He reached into his top left desk drawer for a rumpled pack of Marlboros. He shook one out and raised an inquisitive eyebrow. Alex shook his head. Roberts found a green plastic gas lighter and lit his cigarette. He pulled an ashtray from another drawer and set it on the desk on top of some papers. An exhaust fan could be heard starting.

"Then tell me about your plan for playing your perceived game of three-dimensional micro-chess. Must we all simply lead lives of quiet desperation as we flail blindly at our respective board pieces on three levels?"

"We plan to stay focused and limit our scope. It seems to me this is not the first metaphorical game of three-dimensional micro-chess in history, Mr. President, nor even the only one now underway. It is perhaps the particular game with most impact on world society. My plan, or our plan, is to build an approach to Muslim civilization in the ways that have proven to work in a prior game for others. Our plan is to enable citizens to improve their lives, incrementally, and expect them to do what makes sense to their well-being for the long term."

"You speak only of Islam with that statement?"

"I speak only of Islam in the present, Mr. President, and as a model, only the United Kingdom during the period of the Enlightenment. Our effort in Islam seems hard enough and long enough to us, even with those constraints. It is, not coincidentally, a major mid-game problem at hand. The rest is up to the world's leaders, as it has always been."

"True, but don't lecture me. Your vocation or perhaps avocation as a trained killer negatively impacts your credibility with me."

Alex shrugged. "You've twice mentioned that vocation without attribution for the builders, enablers, and utilizers of my set of skills, as I recall. I was a serving United States Marine when I was so gainfully employed, doing for my bosses what you claim to loathe. Someone had the power to order us to stop. Perhaps they judged the gains greater than the cost. Still, I simply want to be clear about my objectives, Mr. President. I have nothing to be gained by lecturing you, and you asked. I have been a killer for decades, with no plans to stop. Some great philosopher once said, 'You can get more done with a gun and a kind word than with a kind word alone.' I live by that."

"That's disgusting, but I'll consider your request, Mr. Cuchulain, and discuss it with General Kelly," the president said as he stood. "I assume that the services of your Emilie system will remain available to us during the few months it will take to make a decision."

"I had hoped for a quicker decision path than a few months, Mr. President," Alex said as he stood. "But we will continue to provide probabilities from Emilie based on information that we have gathered. Her efficacy is a function of how much she gets, as is ours." He walked to the door behind Roberts and went through it when opened. Roberts clicked it shut behind him.

• • •

Alex made his way back to the security desk to pick up his Kphone and started across Lafayette Park for the Hay Adams Hotel. There was an outstanding call from Jerome, his longtime CIA partner in violence, whom Alex thought of as the pointy end of the spear. He planned and took care of most of the organized violence. Alex sat on a park bench, brushed his thumb across the print reader, and hit the Connect button. Emilie worked the connection.

Jerome was standing on the wooden porch of a restaurant tucked along the water, below US Route 50, east of the Chesapeake Bay Bridge. A thick man with close-cropped hair on a wide head, he had a full beard, neatly trimmed and well sprinkled with gray. His arms were trunks that stretched the sleeves of his cotton shirt. They reached well below his waist and were pushed away from his body by the width of his back. His legs were long and in loose jeans. He was leaned against the back wall of the restaurant and watching the working boats make their way from the Bay.

Jerome Masterson was a retired USMC Gunnery Sergeant, marine sniper and master instructor who had been Alex's partner in CIA special operations for five years. He now lived in Tangier. When Alex left the CIA after eight years, Jerome retired from the Marine Corps. They remained close as Alex pursued his formal education; neither had many friends. After a few years of operating several small businesses and participating with Alex and Brooks Elliot in Mac's periodic lethal ventures for the White House, Jerome began to operate a high-tech arms dealership to supply local police forces and approved foreign governments with sophisticated weapons. He was good at demonstrating their use and explaining where they might be unusually useful in protecting the good guys and causing difficulties for the others. It had grown into a substantial business, but Jerome slowly decided he didn't like being an executive; he found it boring. It was difficult for Jerome to manage. He had found it required a fully engaged executive to make any business work well. Jerome consulted Alex and Brooks and decided to keep his firm going, but with a new chief executive. Brooks found a former Seal who had gone to General Electric for several years after his navy time, then to Wharton for an MBA. He no longer had legs below the knee, thanks to an improvised explosive device set off by the Taliban in Afghanistan and he didn't much like to travel. Jerome hired the Seal to run his business while he remained its salaried director of development. He soon moved to Tangier to lead security efforts for Kufdani Industries and to be the Middle Eastern contact for his firm.

For some time, Jerome had nurtured the idea of building "super squads" to provide offensive and defensive capabilities for Alex and Kufdani Industries. Jerome had long been troubled professionally by the failure of trained combat troops to hit enemies with rifle fire at ranges beyond two hundred meters, especially in a high-stress environment. For the past several months, he had been training squads of twelve Bedouin men employed by Kufdani Industries, each led by an experienced special operations warrior and fully trained sniper hired from the retiring ranks of the SAS in the United Kingdom. Each Kufdani squad member was trained in marksmanship as a sniper, but without the long months of training required to get a sniper stealthily in place. They were provided with appropriate weapons. Some weapons were standard, others were experimental. Jerome's theory was that, with a full array of weapons and training, a squad could deliver the effective firepower of a far larger force, due to the training and accuracy of each squad member compared to a conventional, lesser-trained soldier. As he had explained to Alex when pitching his idea, a well-trained marksman with a sniper rifle could put a bullet every three seconds or so into the chest of a man-sized target nineteen times out of twenty at a range of up to four hundred meters, while under stress. With twelve riflemen per squad, each with three twenty-round magazines, they could kill nineteen men per minute, per man. There were to be three squads. They had an unfair advantage. Jerome was fond of unfair advantages.

The rifle squads were to be supplemented by a weapons squad of eight men. The weapons squad was issued semi-automatic South African 40mm grenade launchers with a laser range finder. It allowed an air burst of hot shrapnel at ten feet above the ground across a five-meter radius, rather than a burst upon ground impact that was largely absorbed by the earth beneath it. The launchers could each shoot five rounds of 40mm grenades before a magazine change. Another standard issue to the weapons squad was the MBT LAW, a disposable, shoulder-fired, light anti-tank weapon developed by Saab for the Swedish and UK armed forces; it could attack armor from almost any angle. Ground to air missiles were effective, simple to use and would be issued if needed; the Israelis had particularly effective hardware. Jerome had two fully trained squads of riflemen and one of weapons operators, cross-trained. Perimeter security was an easier task and had long since been designed and manned for the Tangier offices. Spots were assigned for each of the riflemen in the city, near Kufdani headquarters, with accuracy-enhancing range cards for several key points in the distance. Kevlar padding was installed around each spot to protect the riflemen from counter fire.

Jerome keyed his Kphone and heard Emilie working the connection.

"Hey, Jerome. Here you are in the land of the round doorknob, once again," Alex said. "How are you amusing yourself?"

"I'm at the Narrows restaurant. I just destroyed three bowls of crab gazpacho, half a loaf of French bread, and a couple of draft beers for lunch. I'm about to drive over to meet Brooks and Mac at the boat. It will be fun to see General Kelly again after so many years. I spent a couple of days in New York taking care of business, then I drove the long way down through New Jersey. I stayed over at the Coast Guard station in Cape May last night and caught the first ferry over to Lewes, Delaware. I drove here for lunch."

"I'm sitting in Lafayette Park," Alex said. "I just got out from talking with the Man about our little venture. It was interesting. I'll tell you about it when I get down there. General Kelly is giving me a ride to Elliot's boat, once I get changed. You guys are picking us up at the Naval Academy dock, I think."

"I'll be at the boat in a half hour or so," Jerome said. "I'm the designated deckhand and winch cranker, I think. I have the mooring on my GPS. It looks like about twenty minutes from here."

Alex laughed. "Don't let any marines see you at that manual labor. That's squid stuff. At least you'll have a colonel and a Seal to supervise your work. Don't bend it."

"Roger that. Elliot would not be pleased if I wrinkled his toy. Later." Jerome terminated the call. He walked to his rental car and fitted himself into Mr. Hertz's Hyundai. Westbound traffic on the Bay Bridge was light as Jerome pulled from the service road. He crossed the bridge and drove west on Route 50. The Edgewater exit came quickly and he turned north on it. After one wrong turn, he found the Edgewater Yacht Club and turned into its parking lot. There was no shortage of parking places.

125

Ten minutes later, Jerome dropped his bag and was shaking Mac's hand on the deck of *Old Fashioned*. Brooks and Caitlin were sitting at a table near the stern and both stood as Jerome walked to them, smiling. It was handshakes again. Caitlin didn't like the huggy, kissy stuff. Jerome wasn't crazy about it either.

• • •

Alex walked into the lobby of the Hay Adams Hotel and waved five fingers at General Kelly, who was sitting in the lobby with a laptop computer on his knees. He grinned at Alex, happy to wait. Within fifteen minutes Alex was back in the lobby in shorts and a light-blue, button-down, long-sleeved cotton shirt with his hanging bag luggage over his shoulder. When he walked to the government car waiting for them outside, General Kelly was standing at the curb by a dark green sedan.

"The Naval Academy dock, Corporal, if you please," Kelly said with a grin to the driver. "This could be fun."

• • •

Four hours later, *Old Fashioned's* sails were furled after a short sail from the Naval Academy dock. She was swaying in a gentle, westerly breeze in a small cove on the east side of the Chesapeake Bay, anchors set fore and aft. Powerboats, some with water skiers towed behind, screamed up and down the main channel in the Bay. The roiled water provided a frequent bump from their wakes to shake glasses. The noise was an occasional irritant. A small sailing vessel slid gracefully in and out of sight, heeled over and quartering into the wind. It was early evening; the sun had not yet set. Six people sat on her open deck beside a table at the stern, having cocktails before they started prepping for dinner. Mac, Jerome, and Patrick Kelly were having a few fingers of scotch, comfortable in khaki shorts and polo shirts. Alex, Brooks, and Caitlin were each drinking a glass of Rudd Vineyards Bacigalupi chardonnay. A magnum of Dancing Hares red wine from Napa, Alex's favorite, had been decanted and was sitting to one side, drinking air and waiting to accompany the lamb chops bathing in Alex's secret Moroccan marinade, said to include preserved lemon, anise, and coriander. Alex had been bullied long ago by Freddie into giving him the secret recipe, so he had begged a quart from Freddy at Tagine as he and Abdul left their meal. Caitlin was wearing an old pair of denim shorts and a modest bikini top, no shoes. A bead of sweat formed in the hollow in her neck and meandered down her chest between patches of cotton to her flat stomach before vanishing into her navel. Patrick Kelly was having trouble keeping his eyes off her and uncomfortable that the others seemed amused by his discomfort. As MacMillan had implied, she was other than ugly.

"So, General," Caitlin said as she fixed her unblinking gaze on him, "what do you think of Emilie? Is she doing it for you?"

"Oh, Emilie is doing the job, all right. She is truly a magnificent intelligence system," Kelly said. He wondered when another bead of sweat would show itself and had the random thought that he was acting like a randy thirty-year-old. "I'm surprised at how quickly she came up to speed on dealing with all that data."

Caitlin smiled. "You get the prize, General," she said. "Emilie doesn't do it all herself. She's mostly a correlation and probability engine. NSA has a classified system supplied by Boeing called Narus. Narus cranks through enormous amounts of data looking for specified keywords, names, areas and things like that. When Emilie gets those files, they are already filtered, narrowed for the designated problem of interest. Today it is often Iran. Tomorrow it might be Nigeria or Newark that's of interest. She takes the filtered data set Narus provides and figures out the correlation between disparate data items. The things that pop up of interest to Emilie go into the Narus filters for the next pass on the data. Things get more precise then, and probabilities of events become reliable."

Careful, laddie.

Just then a large, bearded man rose above *Old Fashioned*'s teak rail facing the Bay and vaulted over to the deck to land lightly on his feet. He swung a shotgun over his right shoulder with drama, its barrel pointed to the sky. Two more men landed on the deck a moment later, on either side of the first. Both were grinning, armed with pistols they held pointed at the deck.

"Howdy, folks," the middle man said with a small bow. "I'm Jimmy-Lee Butruss from Edgewater, Maryland, and we're going to have us a party. First we'll have a cash and jewelry collection, and then Blondie there and me are going to have a little fun." He turned his head to the man on his left and said, "I might let you have a little if you're nice."

The hilt of a knife suddenly appeared, protruding from Jimmy-Lee's throat, thrown by Alex from its holster at the back of his neck. The follow-through from throwing the knife brought Alex to his feet. He sprinted straight at the dying Jimmy-Lee, a howling scream exploding from him, his hands held low and palms up. Jerome dove to the deck and crabbed hard toward the cabin. The howl from Alex froze the other two men for a moment with its volume and suddenness.

In two steps Alex reached the men as they began to swing their pistols up. He dipped momentarily and then drove from his legs to hit each of them on the chin with the heel of a hand, lifting them up and over the rail with the force of his blow. The crash of them falling into the boat below that brought them was loud, with shouts from the boat a moment later. Alex drove his knee into the lower stomach of Jimmy-Lee to further slow his rush, then grabbed the shotgun with one hand and pushed the face in front of him over the rail. He could hear Butruss crash onto the deck of a boat. Alex dropped to one knee and clicked the safety off Jimmy-Lee's Remington Model 1100, 12-gauge, gas-operated shotgun. With a roar of outboard motors below, the boat that had brought the men accelerated away from the scene with the detritus of the failed boarding party. A fourth man who had just dropped onto *Old Fashioned's* deck a few feet from the bow spun and dove off with a loud curse in some language other than English.

Alex had the shotgun tucked into his shoulder. His right cheekbone was welded to the stock as he swiveled his body to change his view down the shotgun barrel and across the deck. What he saw he would hit if he pulled the trigger. Dain spoke quickly: ***The chamber, laddie. Be sure.*** Alex slapped the 1100's slide handle back. A shotgun shell hit the deck rolling, as a new shell was plucked from the storage tube beneath the barrel and rammed into the chamber by the slide-spring driven bolt.

It had occurred to Dain that maybe Jimmy-Lee had not chambered a round in the shotgun since he had been foolish enough to leave the safety engaged. There was the splash of someone swimming hard beneath the bow. Alex stood and ran forward, turned to the water, and shot twice into the back of the swimming man who had dived away. He crossed the deck and looked over the port rail into the water there and the shrubbery beyond.

Mac put his hands behind his head and smiled widely.

"That appears to be the lot, Alex. Have a seat. You spilled your drink when you took off for them. I caught mine, but yours spilled."

"Patrick," Mac said, still grinning. "You've met Alex. Now meet Cooch. He's like the Buster Brown shoe ad: That's my man, Cooch, he lives in there too."

Alex walked slowly back to the stern. His face had taken on a serpentine cast with flesh bunched outward around his eyes, hooding them. His breathing was loud as it whistled through his nostrils. He looked over the rail for the swimmer who was still, floating with scarlet tendrils streaming from his back. Alex turned to face the group. His face started to transform back to its usual form. Dain settled back into his special place in the subconscious. Alex's hands shook as his adrenaline began to drain.

Kelly leaned back and whistled through his teeth, then started to laugh.

"Jesus, Mary, and Joseph," he said. "Now I understand why so many people wanted him beside them. This is what you might call a well-trained warrior. A fine fellow to have watching your back. And you'd never know that Alex could act in such a fine fashion."

Mac almost giggled when he said, "He's old and slow now, but by golly, I think his instincts are fully intact. Give me eight years, full time, with any gifted athlete, and I think there will always be good instincts as they age."

Alex racked the slide on the Remington once more, and the bolt locked back, exposing the chamber and showing evidence the gun was empty. He caught the final ejected round as it spun in the air and looked at its base.

"Asshole took the plug out," he said. "Only three rounds are allowed by Fish and Game; there were four in this gun. Double-aught shot; an amateur's choice. He's lucky the game warden didn't catch him. Stole my knife too." Alex plopped into his chair at the table and laid the smoking Remington on the deck.

Kelly was grinning, slowly shaking his head. He had been a marine for thirty-two years and had seen much combat, but had never seen anything quite like this.

"Where the hell were you, Elliot?" he said. "You're a goddamned decorated Seal. I'm a four-star general; I could have been hurt."

"There weren't enough of them for me to bother, General," Elliot said. "Our man Cooch seemed to have had matters in hand without me, and I might have gotten in his way. Getting in his way can be painful. Besides, I mostly shoot people. Cooch isn't picky about how he kills people, as you may have noticed. He is sometimes undignified in his actions. I find that unwholesome."

Jerome was standing on the ladder to the galley with his head and shoulders visible above the deck. He had a compact Kimber .45 semi-automatic pistol in his hand, hammer back, pointing up.

"Don't look at me," he said. "They were way too close for me to bother. Cooch does the close-up stuff. I'm just here in case he trips or something."

Kelly had begun watching Caitlin again. She should have been hysterical, or offended or something distracting. Her eyes were wide and her breathing fast, but she was coping.

"You seem relatively unshaken by all of this, Caitlin," he said. "I'm surprised."

"I date Alex occasionally, and sometimes Cooch pops up. I've seen it before. He's handy to have around when I decide to go slumming. He had to bail me out of a biker bar a while back. It was ugly. I've never quite gotten used to the sudden change in behavior and the scary face, but I've known Cooch was in there for a long time. Most of the time Alex is a very nice boy."

"It's true," Alex said with a smile and a modest nod of his head. "I'm misunderstood. Rhodes Scholars and other lowlife types spread nasty rumors about me to cover their envy. Lies, Elliot! They are all lies."

"Oh, spare me the comedy routine," Kelly said, smiling. "Let me get you another glass of wine, Cooch. My scotch appears to have spilled as well." He stood and walked to the wine bottles.

"Age, I'd guess," Elliot said. "Spillage is often the first symptom of impending system failure. Balance goes first."

"Probably," Alex agreed. "He's no longer young and he drags his left leg just a bit."

"And the horse you rode in on, the both o' you," Kelly said as he raised his middle finger and laughed. He still had a bit of shrapnel in his left leg—few noticed. He poured a glass of wine and handed it to Alex, then reached for the scotch bottle.

"If you want to talk about your meeting with the president, we can," Kelly said. "I'll have to report back anyhow, as will Mac, if you want any traction with your funding ideas."

"We should do that soon," Alex said. "He was a tad hostile at first and is in no hurry. It was a surprisingly thoughtful conversation in its later moments. He's thinking about things, I imagine. I need to get out of here sometime soon and make my way back to Morocco."

"I think I'll tag along," Caitlin said. "I don't have anything else on my to-do list here, and I'm never caught up in Tangier. I need to get to Spain too. You do our reservations to Tangier. I'll get to Spain a little later."

"Let me get dinner started, then I'll work on that before we settle in to talk," Alex said as he picked up his wine glass and walked to the grill. "Enough of this barbarism."

"Brooks, why don't you take the dinghy out and see what our swimmer might have on him and get some prints on a glass or something," Mac said. "I'm curious about him. That curse as he spun and dove sounded Slavic. Push him to the shore and secure him before he floats into a water skier and ruins our evening. I'll send someone for him. He may have forensic tales to tell. He didn't look quite like the others." He picked up his Kphone and hit a few buttons as Brooks moved to the stern ladder, picked up a line that was secured to a stern cleat, and began to pull in the dinghy, the small utility boat with a little outboard that was towed behind. Jerome ducked back to the cabin and returned with a black plastic folder and handed it to Elliot.

"Here's a decent print kit," Jerome said. "I'll ride along to keep you company." The butt of the compact Kimber showed from his waistband, its hammer now down.

After dinner dishes were washed by Mac and Jerome, a bottle of 1994 Dow vintage port was opened. Elliot dug appropriate glasses out from the cabin as the port breathed. A black Chevy Suburban with tinted windows and several antennae showing pulled up to the shore. Two muscular men got out, and walked along the bank with a stretcher, looking for the floater.

Silver Springs, Maryland
The Beltway, I-495

The following morning Alex was driving back to DC when the call came.

"I don't have great news," Jerome said. "It has begun, finally."

"Oh?"

"Yeah, our office in Yemen got blown up this morning just as it opened—demolished," Jerome said. "Suicide bomber, it looks like."

"Our people?" Alex said.

"Everyone in the office is dead, including eleven kids in school. Thirty-three in total. The building may be totaled. They got our top training guy too, Nijad, who was over there for the week. There's another fifty-eight of ours in Aden, out and about, wondering what to do."

"Aw, jeez," Alex said. "I just sent Nijad a wedding present a few weeks ago. Good guy, nice wife. Any warning, other than the Al-Qaeda rants about the child care?"

"No," Jerome said. "But Al-Qaeda in the Arabian Peninsula claimed responsibility an hour or so ago."

"Did they now?" Alex said. "I guess it really has started, and Al-Qaeda in Yemen started it. I heard just this week they were getting ugly. Blowing up a bunch of noncombatants, including children, just pisses me off. They view their battlefield differently than we do."

"Yeah," Jerome said. "We all kill to create political impact, but they go too far for me. Besides, a few successful bombings will tend to discourage our folks. They'll get scared."

"They should get scared," Alex said. "They depend on us for security. We failed them, and now they're watching us to see whether we're worthy of their loyalty. We'll need to put up a new office in Aden. And we'll need to return the message somehow, in an out-of-proportion response. If we can figure out who did this, it's combat time. We need to hurt them."

"Might be time to let Dain out," Jerome said.

"Yeah, it is," Alex said. "I'm sure he's watching. Gear up. Get the boat relief working and take the Hog. She's in port, I assume."

"She is," Jerome said after a moment of punching a few buttons on his Kphone. "She'll need a few days to load, fuel, and go. I can get back there in a day or two."

The Hog, named *Ghania* by registration, was a 475-foot freighter that looked old and tired. She hadn't been painted in years. The rest of her had been extensively and unobtrusively refitted in Newport News, Virginia, several years before under a large contract from the US government for "weapons testing." She was owned by Jerome's company and leased to one of the CIA front companies in Morocco. Kufdani Industries had the contract to operate her. She had a complement of electromagnetic-pulse hardened electronics and armaments far beyond those found even on most government warships in the Middle East. Mac had once said, "It seems wise to have *Ghania* equipped to survive a nuclear exchange, even if I'd rather we didn't have one."

Most of *Ghania's* deadly weapons systems were kept in hardened high-tech containers within a well-guarded storage warehouse next to the pier where the Hog was berthed. Loading was mission dependent, and routine cargo could be loaded as well with large cranes that did double duty, to maintain the veil of banality that made the Hog so valuable. New engines could take her to thirty knots and cruise at twenty. The few who had seen the weapons demo were stunned by the sight of four sides and a roof on a large, apparently benign container falling to the side and a battery of advanced, radar-guided surface-to-air missiles active immediately on the site. Tops of containers could move to the side and a pod of surface-to-surface missiles could pop up, radar guidance enabled. Brooks had once observed, "What a handy, lethal gadget she is, our *Ghania*. A stealth pocket destroyer."

"Take two rifle squads and the weapons support team, along with the Rulon construction gear to get a new office going," Alex said. "We should get construction moving and this time put it behind some wire with some toys on it. Maybe we'll get lucky and find out to whom we should send our violent message."

"Yeah, and I'll take a Hog security team to keep our fat baby safe," Jerome said. "We need the practice anyhow. I'd like a chance to test my super-squad theory."

"I'll go over there a couple of days before you arrive, to look around. What do you figure, two weeks?"

"It's about four thousand miles to Aden," Jerome mused. "At twenty knots, that would be two weeks, more or less. The traffic in the Suez Canal might be heavy this time of year. That would slow us a bit. I'll post a message to you when we enter the Red Sea, with another thousand miles or so to go."

"I'm heading to Tangier this week," Alex said.

Tangier

Late afternoon in Tangier was Alex's favorite time to think. It was just before things slowed dramatically in the harbor. The wind-driven craft were motoring their way to shelter or beating into the wind to save a last drop of diesel before tying up for the night. Behind him, a backdrop of dry hills rose above the city and the offices of Kufdani Industries. Alex sat in the shade in a cushioned chair on the balcony of his office, looking across the city to the water. The flat waters of the Mediterranean shimmered pink as he looked northeast past the fading afternoon sun to the hazy image of Gibraltar in the distance. People eager to close their day scurried beside the walls and gates of the Kasbah, the site of the ancient Roman ruins. The octagonal minaret of the Kasbah mosque stood high over them; a call to prayers would soon be broadcast from it. Alex's quarters adjoined his office, since his hours blended into some sort of a continuum. He seemed to be always on duty, but had no specific duties. There were two separate, fully equipped guest suites with their own security beside his office. At the far end was a large office and suite for Caitlin. A lap pool had been built beside it at her request. Alex had long since decided that

Caitlin would get pretty much anything like that she wanted, since her contributions were so outsized and her security so important. She brought in millions of dollars a year from NSA alone in contract dollars and bonuses that Brooks had negotiated.

Tangier felt increasingly like home to Alex. The offices of Kufdani Industries reached well behind him into a maze of caves that wound through the hills behind the port. The mass of the hills provided a natural barrier that enabled a person like him to indulge a bias toward physical security, given the existence of the touristy Cave of Hercules ten kilometers away and all of its little-known side channels that burrowed their way deep inside the hills. Sheikh Abu Kufdani, his maternal grandfather, had given him a full day tour of the caves long ago, and then had given him a very old, hand-drawn map. Over time Alex had supplemented the old map with grid coordinates from a modern GPS and the results of surveying teams. After several years and much thought and consultation, he had hired a few top engineers from ABB in Switzerland to build a plan. They had designed and slowly developed an operating headquarters within the cave complex that was fitted with the modern conveniences of commerce, and quite a bit more. It was a formidable, high-tech mass known to few, with security and technology designed into its every facet. Thoughts of defense from attack, both physical and electronic, were fundamental to its design.

Achmed, also a Bedouin of the Yahia tribe, was Alex's oldest friend and the top operating executive at Kufdani. He ran it well. Achmed walked from the balcony door and sat beside Alex in a chair with lush, red pillows and a cushioned footstool. It was Achmed's chair. They were ready to do their catch-up bull session, which was usually held on a weekday evening when Alex was in Tangier. For many summers Alex had traveled from his boyhood home in Audley, South Carolina, to Tangier, Morocco, to be with his maternal grandfather, Sheikh Abu Kufdani, in both the city and the desert. Alex and Achmed had been childhood playmates. Alex was the last male issue of the Kufdani family of Yahia Bedouin. Despite Islamic custom, he was to inherit everything his grandfather had accumulated and everything his male ancestors had accumulated before him.

Achmed's father had been the senior servant of the sheikh, "given" to Abu Kufdani by his father before him. The sheikh had, in turn, "given" Achmed to Alex long ago, when Alex graduated from Carnegie Mellon in electrical engineering and computer science, as what the sheikh termed an "adequate" graduation present. It wasn't a matter of slavery or indentured servitude, but rather a vow of servitude without question; Achmed was enthusiastic about being "given away." Abu Kufdani had been a leader, a sheikh, of the Yahia tribe, a group of more than one hundred thousand Bedouin living in Morocco. In the Bedouin way, a vow of servitude had two components. The first was the obvious obligation of the servant; the second was the unspoken but recognized obligation of the beneficiary of that vow of servitude to make the life of the servant a better one than was likely had the vow not been given. Achmed laughed often that being a servant had made his life wonderful, more meaningful and more fulfilling than anyone could have predicted.

The transition of Kufdani Industries to modern management had begun in earnest one evening a number of years earlier, just after Alex completed his studies at Oxford. Alex and Sheikh Kufdani were in the sheikh's sitting room, with a fire blazing in an already overheated room. Rugs were strewn about the stone floor. They sat on pillows, drinking strong mint tea.

"You will soon inherit the business that has been built for you over a period of more than a hundred years," Sheikh Kufdani had said. "I ask only that you use what you have learned to make the world a better place for the Yahia tribe, the Bedouin, and all of

Islam. There is ample cash. You are young, so don't feel a need for haste. Go, consider what needs to be done, decide what must be done first. We will then begin. Some things will no doubt take far longer than others."

"I've already thought of a few things that will take many years to implement, Grandfather," Alex said, "and you may disapprove. Without education and critical thinking skills, Kufdani may prosper in the short term and look good in Morocco and Islam, but we will lose ground to societies that can manage and grow talent. We must begin to build the skills we need to prosper. Our first few years must be devoted to building a cadre of thinkers and doers. I will consider carefully how to get to where you would like us to be and where I would like us to be. I've not yet thought things completely through, but having thoughtful, loyal workers is the first step."

One of Alex's first decisions was that Achmed be sent for a graduate program in international business at IMD, a good school in Switzerland, and that scholarships be established for the top 5 percent of Kufdani employees or Yahia tribesmen who had finished high school, an annual total of about two thousand persons per year if fully allocated. The scholarships were to improve skills for which an aptitude had been demonstrated, and recipients would be required to work in Morocco for Kufdani for a period of five years to earn back the loans granted for the scholarships.

When the sheikh was first informed of Alex's decisions, Kufdani was silent for several minutes, sipping his tea, then shrugged and said, "That is not, or course, what I would choose to do. It seems such a long view for any benefit and quite expensive immediately. But I don't presume to ask for changes to your budding plans, as I said.

"On another topic," the sheikh had continued, "I am aware of your skills in, or perhaps it is your penchant for, violence, from this Cooch business of yours I followed for so long. You have done violence for others, to such a degree that you have gathered renown among commandos. May I assume you are capable of controlling this violence until it is needed?"

Alex raised an eyebrow. "I assume that my violent nature is one of training rather than a control problem, but that assumption hasn't been tested much in the Kufdani environment. I do have a violent nature. There is a different person within me that was a part of my father before me, who is released from time to time. I think I can control him. Still, if I am to accomplish what we hope, there will be resistance from the dark side of the Muslim world, from people who don't want progress, but rather to interpret Islam to their selfish ends. The fanatics may attack anyone who interferes with their plans. I plan to interfere. If they come, and I think they will, there will be violence."

"There will be violence then, at least from the Shiites," Kufdani said. "Plan for it, use it for gain. There has not been an attack on our headquarters for nearly one hundred years. That is perhaps because the last attack ended so badly for the aggressors."

Alex smiled. "I studied that battle when I was ten or twelve. It was one of the lessons of Yahia culture that you made sure I learned. It was nicely done."

"Do you refer to the battle or the lesson?" Kufdani said with a grin peeking from his full beard.

"Both, of course," Alex said. "The lesson was useful from time to time in my violent past."

"Good, good," Kufdani said. "I am fond of things going according to plan. Plans are good, so one can adjust thinking from some considered foundation while under stress."

"Yes," Alex said. "I've learned that. Thank you for the early lesson."

"It was indeed my pleasure."

Alex and Achmed had sat many times over the years on a balcony in this same complex as it grew. They had discussed the future of the Kufdani business. Achmed had finished graduate business school at IMD several years after the sheikh's shrug, worked a few different executive jobs, and finally had become Kufdani's executive vice president, reporting to the sheikh. Alex had long since finished his master's in Islamic studies and history at the College of Oriental Studies at Oxford University, followed by graduate studies in business at New York University. He spent several lucrative years as an investment manager in New York, concentrating on technology. The investment in Caitlin's company, Axial, had been made from that fund. Kufdani owned many of the shares remaining available on the market. Axial was still public and independent, albeit with fewer employees than earlier. The product upon which Emilie was based had been developed there and was first offered to the commercial market, where it did poorly. The cost of product implementation was a hindrance to growth. The government market was far more lucrative and now provided the bulk of revenue for Axial. Caitlin had hired a president to run her business while she dealt with the government and built Emilie. Axial's president had a big salary and not much stock. Cailtin had a small salary but still owned ten percent of Axial, which yielded a huge cash dividend each year.

Alex had decided that Bedouin women should be the administrative bones of Kufdani as it grew, and so instructed Achmed. It would be in his interest to have capable women available and trained, even if underused, Alex told Achmed. In response, Achmed said, "Your wish is my wish, Alex. That's our deal. But tell me what brings you to that decision. It may help my thinking on how to carry out your wishes."

Alex was quiet for a few moments, then said, "The expansion of the roles of women in executive ranks of United States commerce was stunning, beginning in 1975 or so. I looked into it and talked to Caitlin. She thinks it is first that the invention of the birth-control pill allowed women to control the rate at which they procreate, if at all. They were thus able to hold jobs for longer periods and to compete better with men. They were at first willing to work at slightly lower wages in nearly any job held by a male, given a decent education comparable to the group of men whose jobs were coveted."

"And the second reason?" Achmed said.

"The second of the reasons is a little more farfetched, perhaps. Caitlin believes that women's executive success was also enabled by Title Nine, the American law that ensures that women are given the opportunity to play in team sports, rather than only those that emphasize individual performance, such as tennis, swimming, golf, and so on. The benefits were enormous that came from learning to win and lose as a team and from assessing the skills, strengths, and weaknesses of others on the team as well as those of the opponents."

Achmed was quiet for a few seconds, then leaned back in his chair and gave that throaty hoot of laughter that was so well known among the soccer players of Tangier.

"I hadn't thought of it, certainly, but it seems true in my eyes," he said. "It makes sense. I shall be enthusiastic, O Master, and may Allah have mercy on our competitors."

Alex smiled and said, "Anyhow, back to the path for organizing our women. First will come our leaders for the future. We must identify them when they are young, no older than eighteen, because they must be well-educated somehow, somewhere for them to be useful. Later will come the actual workers and their training. Caitlin has proposed a scheme that sounds as if it should work. She is looking now for appropriate US institutions to provide an undergraduate college education. She says the school must be primarily for the working class, and have a component that teaches critical thinking and another that teaches what Brooks calls modern philosophy, the thinking that led up to Adam Smith's work a few hundred years ago. Finally, there must be a component that allows a specialty of study."

"An academic major?" Achmed said, smiling.

"Yeah, thanks." Alex said. "A major. So that they learn to do something concrete that is useful to us. We don't yet need a bunch of kids leading a life of the mind and working for Kufdani. So, those are the criteria for an American college. Caitlin has found one in Western Pennsylvania. We've sent a few people and the results have been good."[3]

"There is another issue that needs your attention," Achmed said. "One of those first Pennsylvania students is the widow of Nijad, our executive killed in Yemen. She has asked to speak with you in private. Her name is Hala. You may have met her."

"I went to her honors college graduation and spoke to her briefly with four others that we sent. I saw her at her wedding with Nijad. We talked for a few moments. She seemed very bright and aggressive. Do you know what she wants?"

"No," Achmed said, "but I would guess it is not to ask for sympathy. Hala is very strong. She has a graduate degree from the IE business school in Madrid and was recruited by the Saudis and Kuwaitis when she graduated. She is two years into working off the Kufdani loan for her education. She is quite capable and well respected, if free with her opinions. Her departure would be a loss for Kufdani."

"Well, set it up," Alex said. "Tomorrow at two should work. Call it forty-five minutes. I'll do what I can, whatever it is."

· · ·

3   For context, see: www.robertcooknovels.com/footnotesPatriot

Alex sat at a desk in his office, a keyboard in front of him and a small display on the corner of the desk. His Kphone was on another corner of the desk, controlling and recording. The room expanded to the east into a conference sitting area with a couch and three easy chairs. There was a slight knock on his office door, just before two. "Come in," Alex said.

A woman in her midtwenties dressed in a long skirt and long-sleeved blouse walked in. She was tall and dark, with black hair beneath a head scarf, large dark eyes, and a prominent nose. No makeup. A large multicolored bag woven of goat hair hung from her left arm. The Goat bags were popular gifts among the middle class of Tangier and the employees of Kufdani Industries. Achmed's wife bought many of the bags and used them as gifts. They were usually bought from women who tended goats in a traditional Muslim marriage where money was badly needed. The children gathered the goat hair, the women made the bags.

Alex stood when she entered. The woman made firm eye contact as she reached out with her right hand.

"There is no need for you to stand," she said. "I am Hala, the widow of Nijad. We met in America at my graduation and again briefly at our wedding. Thank you for seeing me on such short notice."

"I remember the conversations and I'm sorry for your loss," Alex said, shaking her hand as he gestured to a chair. He sat again behind his desk. "Nijad was a capable and intelligent man. Both Achmed and I held him in high regard."

"He was many good things," Hala said. "I miss him. I waited many years to find a man suitable for me. Now he is gone forever. Time has not yet begun to close the wound."

"We miss him as well," Alex said, "and we would like to help you. How can we at Kufdani make your life easier? We feel somewhat responsible for his death."

"Of course Kufdani is responsible for his death," Hala said sharply. "He wouldn't have been in Yemen if not for Kufdani. One can but pray for vengeance, however unlikely."

"Perhaps a pension would allow you to live comfortably in your grief. Some sort of monetary settlement to help you live more comfortably without the salary of Nijad?"

"I don't want your money. I have a job at Kufdani and I am good at it. The pay is acceptable and will no doubt increase as I prove my worth."

"No doubt," Alex said wryly. "That's fine with us. I just want you to know that we feel an obligation, since Nijad's death came as part of what we do. You are very well thought of. You're his widow and you lost something irreplaceable. We owe you."

"Ah, the debt," she said. "What do I have and what have I lost? I am a widow and used, not a virgin to be pursued. Virginity is valued greatly by Muslims. As the Americans say in Pennsylvania, 'The first time at bat is gone.' I'm destined by our custom to spend the rest of my life alone, or with a man who takes me for scullery work as a multiple wife. Nijad is indeed irreplaceable, as is the new life I began just a few weeks ago."

"I understand, at least a bit. But I don't know how to fix that," Alex said, uncomfortable and not sure where the conversation was going.

"You can't fix it," she said. "But you can provide a very discreet personal service for me that may make things somewhat better."

"And that is?" Alex asked warily.

"It is complicated," Hala said, and her face flushed scarlet. "But I have decided to ask it. Simply, I may be pregnant by Nijad. If I am not, I may never be pregnant, except to an aging Muslim who expects duty from his wives."

"How does this affect Kufdani? What is it that you would have us do?"

"Not Kufdani," Hala said. "You. I have done my research. It is the time of my monthly cycle that I could become pregnant. For some women the optimum moment is earlier in their cycle, and for some later. I would like you to have sex with me for each of the next three days, to maximize the probability that I bring something of value from my marriage. Nijad admired you and thought you a great warrior; I knew your grandfather slightly. I have been told your father was a warrior of note. Your seed should be adequate."

"We all hope to be adequate," Alex said, smiling and a bit flustered. "But there are ways that will serve the same purpose, without going through the embarrassment of having sex with a near stranger."

"No!" she said, eyes locked on his. "As I said, I have done the research. That way is too public, which would defeat its purpose and would be even more wrong, I think. If I am to conceive a child, it must be done in the way that is natural in the event that the seed of Nijad was ill-timed, and be a secret between the two of us. I choose you to do that. It is not so much to ask, do you agree?"

"When do you plan to start this little effort?" Alex asked.

"From the swelling in your trousers, I would expect you would choose to begin right now," Hala said sarcastically. "Do we have an agreement?"

There was an urgent beating against his thigh. "We have an agreement. How would you like to do this, other than secretly?"

"I will move to your couch. I think it would be best if we are clean, given the objective at hand. I will wash and inspect you before we begin and I will wash myself. I have brought a lubricant that should make things a bit less unpleasant when we begin. Walk to the couch and turn your back, please."

Alex walked to the door and set the lock with a click. He turned and walked to the couch and stood by it as Hala sat. He turned away, and heard her open her bag and rustle round in it. There was the sound of a liquid gurgling onto something.

"You may turn around," she said after a few moments, her face again scarlet and her eyes defiantly on his. She sat on the couch with her bag open beside her.

"Please remove your trousers and expose your manhood," she said. "I will then clean and lubricate it and we will begin."

"Just like that?" Alex said.

"Yes, just like that," she said. "I am quite uncomfortable with this, but I have made my decision and have but one fleeting opportunity. Remove your trousers, please. I will assist you if the application of the lubricant fails to bring you to readiness to accomplish this task. Nijad needed no extra encouragement, but we were in love. I will understand if you are less eager. You are older and past your prime for this kind of thing, perhaps."

Alex unbuttoned his trousers and dropped them to the floor, then worked his boxer shorts down over a surprisingly raging erection. He stood just in front of her.

"You appear to need no encouragement," Hala said.

A small washcloth was beside her. She picked it up and reached for him, then scrubbed. She again reached into the bag and drew out a small bottle of lotion and applied it to her hands, then to him.

"Would you find it easier to mount me from behind, or must I see the face of a stranger during this most intimate of moments?" she said.

"From the front is easier, particularly on a soft couch," Alex said. "We would both find a hard floor uncomfortable. You may close your eyes."

She lay back on the couch, closed her eyes, and raised her skirt. Alex raised her left leg and put it on the top of the couch back, then positioned himself between her thighs and put his left foot on the floor for stability. Hala reached for him and said, "Perhaps you should proceed slowly. I am new at this and Nijad was of a more modest girth than are you. I will assist."

There were a few moments of trial and error before they first coupled. Early discomfort slowly slid away as the rhythm of the act became more routine. After a few minutes, she opened her eyes and watched his face. She pulled his head down to hers and turned it.

"It has become tolerable, maybe even pleasant," Hala whispered. "Is that normal?"

"That's normal," Alex said. "Kissing makes it even better."

Hala's eyes opened and widened. "We will not do that, but we shall proceed until completion of what we have begun."

The sounds of the couch springs groaning were loud in the room and the ancient cadence unmistakable if heard by an adult. Her face relaxed into a slight frown; her eyes were still closed.

After a few more moments, Hala's eyes opened about halfway, and she smiled for the first time, almost lazily. "Will kissing help it be over sooner? We make too much noise."

"It would help," Alex said with a smile.

"You may kiss me then, but I have little kissing experience," Hala said.

Alex lowered his face to hers and kissed her gently. Her lips were tight, mouth closed.

"Loosen your lips," he murmured into her left ear, "as if you taste a ripe date, or an orange that has been partially sliced."

"It's hard to concentrate with your hips moving so forcefully that way, and your face nearly still," she said. "But don't stop just yet with what you are doing. It has an ending yet to come, at least for you. That is why we are here."

Alex nibbled on her lower lip, then ran his tongue along it. She began to relax her grimace, and her lips softened and parted. Alex touched the tip of her tongue with his and teased it. Their tongues tangled, the kiss deepened, then she turned her head to whisper, "I feel quite strange. It is as if there is a teakettle low inside me, about to boil. Is that normal?"

"That is both normal and good," Alex said softly, continuing. "The goal is for you to let it simmer and keep it there for a bit. Don't let it boil. It takes practice to do that, so let it boil if it must."

A bit later, Hala's jaw suddenly tightened and her eyes widened.

"Oh my. I boil," she gasped. He could feel her convulsively squeezing him as he moved. Alex groaned suddenly. After a few moments, he rested his head on her chest, heaving for breath. His hair was matted with sweat as Hala pushed it gently back with her fingers, a contented smile on her face. As he began to pull from her, she reached down for him and squeezed as he slid through her hand.

"I almost forgot that," she said dreamily. "As I was about to be married, my mother told me to do that, if I expected offspring. She gave me the lotion too. Now I am to lie here for a bit with my feet up. You should go clean yourself." As he stood, she pulled her skirt down, swung her right foot to the top of the couch back, and closed her eyes.

A few minutes later, Alex walked back into the room. Hala was on the couch, eyes closed, feet still propped on the couch back.

Hala opened her eyes and said, "I could nap, but I must not. Now I understand all the commotion about sex. It can be quite pleasant, once past the discomfort."

Alex sat in an overstuffed chair and smiled.

"Pleasant indeed, at least for me," he said. "Do you still plan to return for days two and three?"

Hala's head snapped up. "I do. Is that acceptable?"

Alex laughed and stood. "It most certainly is," he said. He walked to his computer and made a few notes. "What time works for you?"

Hala smiled and then was serious. "Two o'clock is again acceptable. Perhaps you should add thirty minutes to talk about my posting with Kufdani. I would like to go to Spain to work and live; there is nothing for me here."

Alex nodded. "I blocked an hour and a half," he said. "I'll take a look at Spain in the meantime and talk to Achmed."

"Fine," Hala said. "I shall endeavor to be more efficient for our next two efforts. I shall research conception further. Perhaps there are methods to be employed that will enhance my odds of a successful conception, if I search in English. There will be no guidance in Arabic."

"I'm at your service," Alex said, eyebrows raised and with a wisp of a smile. "Now that we have once tried, would you rather take another approach to your conception? I'm concerned that it was excessively unpleasant for you today. I can make a necessary donation without making you uncomfortable."

Hala raised her head and looked directly at him.

"I didn't and don't expect pleasantness," she said sharply. "You performed as expected and your donation, as you call it, seemed as expected and abundant. I now know how to mitigate some of the unpleasantness. You will have to do this only twice more. We have an agreement. I expect you to keep to your word."

"And so I shall," Alex said. "See you tomorrow." He walked to his desk and sat down as Hala picked up her bag and walked to the door. She opened it and went through without looking back.

Just before two on the following day, Alex pressed a key to save the employee file on Hala. She had been a top student in high school.

She had indeed been one of the early students who received a grant from Kufdani to attend Caitlin's chosen American state university in Western Pennsylvania. It had a unique program for talented students, was reasonably priced, and was but fifty miles east of Pittsburgh, where there was a good airport. Muslim students didn't do well when surrounded by great wealth, as in the Ivy League schools, so the Pennsylvania school had proven a good choice for a number of Muslim students. For their first two years, students there learned critical thinking and written and oral communications skills with the Western Civilization classics as the teaching foundation. If one studied David Hume, the Scottish Enlightenment philosopher, and wrote a paper favoring his thinking, one was expected to write and defend the next paper criticizing his thinking, citing another philosopher's work. The ability to argue either side of an issue proved a useful skill to develop for business. Brooks Elliot had done several fifty-minute videos, extolling the virtues of the Enlightenment viewed through the prism of economics. They were a summary of what he had learned about philosophy and economics. Students on Kufdani scholarships studied them over the course of the four undergraduate years.

At the end of each school year, they were required to write a paper that compared current Muslim life in the Middle East to various periods in seventeenth- and eighteenth-century Europe. The students' second two years were spent in an academic major, utilizing the depth of the larger, less rigorous university that housed the honors college. Hala had chosen computer science and graduated with high honors. A sophomore summer internship at Carnegie Mellon University in Pittsburgh, Alex's alma mater, had been a bonus that was repeated in her junior year.

Alex had a post in mind for her in Spain and had called Achmed to discuss it. He was enthusiastic about the idea and had promised to make the arrangements quickly.

Precisely at two o'clock a quiet knock on his door caused him to stand as his erection leaped to life. "Come in," Alex said, embarrassed by his quick physical response.

Hala walked into the room with her large Goat bag over her right arm. She closed the door, set the lock, and walked to the couch.

"I have read on Google the English advice on conception," she said primly, "and then on sex because they are, of course, related. Advice was quite extensive, and some was surprisingly thoughtful."

"And?"

"It seems there is a very wide and thoughtful online discussion of the sexual metaphysics of female orgasm," Hala said as she opened her bag.

"On the sexual metaphysics," Alex said, eyebrows raised and shaking his head.

"Yes," she said, with just a hint of a smile. "Metaphysical teapots."

"Nothing about men, then," he said with a faint smile. "Just the teapot's varying view of things."

"Your sarcasm is unkind, chauvinistic, and condescending," she said. "We're also wasting time on our ninety minutes that I expect you to make up."

"Cool. I'll make it up," Alex said with another slow shake of his head. "But I'm curious. What did you find out about female orgasm?"

"Ugh. I simply detest that Western argot. Cool, indeed!" she said. "But beyond endless superlatives as to the experience, I found that men are not necessary to female orgasm, particularly since the advent of electricity flowing from wall sockets and the discovery of lithium batteries. Strangely, I found that the creation of multiple, shall we say teapots, has been shown to increase substantially the probability of conception within the time window of ovulation, for reasons still unclear. We should discuss that possibility, if you feel confident that you can assist in the creation of that situation."

"You're getting goofy," Alex said. "You sound like a goofy westerner. I will not discuss the possible intersection of orgasm and ovulation with you."

"And part of me is indeed 'a goofy westerner,' praise Allah," she said. "At least in my brain, which is kept mostly separate from the dogma of my religion. My undergraduate honors college experience in America and that of my graduate program in Spain were enlightening. It may not surprise you that I found I don't like being the Bedouin woman. I dislike the whole female subservience component. But I am both Bedouin and Muslim until I die. I work within that construct and look for opportunities to make things incrementally better for me and fellow Muslims; I believe that is what good Muslims do. That doesn't make me stupid. I'm a believer, not a robot. *Cogito, ergo sum,* or some such."

"You quote Descartes in a discussion about ovulation and conception? What the heck?"

"And you have a fresh erection deforming your trousers. Is it the talk of Descartes that arouses you?"

"I'm being sexually exploited!"

"Indeed you are, just as you agreed," Hala said. "But you seem to prepare readily for exploitation, and participate enthusiastically. I read of this orgasm I had, the boiling teapot. The experience was surprisingly pleasant, with enough history that comments to be found in online research were plentiful."

"Did you?" Alex said. "I thought about that. I was curious about your research."

"Indeed I did," Hala said. "I also discovered that you are somewhat deformed, at least by girth, which caused me substantial initial discomfort. I can deal with that, I suppose, but do you have suggestions as to how a multiple teapot would be made possible?"

"Even deformed men have opinions," Alex said. "But I'm no expert. It has to do with the preparation for the act, rather than the act itself, I would think, but each person is probably different. I imagine you read about preparation, foreplay, in your research. It could mitigate the impact on you of my deformity, as you describe it. What would make you comfortable?"

"A diameter shrinkage would be best for comfort. Excluding that, I am certainly not going to do any of those disgusting things to you that I read," she said. "It is I who would most benefit from these things, if stimulated. But most of it is so fundamentally foul in nature that I would not want to experience it."

"I'd say that foulness is a matter of personal perspective, but no matter. Let us proceed as we last did, but more slowly," he said, with a slight smile as his erection again pounded impatiently against his trouser leg. "The kissing thing is not so disgusting and perhaps we can explore each other a little as we practice kissing. Exploration can be stimulating."

"Perhaps," she said. "But I must be in control. When I say stop, you must stop."

"Agreed."

"Remove your trousers, please," Hala said. "I shall prepare you."

In a moment Alex stepped forward as she turned for the lubricant in her bag. As she turned back, she put some lotion on her hand and reached for him, making eye contact with Alex as she applied it.

After a few minutes, as they lay together on the couch, she pulled her mouth from his and said, "Perhaps that is enough exploring on your part, although it was more pleasant than I anticipated. I seem aroused, as the writings describe. You again seem adequately prepared. Please get on with your duty, but this time proceed more slowly and gently at first, if you please."

Later Alec walked from the restroom, drying his hands. As he tucked his shirt into his trousers, she opened her eyes, brought her feet down from the back of the couch, and said lazily, "That was better, with two of the teapots. You are an acceptable student. Once more should be adequate, perhaps with three or four teapots. I am learning to control the simmer. Then I shall get on with my life, as we have agreed."

Alex turned and walked toward his desk, shaking his head.

"I'm pleased I was able to be of service, in my own secret, humble way," he said wryly. "Does two o'clock tomorrow again work for you, for the final of my duty sessions?"

"I think perhaps we should skip one day," Hala said. "I have read that your seed, even at your age, should have enough life that a longer period of ovulation probability should be covered with an extra day's wait. I first will gather my things, close my apartment, and prepare for my move to Spain. I have discussed my new position with Achmed and find it acceptable. He suggests I move there quickly."

"That's fine with me," Alex said. "Check tomorrow with the Kufdani People Office for overnight housing if you need it."

Alex hesitated, then said softly, "Are you sure you want to even do this a third time? Does it make that much difference?"

Hala glared at him and finally said, "We have an agreement. Cancellation of that third encounter is neither a decision for you to make nor a situation for me to explain decision parameters. If you want to know about the changes in the probability of fertilization with a third insemination during a given period of ovulation, look it up. You are not acting in the spirit of our agreement."

"Well said. I apologize. What shall we do?"

"I'll come to your office at four o'clock, day after tomorrow, and we shall proceed from there."

Southwest Texas

A lone turkey vulture soared lazily on a thermal rising over the border between West Texas and Mexico, alert for movement and seeking a whiff of a ripening meal. A thousand feet above it, a small, unmanned airplane called a Predator soared a similar pattern and sent signals back to its minder, with her controlling joystick. She in turn forwarded them on to the Pentagon and the White House, where they turned into graphic photo images. MacMillan and General Patrick Kelly sat in Kelly's office watching the scene on a large flat screen.

"Damn, I should've brought popcorn," Mac said. "Wish Clint Eastwood was here. We could show him some shit. Those pictures of the mortar tubes on the mules were hot. It helps to know whether we should shoot first or later. I like shooting first."

"Eastwood has women," Kelly said. "He doesn't need this shit, and he shoots first whenever he wants. The women don't care about his wrinkles."

Mac nodded. "The wrinkles on his face don't need to be treated."

The ragged line of eight mules stretched for sixty yards of arid soil. It curved along a narrow trail that led north to the Texas border. Eight Mexican mule handlers walked beside beasts loaded with bulky tubes and bags. Another fifteen men walked in front and behind, some with rifles slung over their shoulders and others with rifles held in front of their chests. It was late in the day. Small puffs of red dust rose from the trail as the men shuffled wearily. They were ready to stop for some water and the evening meal as the falling sun cast deepening shadows from the hills to the west.

The trail straightened as the hills leveled, and the last of the men following came around the curve from behind the mules. The last of the mules in the line jerked suddenly. Another of the mules pulled against the lines of its handler. Two others brayed loudly. There was suddenly loud conversation among the handlers. Some of the men in front and back began to unsling their rifles, unsure what had transpired, if anything. A ragged volley of shots rang out, and men other than the handlers began to fall, rifles partially off their shoulders. Two of the handlers tried to calm their frightened beasts. Others turned to run back down the trail and abandoned their mules. As they ran, one stumbled and then another as tranquilizer darts fired from Delta Force rifles hit them in the back. The mules began to go to their knees, and then slowly roll over.

"Halt! Throw down your weapons," an amplified voice said in fluent Castilian Spanish. "Put your hands behind your heads."

There was silence, then two men in silver hazmat suits with Delta Force sleeve decals below an American flag imprint began to work their way down from a small hill to the fallen beasts. One raised a gloved middle finger in the direction of the amplified voice.

"They mock me," said one man in desert camouflage to another lying beside him with a rifle bedded on an improvised sandbag. "Why? I have done my duty with the warning. This time I don't have to wear that smelly sauna suit. Let the gringos do it."

"Stillman, *you're* a fucking gringo. Your mother is a Cabot. You learned Spanish at Yale. And if you had called that warning out early, I'd have shot you."

Stillman grinned. "Yeah, and a little Spanish in prep school. That doesn't make those hazmat suits any more comfortable. I'm glad to not wear that thing as a junior man on the team. I'm a Yalie, and I will testify that I gave the warning long before any of those shots were fired, and in impeccable Spanish. I'm credible."

"Uh-huh. So was John Dean for awhile, back in the Nixon days. If you get called in front of Congress to testify, watch out for your brownie. Those crooked bastards will put you in jail if they catch you in a fib. They'll think you're cute."

"I am cute. You mean Congress or the jailbirds?" Stillman said.

"Both, Stillman. Watch out for the one from Massachusetts."

"Jablonski, you went to some school in Pennsylvania named for a slimy stone or another state or something, and full of people with too many consonants in their surnames. If they want someone for a trophy, they'll take you. You shot an innocent civilian, long before I gave the warning."

There was a chuckle. "Yeah, I got a handler and two mules with darts. The gomer I shot was a cool shot. I think I got him low left on the chest with only a second delay after the magazine change from the darts. He dropped like a stone."

"Yeah, I saw that. Good shot," Stillman said. "It doesn't look like there was any leakage of anything down there other than bodily fluids, but our cute little hazmat boys are furiously taking pictures of the cargo and none of the gomers. This could get interesting."

Jablonski looked into his four-power rifle scope. "Yup, you're right. The civilians will be along to take over soon, I betcha. Those images are probably already back in the Pentagon, thanks to our silent friend circling up there somewhere. We'll get to provide perimeter security all night to make sure nobody molests the corpses down there beside the mules. The handlers are going to wake up in a couple of hours. They are not going to be mellow."

Stillman looked down at the activity. "Not our job, bro," he said. "We'll serve and protect from up here. The stink won't be as bad."

The turkey vulture tightened the arc of his search. There was food just below, ripening.

. . .

At the White House, Kelly and Mac were busily forwarding the photos that had been relayed through the Predator, looking for a good identity on the cargo recovered.

"Talk to me, Mac," Kelly said as he put his red phone down. "You used to do this shit for a living."

"I imagine the six mortar tubes hold 120 millimeter rounds armed with binary sarin from the green bands on the transport tubes, stolen from the Russians or maybe bought from them. Forty rounds were stolen that we know of. We're still missing twelve. This could be six of them. That would be a huge win."

"Yeah," Kelly said. "But what about those steel boxes? The steel boxes worry me."

"Uh-huh. Me too. What the hell is more valuable to an Arab nutcase than nerve gas that could kill fifty thousand people? It has to be something with a very nasty long-term view."

"Any ideas?" Kelly said.

"Nope. This is outside my pay grade. But I'd sure like to know what it is. It scares the shit out of me. We need to police up those guys at the cantina in Texas and read to them from the good book."

"I'm a United States Marine. I know not fear," Kelly said as he picked up his phone again.

Mac snorted and said, "Fear has kept us alive all these years, bro. It ain't gonna let us down now, I hope."

"Execute Longhorn Loudmouth. I say again, Execute Longhorn Loudmouth," Kelly said into the phone, heard a confirmation, and hung up.

West Texas

Near the border with Mexico, armed men slid silently through the night to surround the cantina named *Dos Amigos*. Their target had entered the cantina seventeen minutes before from a small adobe shack now guarded by two other Delta men. They had orders to take the target alive, if possible. His companions were expendable. When the designated shooter shot through an open cantina window to hit the target in the chest with a tranquilizer dart, the leader tossed a flash-bang grenade through the same window. There was a horrifically loud explosion. The flash-bang was designed to stun the occupants into inactivity while the Delta Force men stormed inside, ready to engage any threat that arose. Inside, one man pulled a revolver from his belt and was shot twice. Two other occupants reached for their waist and were killed instantly. It was neither the right time for a resident to get a note from his belt, nor for Delta to discern friend from foe.

The target stood, reached inside his shirt, and pulled from it a small automatic pistol and put it to his head. Another dart hit his chest.

"*Allahu Akbar*," he shouted and pulled the trigger, spraying brains and matter across the room, then collapsed dead to the floor. The others in the room were thrown to the floor and had their hands cuffed behind them, awaiting interrogation.

Outside, the two Delta watchers burst into the shack that had housed the target. It was empty. A maroon Samsung laptop computer sat on a small dresser.

Washington, DC

Several days later, in the situation room of the White House, Mac and Kelly sat with an Army chemical warfare expert, a Lieutenant Colonel Ronald Fielding dispatched from Fort Dietrich, Maryland, and David Glotz, a civilian from the Department of Agriculture's Cereal Disease Laboratory at the Agricultural Research Service. Both held PhDs in their respective fields and the highest security clearances possible. Early reports from the analysis of files from the computer captured in West Texas by Delta Force troops sat in front of each for reference. They had been translated earlier, then studied exhaustively.

Fielding, the colonel, opened and said, "There's not much mystery about sarin, since it was invented in 1938, and I have no new news based on an analysis of the rounds recovered. It is an ugly weapon. The 120 millimeter mortar rounds that were recovered in Texas have the same characteristics as those captured earlier in Iraq and are, in fact, of the same manufacturing lot. In binary form, sarin is sufficiently stable for routine transportation and becomes highly toxic only when its primary two components are mixed. That occurs usually from the concussion of firing the round and detonating it or from a rupture of the membrane separating them, causing hydrolysis of the bond between its phosphorus and fluoride components. It is highly toxic, about five hundred times that of cyanide. One diffused drop is sufficient to cause death in a human. Inhalation and absorption through the skin pose a great threat. Even vapor concentrations immediately penetrate exposed skin. People who absorb a non-lethal dose and receive no immediate appropriate medical treatment may suffer permanent neurological damage. Tests of the earlier captured rounds showed air detonation at twenty meters, as they apparently were set at the factory. That setting allows a thirty-meter radius of lethal dispersal of sarin in a windless environment for unprotected skin and fifty meters for inhalation deaths and non-lethal injuries. A five-knot wind would reduce the spread and lethal impact by thirty-five percent or so. Standard practice calls for a windless target environment."

"What would you guess? A shopping center, a theatre?" Kelly asked.

"There are few windless days in Texas, and penetrating a roof to reach a target would greatly reduce the efficacy of the sarin round," Fielding said. "Mortars are notably inaccurate compared to artillery, which is why they were chosen by the Russians for delivering sarin. Multiple rounds cover a large swath of a target area just by virtue of their inaccuracy. I'd guess the target is some partially enclosed, open-top forum, like a football stadium. Sarin is not persistent, so its effects will diminish quickly in the open. But the first few minutes will be horrific."

"There are a lot of stadiums in Texas," Mac said, "and we're still missing six rounds from the batch, and one from the old batch of a few years ago."

"Yeah, and the sarin profile doesn't match the expected attack profile for the other weapon, right?" said Kelly, looking at Glotz, the man from Agriculture.

"A stadium wouldn't be the ideal dispersal venue," Glotz said. "Spores are best released into the wind, to be carried along. The material recovered is a weaponized wheat disease, the Ug99 fungus, called stem rust. Ug99 has destroyed about eighty percent of the crops it has infected and is moving from Africa into the Middle East. It will reach Pakistan within five years and Russia within ten, if not stopped; both countries are major global wheat producers. That same eighty percent destruction impact is likely if this stem rust gets a foothold in the US. We have been racing to breed resistant plants before the rust reaches the US by natural means, but we're not close. An introduced stem wheat rust that has been weaponized to resist treatment is likely to decimate wheat production in the US within five years and consequently cause starvation for hundreds of millions of people, perhaps billions, around the world. It will reach Canada within a few months if established here, and will decimate their crop as well."

Kelly looked at Mac and grimaced. "We need to find out how much of this stuff they made and how much is missing. Any ideas?"

"Do you have professional relations with any of the labs in Russia that may have produced this rust, Mr. Glotz?" Mac asked.

"We do not," Glotz said. "They were disbanded after the breakup of the Soviet Union. No one at Agriculture has heard from any of them since, to my knowledge."

"Any personal clues as to how we could run this down or get a lead?" Mac asked.

"I imagine I can narrow the list of scientists who could have built this weapon to three or four men," Glotz said. "But I have no idea how to reach them, nor even if they are still alive. We have no communications with anyone who was in that business in the Soviet Union."

"Well, I guess we will just have to figure something out," Kelly said. "Stay close, gentlemen. We may need you again. We've blocked rooms at the Hay Adams, because everyplace else nearby was full, so live it up. I'd like that list of possible creators as quickly as you can assemble it, Dr. Glotz."

Mac sat back in his char and looked at the ceiling, transfixed. Then he stood and followed Kelly out of the situation room.

Kelly turned to Mac and said, "Got something, I hope? This has the signs of a major cluster fuck."

"Maybe," Mac said. "Let's talk about our Russian visitor on *Old Fashioned* at the Bay."

"The one Cooch shot in the back with double-aught, twice, after he dove off the boat? You have the word back from the autopsy? He's a Russian?"

"Yeah, or at least he was. His name was Boris Kasmarov. His passport prints are on file, from an entry four years ago for employment by the Russian diplomatic force. He has the Speznatz tattoo, so he is or was Russian Special Forces. He had the clap too, and atherosclerosis."

"You're over sharing, but I wonder what the hell he was doing with the low lives on the Bay other than screwing their women," Kelly said. "You think there's a story there?"

Mac said, "I do. I think it has to do with the two killings on the Bay where someone valuable to US security got butchered. From the way their families were treated before they were killed, it makes sense to me that our scientists were questioned. Motivation for answers was provided by concern for their families, one brutal act at a time. One of the female victims showed evidence of gonorrhea mixed with the semen in her. I'll know soon if our Speznatz buddy was the owner of that semen."

"That flat pisses me off," Kelly said. "But I don't see any way to tie the Russians to it. He's dead. They won't talk to us about it, even if they did it."

"Like you point out," Mac said, "it seems unlikely that a Speznatz guy would buddy up with a bunch of lowlife Bay trash for no good reason, at least initially. If it was a planned operation, it was a poorly planned one. That's not like the Russians I know."

"I suppose you know someone to talk to," Kelly said with a smile. "Your CIA days seem to have left you with a big Rolodex."

"I don't just want to talk, I want to discuss their shitty planning and lie to them a little bit. I know the top intelligence guy there and there's no way he planned this cock-up. I'm going to tell him a story."

Kelly smiled and leaned back in his chair. "Tell me first," he said. "Maybe I can help from stage left."

• • •

The following evening Mac was uncomfortable in his tux. The ten-year-old dress shirt was a bit tight in the neck, and his bow tie felt crooked despite having been twice retied. He had invited himself to a reception at the residence of the Russian ambassador on Sixteenth Street that celebrated the successful performance of a company of the Bolshoi Ballet at the Kennedy Center. It was Mac's first visit to the residence, which was on the National Register of Historic Places. It had been bought and extensively remodeled after the new embassy had been built following the breakup of the Soviet Union. Mac was often invited to events at the embassy, since he was a "person of interest" to Russian intelligence. His reputation had grown over a long period; Mac seemed able to thwart their plans or to help them solve a problem they hadn't guessed he had known, to his inevitable benefit and sometimes theirs. If they had known he was interested in ballet, he would have been invited earlier. He wasn't interested, but here he was. He walked to a servant holding a tray and took a glass of vodka neat and tossed it back. If that didn't alert Sergei, nothing would.

The bulky waiter who held the tray had a tiny wire going into his ear. He smiled at Mac with steel teeth reminiscent of a character from a James Bond movie, and said, "The general would like a word with you, Colonel." He nodded toward an open terrace door.

"Oh, thank you so much, OddJob, my good man," Mac said, earning a puzzled sneer from the man.

On the terrace, General Sergei Orogortov, the senior intelligence officer at the embassy, was smiling broadly and greeted Mac in his fractured English. "Oh, Colonel MacMillan, how very kind of you to spare me a moment, don't you know."

"Cut the shit, Sergei," Mac said. "But thanks for paying attention. We have a problem."

"We?"

"Well, it's actually more personal for you than for me," Mac said. "You have a problem. I'm here at great personal sacrifice to help you solve it."

Sergei roared with laughter, then spoke into his sleeve. A male servant appeared quickly with a bottle of iced vodka and two glasses. He set them on a small table, beside two chairs.

"So, my lethal friend," Sergei said. "What business are we to do today?"

He poured a decent measure of iced vodka into the two glasses and handed one to Mac. "Cheers. To our mutual benefit," he said and raised his glass. They threw back their glasses and drained them. Sergei raised his shoulders with an inquisitive shrug.

"There are a few things going on. First, I suffered a visit from one of your thugs, a Boris Kasmarov."

"Did you?" Sergei said. "I wondered where he was."

"He's no longer with us, but let me tell you a story. A story about scientists and officials who were seen by our enemies to be essential to the new American war effort. They were abducted on US soil and interrogated, while their families were brutalized as an incentive for their candor."

"Goodness," Sergei said with a grimace. "Who would do something like that?"

"You say that, the next guy says something else. Your failure was in not stopping it and now you own the problem. Someone of your acquaintance, perhaps even in your reporting structure, lacks respect for the US. We have an interrogation tape."

"Illegally obtained, of course," Sergei said, frowning and thoughtful. "But embarrassing at the least. How should we deal with this? I could arrange, perhaps, a nuanced public apology. Such a person, if found, could be severely punished."

"At some personal risk to you," Mac said. "Better the devil we know…"

"Let's get to it, Mac," Sergei said. "What do you want?"

"The white-trash family in Maryland that you employed in this venture seems to feel they have discovered an enjoyable and lucrative pastime; there's been another attack in the Bay and our man Boris was there. Since it happened on your watch and one of yours got them started, we'd like you to have them stop—fair is fair. Their leaders seem anxious to play the Russian-involvement disclosure card if we attempt to prosecute them. That disclosure would upset our populace and damage relations between our countries needlessly; it seems unlikely that such gossip would enhance your career either."

"That's most unkind of them," Sergei said. "Tellers of lies often suffer grave consequences."

"Disclosing this situation is a favor I did for you, Sergei."

"As a representative of the great Russian nation, I assure you that you have our undying gratitude. I don't suppose there is a small favor we could do in return?"

"There is one small thing. We found some of your old Soviet bio-war products that were being smuggled into this country. Al-Qaeda had them. The product is a weaponized wheat stem rust that threatens to kill eventually about eighty percent of wheat production in the world. They hoped to start with America, but it spreads and Russia's turn would come quickly. Wind blows west to east. The hungry will become unpleasant."

"*Da*. The hungry often do," Sergei said. He poured another vodka and threw it back, thoughtful. "The bioweapon issue is difficult. Russia cannot be seen as the promoter of such an attack on America and would disclaim any formerly Soviet connections for such things unless we can blame it on the Ukrainians. It will likely be a few months before there can be any formal discussion of the ramifications of your disclosure. I'm sure we have scientists that are concerned with the problem of wheat stem rust. There was an article about it in the *Economist* in the early summer of 2011. What is it you want from me?"

"First, there was no disclosure. I never spoke of it and will deny any allegations to the contrary," Mac said. "But I'd like you to look into how much of this product you managed to lose so that we can tell if and when we get all that's missing. I'm sure you can find someone who knows the story but has failed to tell it, thus far."

Sergei was thoughtful for a few seconds, then pursed his thick lips into a frown. "Perhaps," he said. "But I don't know where to start. It will take awhile to find where it was made."

Mac reached into his jacket pocket and handed Sergei five photos. Four were of the bio boxes; the top photo was of the sarin mortar tubes.

Sergei's face darkened. "That fucking binary sarin again. I thought we had found all of that. Was it with the bioweapon in the hands of the Arabs?"

"It was, and we're still missing six rounds from that manufactured lot of sarin," Mac said. "Please let us know if you locate more. Your country will get the blame if they are ever used, since they were or are yours. What about the boxes?"

Sergei studied the photos for a few long seconds.

"Well, my friend, they were courteous enough to stamp their laboratory address on the boxes along with the warnings. We now know where this nightmare was made. It is a place to start. I'll make sure we have a long conversation with anyone who may know about their loss to thieves and traitors. We would like to know how much of it has been stolen and to whom it was sold, as perhaps would you."

"I should have a guess from our scientists as to which of your scientists is or was a likely creator of the bioweapon within a few hours. It was nice talking to you again, Sergei, and bringing you up to date," Mac said as he looked in the door at the crowd milling around the room. "I hope to hear from you soon. The residence is spectacular. I assume its electronics are equally stunning. Don't forget to destroy the recording of our little meeting here. You have enemies."

He poured two more glasses of vodka and handed one to Sergei. They each raised a glass to the other and tossed them back. Mac walked through the magnificent room to the front door and out.

• • •

The following morning Mac was in his office in the Old Executive Office. He again had his heels on the old mouse pad and

175

the phone to his ear. Mac had connected with his old friend, Colonel Jack Borson of the Maryland State Police. They had served together in the Marine Corps many years before. They remained friends as Borson worked his way up the ranks of the elite state organization.

"Jack, I had a premonition last night," Mac said.

"Shit! I hate your damned premonitions. Nothing to do with fed scientists getting killed on the Bay recently, does it?"

"Premonitions are seldom that specific, Jack," Mac said. "But if you have anyone on the inside of the Butruss clan down on the Bay, it may be time to give him or her a few days off."

"I've been trying to get someone inside there for three years. That's one nasty, closed-up, inbred bunch. I like them for some of the problems on the Bay, maybe even killing the feds lately. The fed hits are a little too sophisticated for them, though. You're not planning something violent in my patch, are you?"

"Nah, I don't operate inside our borders," Mac said, "but I heard a strong rumor they had pissed off some Russians and slipped off with a few of their belongings, some sensitive. I imagine the Russians will ask for them back at some point. I wouldn't want to be there when they ask."

"Couldn't happen to a nicer bunch," Borson said. "Any sense of timing?"

"No," Mac said. "The rumor didn't talk about timing. Just watch your ass. A random patrol car might be undermanned and underarmed."

"Roger that," Borson said. "Thanks for the tip. Let me know if you hear anything else."

"You too," Mac said. "Catch you later."

Mac stood and began to walk down to the White House cafeteria in the lower level of the Old EOB. He had invited Kelly to meet him there. It was not an unusual sight to see them together at coffee.

They sat at a table in the corner, out of earshot of others. "OK, Shakespeare, did you sell our bullshit story?" Kelly said.

"Hook, line, and sinker," Mac said. "I was brilliant. Eastwood should have been there, or Anthony Hopkins. Once we figured out that Kasmarov was Speznatz Special Forces from his prints and tattoo, it made sense. Sergei didn't admit culpability, mind you, but didn't deny and was not thrilled with the prospects of a Butruss clan grand jury appearance. I doubt we got it exactly right, but it was close enough. Some heads are going to roll over there."

"Pity. I gotta go see the Man in ten minutes," Kelly said after a glance at his watch. "You may get a call today or tomorrow, either to supervise my funeral arrangements or to see the Man. Wish me luck."

"Just in case, General, don't forget about the gold Rolex if things go to hell for you. I do admire it. Fifty dollah."

• • •

The special agent in charge of the president's detail was named Jack Goebel. Goebel had been curious when Mac showed up in his office for a rushed appointment. *"Wie Ghets, Oberst?"* Goebel said curiously. He was a Nebraska boy with a German mother. He had worked with MacMillan before.

"Nicht so gut, Herr Goebel," Mac said as he sat down in a chair across from a steel desk. "Things are a bit *upgefucht*, I'm afraid."

Goebel came alert. "Tell me all about it, Mac," he said.

The long story of the Arabs and the Mexican druggies was told quickly. Then Mac told Goebel the conclusions drawn from the translated computer files.

"Whoa! You're telling me you think there is a reasonable chance that some Arab terrorists will shoot high explosive into Cowboys

Stadium this weekend," Goebel said, writing furiously on a yellow, blue-lined legal pad. "You know the president is planning to go to the game, I assume."

Mac nodded. "That's why I'm here. Consider this a heads-up."

Goebel nodded. "I'll talk to the Man. He shouldn't be there."

Mac stood and said, "Keep me posted, Jack. I'll be down that way."

Two hours later Goebel walked into MacMillan's office, looking tired. "He won't buy it, Mac. He says if we won't cancel the game, he can't justify cancelling his attendance."

Mac shrugged. "I'm surprised, but I can't disagree with him. You'll be there, I assume."

Goebel sighed. "I'll be there along with quite a few of my faithful minions, some of whom leave tonight. Three days ain't much warning."

"I'll send frequencies to you when we sort them out, Jack," Mac said. "Give me a number for a cell phone that will be clear. I don't like the feel of this one."

· · ·

The Intelligence Committee on Impending Nightmares was again together and again meeting at the CIA. The number three guy, Klovosky, at the National Security Agency was again complaining about Caitlin and Emilie.

"O'Connor's just so goddamned arrogant. It's like she is the smartest person in the whole world and we never gave her access to Narus. When she starts to explain Emilie, our guys get it for the first thirty minutes, then their eyes glaze over. I just know she does that on purpose to keep us from figuring it out. I had a professor from CalTech sit in on this meeting with her in hopes he would explain it to us later.

Getting him the fucking clearance alone about broke my budget; he thought Ronald Reagan was a fascist and so told my investigators. He and O'Connor actually hugged and kissed when they met, I shit you not. He was beaming the whole two hours she was talking and nodding his head. Later he said he couldn't explain it to us because he understood the basics of Emilie, but hadn't figured out what Dr. O'Connor had done for the past fifteen years, so it would take a slosh of catch-up. 'Quite a challenge to analyze, actually,' this CalTech guy said. 'I couldn't guarantee results. She's quite clever.' He kindly offered up a multi-year research contract to figure out she did what she's doing for only a few zillion dollars, but with no guarantees. Jesus!"

Belvadous, the National Reconnaissance Office executive, reached to the side pocket of his ancient blazer for his even more ancient Meerschaum pipe and loaded it slowly with tobacco from a pouch in the other pocket. He didn't light it, of course, lest he be forever banished from all of Langley, but when he fumbled with his tobacco props, he had something he was going to say.

"NRO feeds digitized satellite images to Emilie; she is increasingly demanding and specific. We learn from her demands, at least as to where we could best direct our resources. We made one attempt to discern how she comes up with her specific requests, with our most capable and driven intellectual. He returned from a two-day meeting with Dr. O'Connor to tell us he had no clue as to the complex decision operations of Emilie, nor did he expect to. He was quite complimentary in his comments about Dr. O'Connor and the quality of her intellect. He said she told him that what we do best is respond to requests for specific information and that we should devote our efforts to responding well to those requests. Our man agrees. So do I."

The CIA man, Arthur Allen, riffled through his notes, then said, "That makes sense to me. Between us, we have made more progress against Al-Qaeda in the past year than we did in the five years before. I like it."

"There's not a lot new on Iran that we have," Allen said. "Emilie keeps asking for more filtered data from Narus, but she's still under fifty-percent probability with any conclusions. She was right on with the terrorist and Mexican connection, so we'll keep feeding her. We're paying new, concentrated attention to the problems in Texas on Emilie's demand."

Mac nodded and said, "We now have the translations from the captured computer on the Texas raid. Good job on speeding things up, Art. The guy who owned the computer was the guy in the e-mailed picture. We knew him from Iraq and he was on our shit list. Among other things, it seems there is an unidentified terrorist living in Dallas who was to receive the wheat stem rust and the 120 millimeter sarin rounds. They wanted him to fire the sarin first and then some high explosive that he apparently already has before he was to drive off into the sunset throwing stem rust spores merrily into the air to be blown east over several million acres of wheat. We can conclude from the transcript that our Dallas boy has a 120 millimeter mortar and four high-explosive rounds for it, since there were none in the mule-borne shipment that we intercepted, but there was a lot of discussion about techniques and best usage of the 120 millimeter mortar in the captured computer files."

The executive from the Defense Intelligence Agency, an Army full colonel, said, "Is there an indication as to when and where it will be used?"

"There is not. As usual, we have to make an informed, situational guess," Mac said. "But the Cowboys play the Giants this Saturday in Dallas. They expect attendance to be close to a hundred thousand. I found out yesterday the president is planning to attend. So far he won't be dissuaded, and the Secret Service is having a kitten. I don't blame them.

The odds are high enough that Cowboys Stadium is the target, and on Saturday, that we have to go zipper down, balls out on that assumption."

"General Kelly informed me I'm going down there tomorrow to liaise with the Texas lawmen and the Texas National Guard. We'll need heavy surveillance support, both visual and signal."

"We'll move another team from Delta Force out there, just in case things nasty up," said the brigadier from the Joint Chiefs.

"Good idea," Mac said. "Delta did a fabulous job at the border. The president is going to do some attaboys for them the next time he is near Fort Bragg."

The meeting broke upon that note and Mac walked to his government-owned, black Chevrolet Malibu. He drove out of the main CIA entrance and turned right on Route 123. After a few miles of stop-and-go traffic through McLean, Virginia, he exited right to link up with the Dulles Access Highway. There was an American flight from Dulles International to Dallas Fort Worth in two hours. Mac had a middle seat in coach. His connection to Austin from Dallas would consume another hour. He had a fresh battery in his laptop and a spare in his carry-on. He'd have plenty of time to think and plot. Kelly could argue with the president.

MacMillan drove just over the speed limit; the Dulles airport cops were notoriously nasty about speeding. In fact, they were widely thought to just be generally nasty, unprofessional hicks. There was usually at least one radar speed trap on the twenty miles or so of road.

The entrance to Dulles International Airport was an impressive one as Mac rode the free bus from long-term parking to the soaring arches of the terminal designed by Eero Saarinen. The flagpoles were mounted in a huge, meticulously tended flower bed and high enough that the wind nearly always ruffled the flags. His flight was on time. One could ask no more, these days.

Austin, Texas

Patrick Kelly was on the videophone. Mac was sitting in front of the chief of the Texas Rangers, Buster Potter, who was unhappy.

"Lemme see, now," he said. "Y'all run a Delta Force operation in my patch or close to it, and fuck it up. Now I'm supposed to convince the Arlington police to spend a trillion dollars on overtime just to be sure that some nutcase doesn't blow up Cowboys Stadium. Is that about it?"

Kelly flushed and said, "We didn't fuck anything up, and this visit is a courtesy to let you know that this nutcase might kill several thousand people with high explosives, in your fucking patch."

"Yeah we did, General," Mac said. "And we should fess up. If we hadn't let the guy in the cantina shoot himself, we might have gotten information sooner and had more time to plan. And that cantina was in Texas, so we should have given Chief Potter a heads-up at a minimum."

Potter sat for a long moment, silent, then said, "Up your giggy, Mac. You're off my Christmas card list. Net it out for me."

"We finally got most of the good stuff from the terrorist's computer. If its owner hadn't greased himself, we might have gotten it sooner and with a bit more texture. But we have it now and it ain't pretty. He was a Yemen-born, senior bad guy for Al-Qaeda in Iraq, so he's credible. There is a terrorist in Dallas who has been there for several years and an operation that has been planned for more than a year. We missed him at a designated pickup point for more goodies because we didn't get the files decrypted and translated on time. They don't identify him other than some handle they awarded for his heroism-to-be. Netting it out, he's supposed to fire four rounds of 120 millimeter high-explosive rounds from a mortar into Cowboys Stadium at halftime during the Giants game. That's soon. As far as we can tell from the computer files, he has the mortar and he has the shells. We'd be crazy to assume he doesn't know how to use them, and pretty stupid to think he hasn't figured out where and when he plans to use it. All you have to do is find him and stop him."

"I'm not going to invite you to the Ranger Gala anymore either, MacMillan. If it had been nerve gas we are talking about here, you have a zillion feds here to find that nut."

"True," Kelly piped up. "We don't need a nerve gas problem, and be glad we don't have one. But still, do you want us to flood metropolitan Dallas with feds? Things there will slow down a tad if we do. On the other hand, four rounds of 120 mike-mike high-explosive airbursts detonating in the stadium at halftime could be a public relations problem. There will be national TV coverage of the game and the Floppits are doing the halftime show."

"I don't give a rat's ass about the Floppits," Potter said. "But there will be a hundred thousand or so others attending that I do care about. This is going to take some planning. Just so I know, what are you guys willing to do in the background to help us out?"

"A lot," said Kelly. "We'll provide drone surveillance support, helicopters as needed, and as much manpower as you need on the high end. If there are to be troops, we'll send a bunch. The president wants to be sure he provides everything humanly possible to support the people of Texas."

"And our thirty-four electoral votes," Potter said. "Soon to be thirty-eight."

"That too," Kelly said. "You know the drill. On that note, be advised that the president is planning to attend the game and so far won't be dissuaded."

"Oh, that's just marvelous to know. My day is now complete. I want copies of the transcript from that computer you captured on my turf. I want as much drone surveillance support as required. I want any high-end bodies that I ask for, and I want some expert staff help in planning all of this. And I want MacMillan full time until this is over, even though I think he's not a nice person."

"I don't know about Mac," Kelly said. "That's too much political exposure for the White House if it gets fucked up."

"If it gets fucked up, I'll be screaming and pointing at you, General Kelly, as the hospitals and morgues fill," Potter said. "Mac is a deputy assistant turdball and he can act really dumb, though I'm never sure if it's an act. He'll lock up in a brace, pull his chin in, stare straight ahead, and say nothing to the press but, 'Yes sir, no sir, and no excuse, sir.' The reporters won't care about him. Do I get him or not?"

"You make a convincing case, Chief. You may have MacMillan until further notice. If it gets fucked up, I'll throw him under the bus."

"Good, you'll have company then," Potter said. "We'll consult and let you know the operational requirements of the great state of Texas with its thirty-eight electoral votes."

"Oh, ducky," Kelly said. "I can't wait. Be happy you don't work in Rhode Island or Wyoming, Chief." The picture on the video console went off and the phone went dead.

"He didn't say he'd give me that transcript from the captured laptop before he bailed," Potter said, cop-glaring at Mac. "Will you commit to that?"

"He didn't and I won't," Mac said. "You'll get a sanitized version of the computer transcript. There's other shit going on. Are we going to work together or not, Buster?"

"Yeah, we are, Mac," Potter said with a sigh. "I can use all the help I can get. We have three days before some nut maybe shoots a mortar into Cowboys Stadium at halftime of the biggest game of the year with the president of the United States sitting on the fifty-yard line and a hundred thousand citizens sitting and standing around him in the open."

"The 120 millimeter mortar is a nasty weapon with a range of up to seven thousand meters," Mac said. "I assume this guy has an SB11, which is an old Soviet version of it that is very popular in the third world. We gotta figure out how to narrow a search for the nutcase, since half of even a thirty-five-hundred-meter radius is too much to search readily. Accuracy is a lot better inside a thirty-five-hundred-meter radius, and I don't think they want to miss, so we'll assume that. The area we need to watch is thirty-five hundred meters squared times *pi*."

"I don't need a geometry lesson, Mac; I got an A. You're not making me feel warm and fuzzy. How do you think we should do the search for this guy, if he even exists? Are you even sure he's out there, for crying out loud?"

"Welcome to my world, Buster," Mac said. "We're not sure he's out there and we're not sure that if he is, he'll do anything. We don't know exactly how much ammo he has, if any."

"Marvelous. What the hell *do* you know?"

"I know the potential casualties are unacceptable, and there is little chance of cancelling a game this big if we don't have an iron-clad case, which we don't. I know a fair amount about the SB11. That's where we start."

"Go on."

"The SB11 is a recoil monster and very heavy. The Soviets used a specially reinforced truck carrier to haul it around and absorb the recoil. So do most nations that use it today. The recoil is said to be forty tons or so, smack-dab on the base plate."

"There's our first search criterion, then," Potter said. "How reinforced does a truck have to be and how big of a truck?"

"Right, and what trucks lend themselves to that parameter? Should be easy to figure out. Also, there are only about five degrees of aiming latitude on the SB11, so the truck will have to be pointed at the stadium."

Potter moved to his keyboard and started typing. "Now we're getting somewhere," he said.

Cowboys Stadium
Saturday, Cowboys vs. Giants

On the field the ball was on the Cowboys' forty-five. The Giants quarterback, Rand Dilling, was dropping back in his human protective pocket to pass while the grunts of huge men at work in front of him were audible to him even above the crowd's roar. Half of those huge men wanted to rip his throwing arm off and beat him over the head with it; the other half wanted to stop them. So far it was a tie, except for one sack where a 323-pound defensive tackle had lifted Dilling's puny 240-pound body into the air and fallen with it, twisting to slam Dilling under him as the combined 563-pound mass hit the hard artificial turf and bounced slightly.

As the Giants receivers ran their planned routes, Dilling held the football poised by his ear, studying the developing situation, waiting for something good to begin to happen. His wide receivers were well covered, and the pocket was collapsing back on him. The outlet receiver was his tight end, who came off a brush block to run a quick post and turn just as Dilling threw the football at the spot where the tight end would arrive in a second. One of the huge Cowboys defensive tackles was hindered in his rush by the Giants center, who had his shoulder under the Cowboy's shoulder pads as he pushed from his legs to contain the rush. He had a hand hidden that was grasping the front of the Cowboy's pants just inside the waistline, keeping him from spinning easily in either direction to avoid the block and to slow any jumps to block a Dilling pass. Both linemen were straining for advantage.

The Cowboys tackle stuck a desperate hand in the air just as Dilling threw and tipped the ball in the air with his index fingertip. The ball wobbled a bit as it lost speed. It was going to be short of target. As the receiver turned for the ball, the Cowboys linebacker who had been a step behind the receiver glanced over his shoulder. The ball was wobbling right for him. He turned to let the ball come to his waiting hands, then tucked it against his stomach and dropped his shoulder to run, awaiting the inevitable hits from enraged Giants. The Giants receiver wrapped his arms around the linebacker and tried to rip the ball loose as he rode the Cowboy to the ground, and the offensive guard got his licks by driving his helmet into the Cowboy's left thigh.

Seventy thousand Cowboys fans came to their feet with a simultaneous roar. The decibel level in the stadium went up even further. President Roberts, Chief of Staff Michael Condi, and the mayor of Arlington, Texas, were also on their feet, yelling with the rest of the Cowboys fans, in a luxury skybox far above the field and exactly in its middle. The roar of the crowd was muted by the glass enclosure as the interception was being replayed on each of four large screens at the top corners of the room. New red, white, and blue bunting was draped across the front of the skybox, just in front of the presidential party. It was not as professional in its look as the rest of the interior design in the elaborate suite. Beneath the cotton with the colors on it was a long sheet of double-layer Kevlar attached to the front of the box, below the wide glass viewing area. It had been installed yesterday in anticipation of the president's visit. A Secret Service agent was standing at either end of the first row, not watching the game and awaiting a radio command from Goebel to grab the president and push him to the floor behind the Kevlar shield. The agents would lie on top of him in case flying glass and debris rained down from an explosion. There was a windowless room outside the skybox and just down the hall that had two more agents standing outside They had open-top briefcases concealing submachine guns that could be grabbed in a second. The walls of the room had been draped with more Kevlar. Another agent, a former Special Forces medic, waited inside the room with a pistol on his hip and an elaborate first aid kit laid out on a table, just in case. The former medic was trained to provide routine surgery to close bleeding arteries and other ripped flesh to stabilize a victim until he could be evacuated. That room was the destination of choice for the president if things got nasty or if they got early warning trouble was coming. Having Roberts on the floor in the skybox was a last choice.

On the field, the Cowboys ran a quarterback draw for a loss of three, while the bands gathered beneath the stadium and on the ramps, awaiting their opportunity to entertain at halftime. The Floppits came from their makeshift dressing room and mounted a moveable stage. They had guitars to plug into the sound system when they got to the fifty-yard line.

• • •

Hussein pulled into the back parking lot of Herman Hooley's truck stop. He drove slowly over a small bumpy dirt path on the lot's far corner to an uncompleted small office site. He could hear things in the back of his truck rattling and bumping around. He smiled; only he could hear them. There was an open dirt lot beside the stark walls of the office-to-be. He pulled in beside a broken-down Dodge truck, turned, and pointed the hood of his truck at the stadium looming in the afternoon haze. Hussein took an olive drab Army-surplus compass from his shirt pocket, got out of the truck, and did a crude sighting to assure the stadium was within the positioning arc of his beautiful mortar.

Helicopters buzzed over his head frequently, but Hussein knew the news coverage of the game would be extensive and helicopters were part of the effort. He opened the back of the truck and climbed inside, then locked the back door. No one would likely approach the back of his truck, but thieves were everywhere and could ruin his plan. He took an old Colt .44-caliber revolver from the metal storage unit across the front of the truck bed. He placed it on the floor beside the tube, just in case. The rounded copper noses of five bullets could be seen peeking from the front of the cylinder. Hussein's four mortar rounds were secured in their tubes and strapped to the floor of the truck. Three of the transport tubes were painted yellow, and the fourth, the oldest of them, was gray with a dark green band around it. Hussein went to his sighting mechanism and tapped in the target data, then read his GPS and entered the position of the truck. He turned some knobs that moved the mortar tube until the red dot inside the sight was exactly over the stationary green dot.

The Cowboys were up by three with one minute, thirty seconds left in the first half. Ninety three thousand tickets had been sold; the stadium was rocking. Hussein could hear the roar from his firing site, more than two miles away.

• • •

Not far away, on the top floor of a nondescript office building, a young Air Force lieutenant in blues sat hunched, looking at her computer screen with her left hand on a joystick that controlled her unmanned aerial vehicle, a Predator surveillance drone. There were three additional officers in the room, each controlling a Predator drone in one of four quadrants they had defined that surrounded Cowboys Stadium. The Predators were separated vertically by one thousand feet and positioned to avoid commercial air traffic.

Twenty-three potential targets had been identified as possible launch vehicles for a 120mm mortar. Two were garbage trucks, four were dump trucks, and the remaining seventeen were three-ton vehicles similar to Hussein's F350. None seemed likely to host the sought bomber, if only because the garbage and dump trucks' cargo areas were mostly open to view and the remainder had closed tops. Four hundred vehicles had been temporarily eliminated from consideration in the past few minutes, as the demand for 120mm mortar accuracy would require that the trucks stop and turn, if not properly oriented to Cowboys Stadium. In the back of the room were four more active computer screens. MacMillan, Buster Potter, the local chief of police, and an Air Force full colonel sat watching their screens, which allowed a view of any Predator quadrant selected or a 360-degree picture of the whole.

On the radio in the background, the half ended.

"It's showtime, folks," Mac said into his headset to the lieutenants. "Be alert. We need you."

There was a slight pause in one picture being transmitted, as the operator zoomed. The white roof of a red F350 had a panel suddenly removed from it and pulled into the truck. The truck bed stood open to the afternoon air.

"Bingo," shouted one officer. "We may have him."

The full zoom picture of Hussein's truck showed a green tube on a tripod, facing into the air above the truck and oriented to Cowboys Stadium. A man looked up at the sky, then ducked down to reach for something.

"Units twelve, fourteen and eighteen," Potter said into his headset. "He is behind Hooley's truck stop in a lot by an unfinished office site. Red Ford F350, white cap, pointed at the stadium. If you see him, kill him. Move, move, move." The State of Texas was more casual about the civil rights of terrorists than were many of the more liberal Eastern states. If someone had a mortar and live rounds pointed at Cowboys Stadium, he would be read his Miranda rights as soon as possible after he had been killed.

Mac pushed a button on his Kphone.

"Get him out of there, Goebel. Possible incoming. Two minutes."

The other views from the UAVs began to shift toward Hussein's truck. All of the controllers wanted to watch the action. Mac spun to look at the Air Force colonel, who was watching him rather than the action. Mac gave a violent shake of his head.

The colonel spoke into his headset. "We may have one. There may be more. Return to your quadrants immediately and search again. Look for another, *now*! This is not a drill." The view on the screens from the three other UAVs moved abruptly away from the truck.

Behind Hooley's, Hussein unstrapped the cases holding the mortar rounds and opened them. Each shell was shiny and proud, as was Hussein. He picked up the oldest shell from its case. If he dropped it in the tube properly, it would fire and create the havoc on the arrogant infidels that he had dreamed of for many years. The shell was a bit wet when he picked it up, perhaps a leak caused by jarring on the bumpy path to the firing site, but there no was time for hygiene and Hussein had a firm grip. He turned and lifted the heavy shell to position it over the mouth of the green mortar tube.

"We're too late," Mac said into his headset. "He's going to get the first round off. Let's kill him before he drops another one into that tube. No warning."

Into his Kphone, Mac said, "Sixty seconds, Goebel. I'm looking at the mortar."

In the skybox, President Roberts was lifted by his biceps by an agent on either side of him and rushed from his seat toward the door. One of the other guests standing by the door held out his hand to stop them and ask what was going on. He was kicked in the shin just beneath the knee by the lead agent, then knocked aside to the floor. The president was rushed through the door and down the hall to the waiting small room. Potter spoke into his headset, urgently, as four police cars slid to a stop around the truck. Men in body armor rushed the truck. The back door was blown away from its lock by the blast of a 12-gauge shotgun. One man ripped the door away, and two others looked down their pistols for a target. They saw a man on the floor beside a large mortar round, still. Both shot into him, twice, then yelled, "Freeze!"

Mac was watching the action on his screen as if he were ten feet away. The mortar round was on the floor of the truck, pointed toward the rear wheels of the F350 as a result of being dropped by Hussein. It was painted gray with a dark green band. He had seen that paint scheme many times in the past few years.

"Get back," Mac yelled into his microphone. "Get back, now! Set up a perimeter defense at twenty-five yards from the truck."

At the truck one policeman squatted to check for a pulse on Hussein's wet wrist, then turned as the order from Potter came, urgently. He moved to get out of the truck, then felt weak. Suddenly he couldn't breathe, and there was a painful twisting in his solar plexus. He fell dead to the floor of the truck.

"Nerve gas, I say again, nerve gas," Mac yelled. "Let him lie. Get back." He couldn't lose the mental image of the sarin round lying on the floor of an old truck, inert yet so ready to kill, as he switched frequency with a click of his phone.

"Hazmat, hazmat, hazmat," he said into his headset and thumbed his Kphone. "Behind Hooley's truck stop. Sarin. I say again, sarin. Coordinates follow." Four miles away an Army truck roared to life and headed at speed toward Hooley's. Soldiers in the rear of the truck began pulling on their protective suits.

Potter was on his radio, working with the team on the ground by the truck. They had lost one of theirs and were edgy, looking for something to shoot.

"Set up a strong defensive perimeter at twenty-five yards," he said, more to keep them occupied than for hazard reasons. "Army hazmat units are en route." The sound of band music blared over the portable radio as the halftime show at Cowboys Stadium got underway. The Cowboys were up by seven.

"All clear, Goebel. I say again, all clear," Mac said into his Kphone. "The president can rejoin the game."

Mac sat back in his chair, looking at the ceiling, trying to figure out how he could have known about the sarin. It was implied on the captured records from the computer, but not specific. The computer transcript said they wanted the oldest round fired first; he should have guessed.

At Cowboys Stadium, the president returned to the skybox with the agents. "Sorry, folks, there was a false alarm," Roberts said with chagrin obvious on his face. "I interrupted a fun day for you. That was terribly rude. I apologize. I promise you I'll find out who was responsible for this fiasco." He again took his chair at the front of the box. The agents resumed their quiet spots at either end of that aisle.

Chief of Staff Condi had a wet shirtfront caused by the vomit that had erupted from him when he figured out he was in harm's way and the president was long gone. The worst of it had been easy to wash off the white polyester Cowboys shirt, but his hands were still shaking.

Special Agent in Charge Jack Goebel was outside the skybox, also waiting for his adrenaline to ebb. After two shaky tries, Goebel got his cell phone back in its holster on his left hip. That had been close, according to MacMillan, who had a reputation for candor. The president had been first terrified, then angry when it became clear there was no immediate threat. Goebel shrugged. That was the job. He'd retire in a few years and fish, full-time. There was something quieting about the perfect cast of a dry fly; it floated above the pool, over and over, until the fish rose to it, or not. You had to pay attention, but not much. Until then he'd stay with the endless hours of boredom punctuated by the occasional heart-pounding minute or two.

Much later that day, Mac and Buster Potter were sitting at a bar at DFW Airport, waiting for Mac's flight to be called. The Cowboys had lost by three.

"Like you said, Mac," Potter said. "We lucked out. I wonder how long that sarin round was in Dallas."

"I doubt we'll ever know, given that we deny any such sarin round was found," Mac said. "But we'll see the report of the investigation if they ever get around to finishing it and know a little more about people who want to do this shit. Your folks did good, Buster. I was impressed with their professionalism."

"Thanks. It could have been a lot worse. If you can find a woman who will have you, you can come to the Ranger Gala."

"I'm out of here," Mac said. "There will be a lot of buzz about this investigation, and I need to keep a lid on the gossip." They shook hands. Potter turned and walked down the concourse to catch the little airport train to parking.

Just as his flight was called, Mac's Kphone rang. It was General Kelly. "It sounds like things went fine down there, Mac, other than the cop that got killed."

"You can thank Chief Potter for that, General. They all done good. I'm heading back your way in a few minutes, so I'll see you tomorrow late morning. It's Sunday."

"Yeah, I'm with the president at Mass at eleven, praise the Lord," Kelly said. "He'll bend my ear about the false alarm, I imagine, and about your proclivity for false alarms. By the way, your buddy from the Maryland State Police, Borson, called for you and settled for talking to me. He said there was a big killing on the Bay last night. Some family down there named Butruss; they're all dead. Twenty-three of them; men, women, and a few kids."

"Imagine that. I guess there is senseless violence everywhere. Any clue as to the perps?"

Kelly snorted, then said, "Nope. Just a big scattering of Ukraine-made 7.62mm casings that had been wiped clean of prints."

"Speznatz does that when they load their magazines, and they blame the Ukraine at every chance. I really must remember to send Sergei a nice thank-you note. Maybe even a magnum of Dancing Hares. I think I could expense that."

"You're a sick puppy, Mac. See you tomorrow," Kelly said with a chuckle, and clicked off.

Morocco

In Tangier Alex walked from the gym within the Kufdani complex back to his office. He had spent ninety minutes in his usual routine, first exercising, then sparring with Tang, his valet and martial arts instructor who had come to him from the CIA's Farm a few years earlier when Tang retired. Tang was of some indeterminate age. He had seemed middle-aged when Alex first met him at the Farm many years before and seemed little older now. Tang's wife had died several years earlier. He was an ethnic Chinese, born and living in the Philippines, with a father who had been hired from China to be an instructor of kung fu and karate. Tang had added a mastery of Philippine Jujitsu to the skill set his father had taught him since birth. Caitlin had discovered Tang and worked out with him at least daily when she was in residence in Tangier; she had a taste for the martial arts. Tang was encouraged to stay with Caitlin when she walked or ran errands in Tangier. Rather than be offended by the presence of a bodyguard, Caitlin welcomed it. Despite her daily practice, she had yet to test her skills in an actual encounter.

"Thieves might steal my purse, but it will take six of them," she told Alex. "If there are more, Tang will handle them."

Hala knocked on his office door just after four in the afternoon. When he opened the door, she said, "There is no time for my third session just now. I suggest you come to my guest quarters just down the hall at some time after the evening meal; shall we say at eight o'clock? There are no other guests in residence just now. You may complete your obligation at that time."

"I live only to service," Alex said with a wry grin.

"I have again been doing research and considering ovulation, sex, and teapots. It occurred to me that this is likely to be the last time I participate in this act, and that I have not yet experienced its full complexity and additions to life experience, as alleged in the literature. Had Nijad survived, we no doubt would have experimented and found our way together. I will not work in Tangier again, so any opportunity I have to extend my, ah, emotional experience base should happen here. It occurred to me that you have the necessary experience and perhaps the skills to introduce me to the mechanics of multiple teapots, beyond our actions thus far."

"Just like that?" Alex asked.

"Yes, just like that," Hala said. "You are again deforming your trousers. It will have to wait."

At eight o'clock Alex knocked gently on the guest suite door nearest his office. It was slightly ajar, and he pushed it open, slipped through, and closed it. He could hear a shower running.

"Hala?" he called.

"I am bathing," she said. "Disrobe, please, and come in here."

Alec removed his clothes and folded them neatly, then put them on a chair near the door. His shoes went beneath it. He turned and walked to the shower.

Hala stood in the stone shower with water cascading over her body. She was lean, with hips flaring and small breasts aroused. Alex walked to the shower and stepped inside.

"May I join you?" he said.

Hala turned and looked at his face and down his chest. She reached a finger to his shoulder and traced the scar there, then down to his navel over each of what warriors called "zippers and assholes," the healed scars of surgery and bullet holes left by surgeons after hurried repairs. There was a birthmark below his navel. It was shaped like an inverted comma and was a deep purple. She glanced at his groin.

"Of course you may join me," Hala said. "That is why I invited you. I am merely adding knowledge to a situation that I have long since accepted and brazenly presented to you. Let me clean you again, and then you will tell me what disgusting thing you would like me to do for you, and you for me. I decided I should not die before exploring a bit more. You are my chance. If you know, teach me."

"No rules?" Alex said with a small smile.

"I suppose I expect you to be civilized, but creative without pain," she said, moving closer to him and soaping his shoulders and across his chest. "How shall we proceed?"

"I am still thinking about it," he said. "Give me a few minutes. Is that acceptable?"

She dropped her soapy hand, then said softly, "That is acceptable. And you have been nicely angered."

After a bit, Alex said into her ear, "The objective is to provide a donation that is teapot enhanced."

"Indeed it is," she whispered, moving slowly with a very firm, soapy grip. "Multiple, record-setting teapots followed by an acceptable donation."

"And no premature donations, so stop with what you are doing." Alex said. "Let's get cleaned up and try to find a creative way to deal with this particular problem."

"You are quite correct," she said and stepped back, again glancing down at him. "Still, I would have liked to have watched the happy ending."

They spent a few minutes soaping each other, then rinsed, stopped the shower, and reached for towels. They dried quickly and walked into the bedroom. There was music playing from a small speaker that now had Alex's IPod now plugged into it, a quiet album of piano and jazz guitar. Hala had turned the bed back.

As they walked, Alex said, "As you pointed out the other day, our agreement concerns conception and how to achieve it. I think I will first address the issue that you think enhances fertility; the old-fashioned way is not going to allow many teapot repetitions. Later I may teach you how best to do some disgusting things to me. Be patient with me"

She looked at him quizzically for a few seconds, then rolled onto the bed and looked at him from a pillow, her dark hair damp on it. "I'd like that," she said, and stretched her arm out to him. Hala soon discovered that Alex's teasing pace was disturbingly slow for her budding instincts when he moved from her lips to her chest. It seemed he took forever to do whatever he was doing at each stop. Then it was better. His pace seemed to quicken. It was still agonizingly slow. The familiar simmer arose and began to grow, then finally reached a plateau. Hala was able to hold the plateau for what seemed like minutes, before it boiled out of control.

Much later, he was beside her on the pillow. She turned lazily and gazed at him.

"Welcome," he said.

"I truly had no idea. Nijad was my first. I thought the commotion and legends were all hyperbole. My jaw is tired and my low back is exhausted. I must learn to relax."

"You shouldn't die without one good experience in this particular world," Alex said. "It was indeed my pleasure."

"A few extra teapots and an enthusiastic donation. I find your performance acceptable," Hala whispered. "I really must buy this album. Now please excuse me for a few moments. When I return, I am to have lessons on reciprocity. And oh, you have bad breath."

Aden International Airport
Yemen

The Yemenia Airline 737 dropped toward the dark strip of runway, vivid against the light scrub of the Yemeni countryside, the storage tanks for petroleum, and the low, white buildings. Aden International Airport, a former British RAF base, was at the outskirts of Aden, the second largest city, on Yemen's southwest coast. After a slight bump from the tires and the roar of reverse thrust from the engines, the plane slowed and taxied toward a building that acted as a terminal. Alex cleared customs with a Moroccan passport and walked inside the terminal to the small desk of a car rental agency. After a few minutes, he opened the door of a tiny Fiat and reached inside to start the car, then jumped away from its sun-baked interior heat. He walked around the car and opened the passenger door, then leaned over the seat to turn on the air conditioning. In a few moments, the heat would be tolerable.

Alex drove west through sleepy suburbs for twenty minutes. He swung into the marked drive to the Port of Aden facility that enclosed the eastern side of a natural harbor. Within ten minutes he pulled into a parking place near a pile of rubble. It was just past a small café with the windows blown out. Several men in traditional dress sat on old steel chairs at an outside table, smoking and drinking tea. A brief walk around the site confirmed his earlier suspicion that the building was a total loss. Thin ribbons of gray smoke rose from several spots amid the rubble. There was a spear of unburned drywall still standing; half was covered with a jagged and lumpy crimson stain. A tiny red sandal with the toe blown away was resting on the edge of a burned desk. Where once stood the Yemeni office of Kufdani Industries, workplace of eighty people, child-care site and madrassas school for eleven of their progeny, now nothing remained except a smoking rubbish pile waiting to cool before being carted off.

The harbor facilities began on the other side of the road. There were several small freighters being unloaded and barriers of cyclone fence and barbed wire on several other spots on the dock.

Alex walked to a gate in one of these fences and waved at a guard sitting outside a small building, beside a crane. When the man walked up cautiously, Alex thumbed a few keys on his Kphone to trigger a proximity recognition signal, then said a few words. He waited while the guard slid the rusty gate to the side.

A few minutes of conversation confirmed that were an adequate number of Kufdani employees available to unload cargo when appropriate, but most remained at home for lack of a place to work. There was rage at Al-Qaeda, the assumed bombers, and fear of further reprisal as well. None of the men had any helpful information as to the location or identities of the culprits. The suicide bomber had been a young girl, but no one seemed to know her.

As Alex returned to his car, one of the men from the café got up and began walking toward him as another walked to a small van parked on the street. Alex tensed as he examined the man approaching. The guy didn't walk quite like he was concealing the weight of a weapon, but something didn't feel quite right.

Careful, laddie.

The man turned a little from his path to pass more than five feet from Alex. Just as the man passed from his peripheral vision and Alex began to relax, he heard a rustle and a grunt. As Alex turned his head to look, he saw the man pointing something at him and felt a sting low on his back. The man began to run. Alex spun and set out to run him down. As he closed on him, Alex felt his vision begin to narrow, ambient noise faded, and he fell to the rough pavement.

The van roared from its spot to stop just beside him. The driver jumped from the van and ran to open the back door. He turned to Alex, inert on the ground, and knelt beside him. A length of strong cord was used to expertly bind Alex's hands behind him and another bound his feet. The driver began to drag Alex toward the rear of the van as the other man returned, panting, and reached to help.

The two of them picked up his body by its clothes, and swung it once, throwing Alex into the van, and slammed the rear doors. They jumped in and drove away. The man outside the Kufdani hut spun from where he had been standing, gape-mouthed, and ran into the building.

· · ·

The freighter *Ghania*, aka Hog, was making good time as she drove through the calm waters of the Red Sea on her way south from the Suez Canal city of Port Said to the port of Aden. Stacked on her deck were tens of containers, but only a few were of immediate interest to Jerome. Three were on wheeled trailers and contained battered, beige Toyota pickup trucks. Most had two off-road motorcycles lashed upright to the truck bed. Two other trucks held support equipment. These five had been loaded last and could be moved by deck cranes that could put them on the dock surface in a few moments, where the back of the container dropped to a ramp with the flick of a switch. The trucks could be driven down the ramp in moments. Several other containers had been loaded, but would stay on board. The most important of these was a communications setup that could talk to Kufdani in Tangier, to the US fleet guarding the Gulf, or to any other site with sophisticated communications gear. There were four commercial tractors aboard that could haul the containers to a place that would avoid comment when they were unloaded. Several containers had been fitted to attachments on the decks and plugged into the communications trailer.

Jerome sat in his cabin with his Kphone, scanning satellite photos of the area around Aden, projected on a large screen. The terrain rose to hills quickly, once beyond the city.

"I hope to hell Cooch finds something worth chasing," he mused. "There's a lot of ugly real estate outside of Aden, and we don't know who the bad guys are or where they are."

His computer lit up with a full-screen alert that said only, "*Flash Message.*" The communications container was active.

Jerome brushed his thumb across the print reader on his Kphone and data filled his screen, organized as planned. The message was not anything planned.

K workers on Aden dock were interviewed by Alpha One. When A1 departed the secure area, he was abducted by two men in a van and was inert when taken and observed by K workers. No license plate. GPS on Kphone active and being tracked. Repositioning tracking for better clarity.

Jerome pushed a green toggle switch on his table to connect him to the bridge.

"Increase speed," he said. "We must arrive in Aden at dawn or before. Report computed arrival time." He felt the surge as *Ghania's* engines increased their power.

Jerome began to consider his operating environment. He had seventy trained men available. The most important were two super squads and a weapons squad. Perimeter security was covered. There were men to provide security as building materials were unloaded and positioned to begin construction of a new office for Kufdani Yemen. A group of others would do the actual construction.

A new flash filled his screen:

Alpha One GPS signal stopped and dropped. Last position noted.

"Well, shit," Jerome said to himself. "I guess I'd better start figuring out what the last position looks like and how we're going to do something around it."

He pulled up a map using last known coordinates for Alex. It was about twenty-three kilometers from Aden, in the northeast hills. Jerome's Kphone beeped and displayed a satellite image of Alex's last known position. When he zoomed in, he found a small structure on a hillside that looked like a residence and a few more, larger, on a small plain just below that seemed more commercial. He played with the zoom until he had a decent topographic map of the immediate area. He saved it and sent a Message Immediate to his squad leaders with the map attached. *Plan for this to be a target. We'll go in near the residence. Calculate ingress/egress security and fields of fire from hillside down. Full combat load. Meeting in 50 minutes, in the conference cabin.*

Jerome sat back in his chair and pondered the situation. After a few minutes, he picked up his Kphone, then punched keys for a bit and waited for the security software to secure the call with his thumbprint and find the recipient of the call. After five minutes or so, a voice answered, "November Sierra."

"Alpha Two," he said, knowing Mac knew who was calling. Caitlin was good at that kind of thing and NSA valued her work, which made things go faster.

"Be advised that Alpha One has been taken in Aden," Jerome said. "Don't know who did the taking yet. He was either dead or unconscious when taken. Kufdani Aden office was destroyed two weeks ago, and Al-Qaeda in the Arabian Peninsula claimed responsibility, see earlier message titled 'ADEN: Kufdani.' A1 was on the ground to review the situation for damage assessment and with an eye to counter. Last GPS was as follows. I plan to follow to site with two squads and weapons support."

There were a few moments of silence and the whisper of keys tapped on a keyboard, then, "I'll alert some assets over there," Mac said. "No manpower support will be possible, but maybe some toys. Keep me informed."

"Roger," Jerome said. "I'll plug you into the data stream if you give me a link. A better set of topos would be handy. See what Emilie thinks about that spot."

"Wilco, wait one," Mac said. "Link coming and I'll jack up our satellite jocks for a better map and maybe some real time if available...OK, Emilie says it is seventy-three percent likely that there are three hundred fifty or so more people in that area than known. Food and staples shipments to the area are far beyond what is normal for the population asserted by the government. It is fifty-three percent likely they are Al-Qaeda. Watch your ass."

"Roger, out," Jerome said as he broke the link. He had some planning to do.

• • •

It was cold and dark. There was the faint rustle of an exhaust fan running. Alex was in some sort of metal chair. The steel slats were cold on his naked buttocks, and his right shoulder ached. As Alex turned, he felt the leather straps across his chest and around his wrists. A quick tug revealed his ankles immobilized as well and a strap around each thigh. He concentrated, then exerted all his force against the wrist straps. They held, with no sign of weakness. After a moment, his legs also failed to make any progress against the restraints. His face was tightening.

The inner voice of Dain erupted. *Well, this is not an attractive situation, is it now? I should imagine we found the bombers, or perhaps they just found us. Sorry about that bloke at the dock. He seemed fat and harmless. I let you down. I utterly despise doing that. It happened once with your great-grandfather. He had a limp for twenty years.*

A dagger of light showed suddenly under a door to his right and there was the sound of shuffling feet, clad perhaps in sandals. The sound was irregular, as if something was being dragged behind. The door opened and light suddenly flooded the room.

"Good afternoon," said an older man in traditional Yemeni garb. "Welcome to my tiny interrogation center. I am Hamza. We are going to be friends, so tell me your name. You have this fancy little telephone; that's my signal that you are one of them. I've been told by a reliable and valued associate in Tangier that having that phone is a signal. It means you represent the firm that has invaded the schooling of our children in Aden and allowed our women to live and work uncovered. I have been told many things about this Kufdani group of Sunni heretics and have questions about them; you will provide answers for me."

Don't talk to this arsehole. This promises to be rather unpleasant.

211

"Ah, a resistor. I do enjoy apostates like you. Allah has given me, in his wisdom, the skill to extract what I want to know and to employ it in his glory. I assure you I am a patient man. You will be my guest for many months. We shall talk about schooling our children and about why you are employing women in jobs men are best suited to do, in defiance of the commands of Allah and Sharia law. You will beg to tell me what plans you have to enable continued Sunni dominance over we true Shiite believers."

Hamza limped to the chair where Alex was strapped and ran a dirty fingernail around his eyes, then poked into his left one. Alex flinched involuntarily. There was a faint chuckle. The ragged nail ran down his stomach, casually traced the scars from a few wounds and then another scar to his groin, and stopped.

"My, my," Hamza said. "What have we here? An oversized seed sack and gourd, I believe. How disgusting. You'll have little need for those in the future, I assure you. Perhaps I'll first slice them down to normal size and see if you become more talkative."

Alex watched the man as he studied his genitals.

"Abrasion would be just the thing to address these ugly, excessive wrinkles and make them smoother, then finish with a little alcohol to avoid infection. Still, perhaps that can wait. I have found it is better for our conversation if you have some time to contemplate the slow loss of your manhood, even though your life is ultimately forfeit. I have twenty strong young women who are dedicated to our cause housed just a few hundred meters away. Perhaps I should have one of them cut on you for a few hours. But no, they are to be martyrs to our cause and such an encounter would befoul their purity. There are sixteen men remaining below, but they would have no interest in postponing martyrdom to ask you questions. There are a number of Iranians visiting with my planners, but they are busy with Allah's work. It must be that it is left to me. I welcome the responsibility."

This wog seems a bit unhinged! We must settle in for some pain, it seems. You go away. I'll keep a proper eye on things.

The ragged nail moved again, down his right thigh, then to his toes as Hamza leaned over, supporting himself on his cane.

"Have you seen someone try to walk without their toes? Quite amusing. We'll get to that, I assure you, but the exquisite beauty of interrogation is for me to bask in your submission long before the end is nigh."

A movement up the left thigh was accompanied by a sudden jab to the scrotum, and a ripping pull through the loose skin. A small grunt escaped from Alex.

"Oh, you have a voice!" Hamza raised the ragged, bloody fingernail to his nose and inhaled deeply. "Ah, the smell of terror is still missing from your blood. Over the weeks, we'll work on that."

Alex let himself fade into a deep meditation. He was aware of everything going on, but removed from it, pushing away thoughts that the time had finally come to pay the piper when no one of his blood remained to help pursue the Kufdani mission. After a few moments, his thoughts went to a conversation he had had with his father when he was first back from the special operation in Iraq. It was there he came to know his alter ego and first got a reputation as "Cooch, that's the guy you want watching your back on the hairy ones."

Alex had been assigned to a Seal team tasked to get a high value target out of the hands of Iraq's Special Guard. There had been some concern by the planners that demolition might be needed to get into a hardened holding site, even though they were going in at 0200 on a moonless night. Since Alex was the CIA's demolition specialist for special ops, he was the answer to those concerns and otherwise a well-trained, if unblooded, operative. The landscape was clear but green through the enhanced night vision goggles they all wore. The goggles paired passive night vision with a thermal imager for seeing the heat of targets through smoke or fog or, more frequently, to detect a hot weapon under a jacket or a suicide vest on approaching persons. As they moved toward a small building, past two dead sentries, the inner voice Alex had been hearing more frequently of late pushed further into his consciousness, more demanding.

This house is too big, laddie. There may be a lot of people in here. They are all the enemy. Your mates are depending on us, and we on them. Remember what your father told you about innocents on the battlefield; it has been true for centuries. We must be aggressive.

Perimeter security men were flowing into their positions and falling prone. They reached to extend bipods on the sound-suppressed M110 7.62mm rifles they carried. The other Seals carried silenced Heckler and Koch MP5 9mm submachine guns.

On either side two Seals set up modified Claymore mines to cover approaches down the dusty road from the other buildings in the village, where they would fire down a long vector, shredding anything in their path. Some fired long and narrow, others fired a broad swath. With both, there was a swarm of hot ball bearings reaching for targets. The key tactic was to delay firing the Claymores until the road was crowded with approaching Iraqis; they were horrifically loud and would attract dangerous attention. Individuals or small groups approaching would be stopped by rifle fire, quietly.

The lead Seal inspected the worn wooden door, tested its door latch, and pumped his hand above his head to signal "no lock," then slammed the door aside and rushed suddenly inside. The others followed closely.

"Hands up, hands up," could be heard shouted in Arabic, then the clicks of a free-floating bolt locking and releasing and of casings ejected from MP5 fire bouncing on the floor.

When Alex came through the door a moment later, the Seals in front of him charged into the next room. Two men lay still on the floor with dark stains spreading on their chests. Alex swiveled his shoulders as he swept the room with his vision- enhanced eyes, his MP5 swinging with his gaze. The other room was quiet now; the only sounds were the grunts of Seals checking bodies and the fluttering stench of releasing bowels.

Alex swung his MP5 back and forth among the mass of people on the floor, looking down its barrel for a threat. The Iraqis were frozen, staring. Two held their hands in the air. Suddenly there was movement, and he saw a woman nursing a baby fumbling with the pin on a fat fragmentation grenade. The pin came out and the handle released with a clack and spun into the air. The grenade was live in the woman's hand. *Now, lad.* His finger stroked the MP5 trigger and two rounds ripped into her chest, one of them through the child. The grenade rolled from her hand to the floor. He felt control being enhanced by Dain.

"Grenade!" Alex yelled almost involuntarily. He reached to grab the woman by the hair and pulled her over the grenade, the child beneath her. *Four thousand, three thousand…*Dain was counting down the six-second fuse on the grenade. Alex grabbed a man next to her by the shirtfront and threw him over the woman, then dove to a corner onto his back. The grenade detonated with a thump and a bang. Hot shrapnel burned into Alex's left shoulder and past. There was more movement among the people on the floor and a faint clank of metal pieces coming together. Alex came to one knee and began to shoot into them from left to right. His magazine change was a blur of sound; he kept shooting into the mass.

On his left a door moved, and he shot into that, then came to his feet and charged through it. There were more people, moving, and some scrambling to their feet. He shot into movement, then shot

215

into the rest of the forms there. The double tap of two rounds from the MP5 was nearly continuous, and empty casings ejected from it chased one another in the air. Another magazine change, and he worked back across the room, shooting into every form.

"Clear?" a voice shouted.

"Clear," Alex said, as he put his weapon on safe. He dropped the half-empty magazine from his MP5 and slammed a fresh one into place. His face began to relax.

Well done, lad, well done.

"Jesus Christ," he heard a voice say. "They're all dead. Women, kids, all of them."

"They were on the battlefield. There are more in here," Alex said coldly, and moved to join the quiet exit force, behind an old man carried across the shoulders and back of a bulky Seal.

Alex had executed the hardest mental feat of them all, and done it well. His father had told Alex that it doesn't matter what or who is on the battlefield against you, whether man, woman, child, or beast, it is the enemy and thus a target. Kill it at first opportunity before it kills you or one of yours. Later, when they were back on the sub that had carried them in, the Seals each found time to go over to Alex and say a word or bump a fist. He was "Cooch" now and the legend had begun.

There was a tug of flesh from Hamza that moved on.

Alex remembered saying to his father, Mick, "There was this voice, telling me what to do, and it was my voice, sort of."

Mick had nodded and was quiet for a few moments.

"He went from me to you. My father called him Dain; so did I. Dain is the voice of experience and violence that lives within a Cuchulain. Maybe we're certifiably schizophrenic, but it works if you're in the violence business. Somehow Dain always seems to be watching, and when you need him, you save a second or two because he made you ready. Listen to him when things get violent, but try to avoid giving him any control otherwise. He's a bit nasty for civilized society. He got involved in a bar fight of mine once. I almost killed three Rangers, and one marine who tried to pull me off almost lost an eye. I didn't have bar fights after that."

Hamza limped to a rough wooden cabinet on the wall on the right side of the door, lifted a crude latch, and opened it. Hanging neatly inside was a crude bow saw, a large bolt cutter, and some knives and scissors. An extension cord was hanging beside what looked to be an old electric soldering iron.

"Which of these should I first employ to assist me in our little conversations, eh?" Hamza said. "Each has its uses. Within a month or maybe two, you will know them all well, and you will sing to me. Your song will beg me to let you die, but I shall not. You are my only guest at the moment, and my only entertainment. I have had a disappointment in the land of the Great Satan, where our attack on an American sporting contest failed somehow, but my time with you will help me await another opportunity there.

"I think I shan't do more than get your attention today," Hamza said. He moved a step to Alex's left and gazed at him, studying. "I know just the thing to allow you to consider the days and months to come while I retire for my evening prayers and a nice meal."

It doesn't sound like Mr. One-Eyed Willy is in trouble yet, that's the good news. I've grown fond of watching him flail around. Those things don't change much. But I don't think we're going to like this.

Hamza took down the extension cord and the soldering iron, then joined them and plugged one end into a wall socket. He reached to the cabinet, took out the bolt cutters, and moved again to Alex's left. In a single motion, he pulled the handles of the cutter apart and put the jaws over the first joint of Alex's little finger. Hamza leaned hard against the handles, and the fingertip fell severed to the floor.

Bugger! That hurt.

A grunt escaped Alex's lips.

"Another little noise, my friend," Hamza said. "How exciting. It is the first of many, I assure you."

"*Inshallah*," Alex said quietly, then went back to his little place, trying to be hidden in a place in his mind.

"*Inshallah*, God willing, indeed," said Hamza. "Allah is indeed willing, as I do Allah's work. It offends me that you invoke his name."

He shuffled back to the cabinet and picked up the soldering iron. A tiny curl of smoke came from it, and it was pink at its tip. Hamza dragged its cord across the stone floor to Alex's left side.

"What shall I do next? It could be an eye. I love the smell of seared eye and the sounds that accompany it. But again, I think I'll save that so you can watch results carefully over the next several months as I reason with you." Hamza held the end of the soldering iron to Alex's remaining fingertip, and rolled it. The stench of burned flesh curled into the air as Hamza inhaled deeply, leaning over the wound.

"That kindness should allow you to avoid infection, my friend," Hamza said quietly. "We don't need any abbreviation of our little outings now, do we? Perhaps I'll send someone later to take care of your personal hygiene."

With a giggle Hamza went back through the door and closed it. Alex could hear him drag his foot up the stairs.

I shall hurt that man. Aye, he will declare dedication to our Holy Father in Rome and fall in carnal love with Dr. Frankenstein.

Dawn
Aden harbor

*G*hania entered the new harbor of Aden just past dawn when there was little activity in the port. She tied up at the pier, bow in, and began her preparations. There were four riflemen in well-ventilated Kevlar pods mounted above the deck. They had laser range finders, a stable, prone shooting position, and a full view of the harbor facilities. On the deck just behind the bow were three large brown metal containers marked with the Kufdani logo, side by side. They were connected by electronics that ran throughout the sub-decks to a Combat Information Center and to the armored bridge. This was one container set of several that wasn't stored inside a building when *Ghania* was moored in Tangier. Inside that benign-appearing three-container complex was an adaptation of a Dutch-built close-support weapon system named Goalkeeper, for the key defensive position in the football sport that dominated Europe. Goalkeeper was comprised of a radar-guided, 30mm hydraulically driven, seven-barrel rotary cannon known commonly as the Avenger, but formally named the GAU-8a. The Avenger had been famously used on the American A-10 Thunderbolt attack aircraft that destroyed from above most of the Republican Guard's vaunted Russian-built tank forces in the first Gulf War; tanks were lightly armored on their tops. The radar guidance was new and had been adapted to surface vessels and used by the Dutch and Royal Navies, among others, primarily to detect and engage incoming missiles and attacking airplanes. Goalkeeper's radar could track as many as thirty targets simultaneously and engage as many as four. The system weighed about seven tons, an insignificant addition to deck weight. When the brown container sides dropped flat to the deck in four seconds, Goalkeeper could engage and automatically fire on target in another three seconds. Each burst, as set, lasted about two-tenths of a second and sent seventy rounds at the target, each weighing from three-quarters of a pound to one pound, depending on whether high explosive or armor piercing. When directed at a building or vehicle, Goalkeeper pulverized the target in a few seconds. A rocket-propelled grenade could be detected when fired and destroyed in the air, followed immediately by the option to destroy the general area that housed the shooter. The advantage that Goalkeeper gave to its owners was overwhelmingly unfair and devastatingly final. *Ghania* sat rusty and benign at her mooring, rocking slightly, apparently just another old, rusting merchantman. Three trained Bedouins and a retired US Navy chief petty officer who had trained them sat in an air-conditioned windowless room just aft of the bridge, equipped with Aegis class electronics and watching the radar screens for any sign of movement beyond the ordinary. First choice was to let the riflemen above engage targets, unless something large was shot at them. *Ghania's* cranes were lifting containers holding trucks to the dock as several dozen men came hurrying down the gangway carrying backpacks. On deck, others were readying more traditional cargo needed to begin to rebuild the Kufdani office, but Jerome's business needed the cranes more urgently at the moment.

As the last of the truck-filled containers was lowered to the dock, the first of them was opened. The trucks were unlashed and backed down to the dock. Before long there was a ragged line of idling trucks beside *Ghania*, the bed of each covered with a mottled brown tarp. In each cab, there was a driver and one other. Jerome mounted the lead truck and drove off. Each of the others followed.

Thirty minutes later, after a stop for a map check and for Jerome to consult his Kphone's Global Positioning System, the caravan of dusty trucks pulled off the blacktop road into a wadi. They drove under a bridge to a deeper wash that was invisible from the road. There were two canvas-covered, off-road motorcycles strapped to the bed of most trucks, while another was loaded with a small 4x4 heaped with canvas bags. Two men jumped from each truck. One began to unstrap the cargo while the other dropped the folding tailgate to act as a ramp to bring the motorcycles to the ground. Three men began to unload disposable, shoulder-fired anti-tank missiles and several 40mm grenade launchers from the 4x4. They were the defense force for the trucks and to ensure that all had a ride back to the Hog. After a glare from Jerome, they took two shoulder-fired ground-to-air missiles from the truck and added them to their load.

The remainder of the men shouldered small packs and then slung rifles over their backs. At a wave from Jerome, they set out behind him on the motorcycles, north through the dusty ground toward some hills rising from the dry flood plain. The motorcycles were well muffled and made little noise. Within twenty minutes or so, Jerome slowed, then parked his bike against a bush and crawled on his stomach to peek over a low mound on the side of a hill. Alex's last position shown was about seventy yards from where Jerome lay on his belly, studying the terrain with his binoculars.

A small stone house with a rough wooden roof was situated on the side of a hill near the top, above a plain. There were several flat buildings at the bottom of the hill. A truck was pulling up to a hillside entrance, a large hole gouged into the hillside with enormous folding gates standing open. Several men came out to the truck and began to unload it. Jerome studied his terrain map, considering the path that relief forces for the house would likely take, then spoke into his phone.

"Squad one, set up on the west slope and find and dig cover. Squad two, take the east. Move slowly until in position. There is no hurry. The down angle on the shot is thirty degrees to the bottom and twenty degrees to the hillside gate. The wind is steady from the south at five."

Jerome began to work his way toward the house, moving slowly and utilizing what cover was available. He could see two men sitting in chairs overlooking the valley, one nodding at the other. Suddenly, his foot caught a concealed wire and several cans attached to it clanked loudly.

Shit! Jerome thought. *Of all the damned amateur mistakes.* He fell to his knees, then chest, and pulled his rifle to his shoulder in a single fluid motion and immobilized his cheek on the stock, as he gazed through the scope. The two men inside the house were looking his way; he froze. Then they looked across the hillside and one man pointed frantically at Jerome's men on the slope and reached for a button on the wall. The other took one look, then turned to hop unsteadily for the back of the room.

Jerome saw the image of a chest in his scope and felt two slight shoulder jolts from the rifle just before the bullets tore through the left center of the man's chest. He swung the rifle to look for the other man. He was gone. "I hope to hell I just killed a bad guy, or we're in deep shit," Jerome muttered to himself as he watched the room through the scope for movement and a third or fourth man.

Jerome spoke into his headset mike, "I think the house hit an alarm, so watch to see if any gomers come charging out of that cave with their AKs and head our way. Dig a hiding place in defilade where you can find a good spot, the deeper, the better. Rifles safe, free only on leader command." He set his rifle against his pack. "I'm going into that house."

He stood and ran for the house in an irregular path, ducking behind mounds of dirt and denying anyone an easy shot. His pistol slid into his hand and was in front of him, seeking.

Jerome hit the door with his shoulder and rolled into the room, then smoothly to his feet, looking for an adversary. There was just one form on the floor, still, bleeding into the ornate carpet. A Makarov pistol was a few inches from his inert hand. The chest shots were within an inch of each other, low and a little left. There was an old phone at the corner of a cheap wooden desk, ringing. At the back of the room there were two openings on the stone wall. One was a full door and the other smaller, standing partially open. There was a sound like sizzling water on a hot skillet coming from it. Jerome stood to the side and pushed the smaller door closed. He latched it. Whatever or whoever was in there could wait. First, he had to find Cooch. At the door in the back, Jerome stopped and stood to the side of the latch, then pulled it open and dropped to the floor. After a moment he stood, pulled a flash-bang concussion grenade from his vest, and held it in his left hand. He pushed the door the rest of the way open, and again waited. Nothing.

"Cooch?" Jerome yelled into the doorway. "You there?"

"Down here," came the faint reply. "There are two known gomers."

Jerome slipped the grenade back into his vest and went through the doorway, feeling for a light switch. He found a toggle and flipped it. A number of bare bulbs lit the stone stairway and the darkness beyond. Jerome went slowly down the stairs with his pistol swinging side to side in front of him, seeking a target. He looked to his right, but there was no light; a quick flash from his vest light showed only stone. On his left in the tunnel were four doors, closed and latched. Two of them had a crude padlock. The others, the nearest, had none.

"Cooch?"

"In here." The voice came from behind the first door.

Jerome put his finger on the latch and raised it, then pushed the door open and spun into the room, his pistol again seeking a target. There, strapped to the steel chair, was Alex.

"You're underdressed, and you stink," Jerome said. He walked to the chair. He picked up an end of the arm strap and pulled. "Let me get you out of there. I thought you were a goner. Who the hell would manage my money if you checked out?"

Alex slapped the loosened chest and arm straps aside and undid those around his legs and ankles. He pushed himself halfway up from the chair and caught his bearings. After a moment, he stood, naked. The left side of his mouth was swollen.

"Any chance you saw an old guy with a limp? I'd like to talk to him a bit."

"There were two guys upstairs when I came in. One won't be talking. The other ducked into a hole up there."

"We should find him," Alex said. "Dain wants a word and there are a few questions I'd like to ask him."

Jerome smiled, and then saw the bloodied stump of Alex's fingertip. There was a black scab on its end, where the soldering iron had cauterized the amputated stump and some blood was running from under it, dripping to the floor.

"Holy shit," Jerome said. "That's ugly."

"Yeah, that's why Dain wants a word," Alex said. "What's the situation outside?"

"It's evolving. There are a quite a few folks with AKs at the bottom of a hill; Emilie says there may be several hundred. We're set up. We have two squads and some weapons types. A test of my combat theories may be in the works. Let's find you some clothes and go find out."

"Let's go find out, then find me some clothes," Alex said, picking his Kphone from the small wooden table where it had been placed, mostly ignored.

"Better choice," Jerome said with a nod as he moved to the door and pulled his Kphone from his vest to look at the screen. "There's no reception down here. I suspect we're gonna have us a firefight outside."

The two of them moved quickly up the stairs. As he entered the room, Alex saw the body of Bazir. He almost paused to spit on the corpse through his fat lip, then decided against it. *I think we're even, Bazir.* He glanced at the now-secured hatch beside the door, and then moved to the window.

"Road security, report," Jerome said into his headset. He listened for a few moments, then said, "Roger. Stay alert and get them off the road."

He turned to Alex. "Road security stopped a truck. They zapped two guys who had weapons. Our guys think they probably got off a radio message."

Alex walked to a pile of clothes at the corner of the room. His throwing knife and harness were on top. He shrugged into the harness, then shook the clothes out and dressed quickly. He slipped his Kphone into its holster as he moved back to the window.

"Well," he said. "We'll know soon enough how many there are, but these are bad guys. We want them all dead."

Suddenly several dozen men began streaming from the cave in the hillside and from the flat buildings nearby. They had AK47s and some had rifles with grenade launchers. A few men, waving their arms and pointing, began to organize the others to go up the hill. Two pickup trucks crowded with standing men waving rifles roared from the cave and headed down the road toward Aden.

"Do not fire," Jerome said into his headset. "Let them commit to an assault. Weapons, move to cover the cave entrance after they start. Break. Road security, you have two shooter-loaded trucks coming your way. Hit the trucks at one hundred meters, then pop some forty mike-mike over the shooters. Put one round into everyone after that. No survivors."

The men at the base of the hill began to move in single file up the hill with a small rise between them. At the base more men rushed from the cave to watch those climbing the hill, ready to join if needed.

"There's more than a few," Alex said. "What's your ammo load?"

"Hey, Cooch, who's the gunny here?" Jerome said with a snicker. "Two hundred rounds each for the rifles and a total of four hundred for the forty mike-mikes. Using the bikes lets us carry a good load."

"Cool," Alex said. "Let's go find the Master Pack and see who we can interest in this. I think we might have found Al-Qaeda's Yemen training center. It's fertile ground for a little sneak and peek. We'll come back here in a bit to look around and find my buddy Hamza."

"I gave Mac a heads up about thirty-six hours ago," Jerome said. "He's interested. I thought I might be looking for a new boss, so I told him you were among the missing and where we last heard from you."

Alex ran behind Jerome out of the house and behind a small mound, where Jerome had dropped a bulky backpack, the Master Pack. He pulled from it a combat vest that was rolled into a side pocket. He dug out four blocks of soft, white putty, a few feet of what looked like a white plastic cord, and from beside them a small, dark plastic bag. He shrugged into the vest. A Kimber .45 had a magazine slammed into the well and a round quickly chambered. It went into a holster on his vest. There was a paperback-book-sized box with a cord hanging from it. He plugged it into his Kphone for a quick field power charge. He turned and looked down the hill. Jerome was on his stomach in front of the mound, with binoculars trained on the developing situation at the base of the hill. The men from the bottom had split into two lines, about thirty yards apart, and were moving toward a pair of long mounds of dirt that would provide a little cover in the event someone from the house shot at them.

"Squad leaders, confirm fire discipline," Jerome said into his headset. "One round per man, center body, front man to back." Some FBI tests had shown a man could continue for ten to fifteen seconds after his chest was blown out if the central nervous system was not hit. The shock of the new sniper rounds they were using was supposed to destroy the central nervous system. Jerome wanted to watch carefully for confirmation. It was not every day he got live shooting dummies.

"One, roger."

"Two, roger."

"Take them now," Jerome said, and heard the orders being given. The two leaders at the base of the hill were the first to fall, dropped by the SAS sniper-trained squad leaders. As a steady stream of shots sounded, he studied the men below who were targeted by the first squad. One by one, their chests exploded at about half-second intervals and the rear most men began to run back toward the cave, only to fall as the shooters with the new bullets found them. The targets of the second squad fell, but some tried to crawl to cover before being hit. A few returned fire. Two men appeared on the roof of the largest building and began setting up a heavy machine gun. One and then another fell to the fire of the squad leaders. There was suddenly silence, and the stench of burned cordite wafted slowly toward Alex.

"Cooch, don't you just fucking love that smell?" Jerome said. He wore a big grin as he rolled onto his back and looked at Alex. "Those new rounds you designed seemed to be just the ticket."

"They do," Alex said. "My nostrils are having a homecoming party. I do love this shit, and I'm so very pleased my bullets perform to your satisfaction."

"Well, hell," Jerome chuckled. "It took you a bunch of years to get it right and the Army weenies got there first, mostly. We'll find out about the AP rounds when we get back to the truck."

The cartridges issued to the first squad for their M110 rifles looked like 7.62mm hunting rounds rather than new M855A1 military rounds, but were built with a tiny piece of complex explosive behind the tip of each. The explosive was armed by the acceleration shock of leaving the rifle barrel and detonated by the deceleration at impact. The 180-grain bullet expanded instantly into a grotesque splay of copper and lead that tore a four-inch gouge in the torso of a man. It never quite left the target. Energy was depleted by the new breadth of the mass it had projected as it forced its way through tissue and bone. A head shot was likely to make the head nearly disappear from the torso in a single, viscous pop. The tips on those rounds were painted green. There were also black-tipped armor-piercing (AP) rounds that were used for vehicles. They had an explosive delay that allowed the bullet to penetrate for a few milliseconds before the explosive detonated, in order to cause the inside metal wall of an armored personnel carrier to peel off into hundreds of tiny molten pieces that bounced around the interior of the vehicle. The same round fired into the radiator of a truck would explode the radiator and shred the drive belts.

At the road security site, Jerome's men were preparing to approach the inert and smoking remains of two trucks that had come roaring down the road a few minutes earlier.

Two of the Kufdani men had been kneeling, fifty feet apart, looking through the plastic, flip-up sights of the Swedish-built MBT LAW, a light anti-tank weapon, waiting for the trucks to get to the mark they had chosen, a small bush on the south side of the road at a range of about one hundred meters. They had heard the trucks roaring toward them. A third man had been dug in, a little higher and to the south, away from the back blast of the LAWs, with his rifle cradled into his shoulder and his right check firm on the dull black plastic stock. His left hand was on the mound of dirt with the rifle resting on it, stabilizing his sight picture. He gazed comfortably through his scope at an area around the small target bush.

From around a turn in the road had come the first truck at high speed, the second twenty meters behind. The first anti-tank missile had screamed out toward the second truck with a roar and a flash from its disposable tube, both front and back. The second truck was hit first because a spectacular explosion and the resultant flying debris did nothing to interfere with hitting the front truck a second or two after the rear one was hit. If the front truck was hit first, the detritus of that explosion was likely to ruin an otherwise fine sight picture for the second shot. Jerome's rage at such a "beginner's mistake" was also a worry.

The second missile followed after a moment, aimed at the first truck. Both hit the middle of the grill of the target truck and exploded a few milliseconds later, driving the front wheels of the trucks into the air momentarily as the engine absorbed much of the blast that was meant to destroy a fifty-ton tank. The shredded wheels spun lazily to the ground and bounced, while the trucks exploded. Men were seen tumbling in the air, launched by the sudden deceleration as the flames surrounded them. The two shooters reached for the semi-automatic 40mm grenade launchers on the ground beside them and double-checked their range calculation, while the third road guard began to fire deliberately from his rifle at anything that moved. Not much moved, so he had methodically shot into the forms on the road that he could see. Two 40mm grenades popped at fifteen feet over each of the trucks, spraying lethal shrapnel down upon the mass that had been trucks and men, then two popped on the trucks' far sides, which were shielded from view by the smoking hulks.

The men placed the two 40mm launchers to the side, picked up their rifles from a small canvas pad beside them, and began to gaze through their scopes at the carnage, looking for movement. The third man shot twice more, then his rifle locked open, empty. With a well-practiced movement, he had dropped the empty cartridge magazine to the dirt and pulled a second from his vest and put it in place with a solid click. The bolt was released by his thumb, and another round was plucked from the new magazine and slammed into the receiver. He brought his left sleeve near his mouth and said, "Six, this is road security. Two trucks down. No resistance yet. No apparent survivors. Two LAWs and a single sniper." He picked up the empty magazine and slid it into a pouch on his vest.

"Roger, road security. Good job. Make sure there are no survivors. Leave one man at the hide for security. Bring two trucks up in thirty minutes."

Jerome turned to Alex, who had pulled a small round device and a tripod from the large pack.

"The two gomer trucks were stopped and dealt with. I don't think we have yet combat-tested the armor-piercing rounds you designed. You may have to give Uncle Sam a refund."

"Survivors?"

"There were none," Jerome said with a grin.

"Pity," Alex said solemnly. He looked at the blackened tip of the second joint of his little finger. "They are such a caring people. Laser that cave entrance and get me a sixteen-digit grid coordinate on the cave mouth." Jerome picked up the small device and set it on the tripod, then looked through a small viewport on its side and pressed a raised button. The laser beam shot invisibly from it, then Jerome moved it so that its bright spot was on the top of the door to the cave. He pressed another button. "Coordinates are on your phone," he said.

Alex nodded, picked up his Kphone, disconnected the charger, then pressed a few keys and said, "November Sierra, this is Alpha One, over."

Almost immediately, the electronic voice said, "Authenticate." Alex brushed his thumb over the reader on the phone and heard the familiar beep of acceptance as a complex encryption mode was entered, thought by NSA to be even more secure than the one routinely used by Caitlin's system, Emilie. Another key pushed allowed Jerome to monitor the voice traffic.

"This is November Sierra," the familiar voice said. "You're just the man I wanted to talk to; nice to have you alive. You can tell me your kidnap story later. We found out what the boys were bringing to Texas from Mexico. It's ugly, but that was a super lead from your Emilie system. We found out who planned that operation from the computer of the rag head that you and Gomez identified. He's somewhere in your neck of the woods. Keep an eye out for him. His name is Hamza. Hey, is that rifle fire I hear?"

"Yeah, it is," Alex said. "We're cleaning up a little and keeping some folks pinned in a cave."

"Anyone I know?" Mac said.

"I'm pretty sure it is the main training center for the Yemen-based Al-Qaeda bunch. Here's the location, in case you'd like to send them a message. I can pretty much ensure the death of Hamza. That should get us a little bonus for our security operation."

"We'd like to consider that message, strongly," Mac said. "Any suggestions, boomer man?"

"I'd say a Hellfire through the door to loosen any roof supports and then a bunker-buster cruise missile on the hillside above would do nicely. We have a target laser active on the top of the door."

The phone went on hold for a few moments, then came back on. "Roger laser. General Kelly just walked in. He says that's a big deal for what may be just a few bad guys. You have a count?"

Alex looked Jerome and raised his eyebrow in question. Jerome shrugged and said, "We killed maybe a hundred and fifty so far."

"We've taken a hundred or two so far," Alex said into the phone. "I imagine there's a lot more inside. I was told there are thirty-six suicide bombers inside the cave, trained and ready for martyrdom. How bad do you want Hamza?"

"We want him pretty badly," Mac said with a chuckle. "Losing him and his staff would mess up their ops for awhile. I'd like to accelerate the martyrdom of the bombers too. There's a missile sub coming your way at flank speed, which appears likely to be a handy thing."

"All this and more is within your grasp," Alex said quietly.

"Stand by," Mac said. After two or three minutes he said, "On the way with Hellfire."

"On the way, wait," Alex said with a contented smile, as he spoke the classic artillery man's response to getting notice that targeted fire was heading toward his chosen target.

Jerome rolled up to the edge of the mound again to watch the door to the cave. Alex dropped to lie beside him. Two men wrestled with the huge door to the cave, trying to close it without exposing themselves.

"Leaders, drop the guys at the cave doors," Jerome said into his headset mike.

"One has no shot."

"Roger, the bleedin' angle isn't great for Two," one voice answered. "Switching to armor piercing." Four shots rang out, each closely followed by another. One man dropped to the ground on the first shot, and a small puff of dirt behind him marked the passing of the armor-piercing round. Three more shots caused the second man to duck back inside the cave, dragging one leg.

"Nice get, Two," Jerome said. The latter three shots had been shot into the steel of the door to cause a shrapnel-like spauling on the back side of the open cave door as sharp steel splinters spun from the door in the direction of the second man.

"Thirty seconds or so on the Hellfire. Tomahawk is sub-launched," Mac said.

"Everyone down," Jerome said into his headset mike. "Incoming, two big rounds, not one. I say again, *two rounds*. Stay down." A few moments later they saw the Hellfire missile that had been launched from a CIA Predator drone fly into the cave, two feet below the laser dot. There was a huge explosion, then two secondary explosions. A cloud of dust and debris burst out from the door.

"Bingo," said Alex into his Kphone. "Got a couple of nice secondaries, probably from the suicide supplies. ETA on the Tomahawk?"

"Looks like about forty seconds," Mac said. "Are you going into that place to look for Hamza?"

"Nah, too dusty," Alex said. "He's hiding. I'll go find him in a minute. But you'll get him, just like I said."

"Send me a finger," Mac said. "Maybe we can get a positive ID."

Alex smiled. "What a marvelous idea. Check your mail."

There was a whoosh overhead and a fast movement, then the side of the hill first exploded out, then in, as the hole caused by the bunker buster's delayed explosion ripped inward. One side of the hill collapsed.

"I'll get back to you in a bit," Alex said. "The target has imploded; there won't be survivors. Three cheers for the Navy and the Air Force. Good shooting. Alpha One out."

He turned to Jerome and picked up the heavy pack, then said, "Why don't you have one of the trucks brought up closer. I'll need a ride to the Hog, and we may find something that needs transportation. Trash and burn those two buildings and drop any runners."

Jerome nodded and relayed the message to the squad leaders and to his weapons squad, then called for a truck.

A few moments later, the first of four 40mm white phosphorus grenades landed on the roof of the nearest building. Three thermite rounds soon landed on the roof of the second. As the white-hot grenades ignited the dry wooden roofs, several more landed and burned. Smoke began to pour from the narrow windows of both buildings. Suddenly a large group of men ran from the first building, shooting wildly at the hillside. More ran from the second building. Methodical rifle fire from Jerome's men sounded and running men fell. More 40mm grenades were now falling, this time loaded with high-explosive rounds that exploded above the men, driving hot shrapnel down.

"Take a watchful thirty minutes before you go down there, then start to clean up," Jerome said into his mike. "We already won this one. I don't want any friendlies killed." He stood and leaned his rifle against the backpack.

Jerome slipped his Kimber .45 from its nylon holster at his belt, then pulled and locked the slide back with his thumb and forefinger. He caught the ejected round with its shiny brass casing as it spun from the receiver. He dropped the magazine from the well of the Kimber with a push of his finger. The ejected round was thumbed back into the magazine. Two fresh pistol magazines from a slot in the Master Pack were found; flat-nosed gray bullets protruded from the brass casings. Jerome pushed one magazine into his Kimber with a click, then released the slide to chamber a new round. He handed the second magazine to Alex.

"I don't want to be shooting any hardball in a cave. Any ricochets are as likely to kill us as a bad guy. This frangible round will break up quickly if it hits something denser than a body. It's a one-hundred-and-twenty-five-grain hollow point that comes out at about thirteen hundred feet per second, so it'll still get the job done if your Hamza buddy shows up; it just won't come out the other side of him. We wouldn't want to waste its energy."

"Let's go see what we can find in this house of horrors," Alex said. He dropped a magazine into his hand, pushed the new magazine into his Kimber, chambered a new round with a pull on the slide, and started for the house. Jerome was right behind him.

Inside the room Alex bent and knocked on the small door. The sound of sizzling water came again, loudly.

"I think we'll wait a bit before going in there," he said. "I know that sound. Let's go look around."

Jerome led the way down the stone stairs. "It stinks a little down here," he said. "It smells familiar, but I can't place it."

"I've been told on good authority that it is the smell of ongoing hopeless, desperate fear," Alex said. "This fat lip was punctuation."

"I'd have killed that motherfucker upstairs with more pleasure, if I'd known," Jerome said with a grimace. "But if that is, in fact, what that odor is, I hope I never smell it again."

Jerome and Alex turned right rather than left at the bottom of the stairs and moved cautiously, each holding a pistol. Alex's flashlights showed no evidence of anything but blank stone. Jerome's was in front of him, held in two hands, searching. A dead end came quickly, with no evidence of a doorway leading anywhere. They turned back to examine the area with the four doors.

They walked past the door to the room where Alex had been held and glanced into the second room. It was empty, with nothing but another steel chair bolted to the stained floor. They stopped at the first locked door. A pull on the lock by Jerome did nothing to open it, so they moved to the second. A tug on that lock did nothing.

"I'm not a trusting soul," Alex said. "So why don't I take a look at this setup, while you go in the first room and get the bolt cutters from the cabinet beside the door."

"Good idea," Jerome said. "I don't want to go boom. You know about that shit."

"Since a long time ago, I know about that shit," Alex said. He again took the small flashlight from his vest, then peered into the gaps around the door. "It will someday blow me up, but probably not today. There is a single trip wire on the door. I think I'll cut it. These gomers don't know how to do a delay trigger and if they did, they would know how to hide it."

Alex reached up with the bolt cutters and severed a wire, then cut the hasp on the first padlock with a strong close on the handles. "I guess I knew these things were sharp," he said. "Let's look inside."

The room was empty. They moved to the last door, cut the wire and the hasp on the lock. Alex opened it. There was a light switch to the right of the door that Alex flipped and three overhead lights came on. On the floor of the room, strapped to a wooden pallet, were six storage tubes for 120mm mortar shells, with Russian markings on them. Beside them, two smaller steel boxes were strapped to another pallet, also with Russian markings.

"OK, O Russian master," Alex said. "What do the markings say?"

Jerome had a facility for languages and had once spent a year at the Naval Language School in Monterey, California, learning

Russian, while Alex had been assigned the far less fulfilling and infinitely filthier duty of learning to put out oil well fires with explosives. Each managed that year with only two missions to interrupt their ongoing education.

"I shall inspect them carefully, and report," Jerome said haughtily. "The mortar tubes say 'Danger, Toxic Matter' and a bunch of other warnings. Then it says 'Binary Sarin!' below. I think we found us some nerve gas rounds."

"Yeah," Alex said. "They paid some real money for these. Mac is going to be *very* happy to get rid of them. What do the other ones say?"

"Well, the warnings are a lot worse. 'Pain of Death for Opening' and shit like that. Some lab in Mongolia was the owner. Here's the address."

"I took some thermite from the Master Pack that will burn up the nerve gas, I think," Alex said. "I have some C6 and det cord too. I don't know about these other boxes. We gotta check with Mac." He held out his Kphone and carefully took twelve megapixel pictures of the lettering on each of the boxes.

"I want to be back on the Hog and out to sea before you start fucking with nerve gas, and I don't want you beside me unless you're empty-handed."

"Deal," Alex said. "OK, let's go upstairs and look for Hamza, then talk to Mac." He walked to the mortar tubes and loosened the restraining straps. He raised each tube and then lowered it. He moved to the two steel boxes, loosened the restraining straps and did the same, then tightened them again and turned to the door. "They're not empty." He picked up the bolt cutters and walked to the stairs.

Jerome flipped the room light off and followed as they walked quickly up the stairs. Alex looked around the small room and saw a dull silver Sony laptop on a battered wooden side table. He went through the desk drawers. He picked up a three-ring notebook in one, then unplugged the computer, picked it up, and set it by the door.

"OK," Alex said. "We're going to stand away from this little door and open it. If anything crawls or slithers out, you shoot it. I'll talk to Hamza. He hasn't heard my voice and your accent is atrocious." Alex flipped the latch and door and pulled it open from its top, then jumped back from it.

"Hamza," Alex yelled in a coarse Yemeni dialect of Arabic, "are you there? We have killed the attackers and come for you."

"I am injured. Get me out of here, but be careful."

Suddenly from the base of the door a short, wide, pear-shaped head appeared, followed quickly by two feet of saw-scaled viper, known to herpetologists as *Echis corinatus*, the snake reputed to have killed more humans than any other. Rather than rattle, the saw-scale viper rubs its protruding scales together when stressed, to make a hissing sound similar to the sound of water sizzling in a hot skillet. It sensed Alex and Jerome and began to coil and turn. There was the sound of three shots a half second apart. The head of the viper disappeared, and then two pieces just behind its head.

"We have killed the viper, Hamza. You may come out and be treated."

There was some movement and a groan from inside the hole; then a head appeared. As Hamza looked up, Alex grabbed him by the hair and pulled him into the room. Jerome was to the side, with his Kimber raised and pointed at Hamza's head, a wisp of light gray smoke curling from the end of its barrel.

Alex took a plastic tie from his vest, pulled Hamza's hands behind him, and secured his wrists. Bad guys were less dangerous with their hands tied behind them. In fact, everyone was.

"Talk to me, Hamza," Alex said with his Yemeni accent. "Did you meet the viper?"

Hamza involuntarily glanced at his right arm but did not speak. Alex pulled his sleeve up. There were two sets of puncture marks on it; the viper had struck twice.

"We have the treatment to save your life, Hamza. I'd like you to answer a few questions, and then I'll provide the antidote to you. You will be sent to a prison named Guantanamo in Cuba by the Americans when we sell you to them. It is filled with your fellow Al-Qaeda patriots." Alex pulled his Kphone from its holster and set it to record.

Hamza felt a bit drunk, the early effects of the viper's venom. It was clear Allah would not want him to achieve martyrdom yet with so much work for Hamza still to do to prepare for the caliphate. A few vague and incomplete answers would not be as harmful as the loss to Allah of Hamza's services.

"What is it you would like to know?" Hamza said. "And do you promise not to tell the Americans?"

"Americans will learn nothing they do not already know, Hamza," Alex said. "Tell me about your friends in Iran and your plans with them."

"There is a new day coming, where the remaining Zionists will live only to serve the Shiites, with just the tools of their ancestors. Palestine will belong to Palestinians." Hamza began to speak volumes with wild claims about infidel casualties and Iran at the head of three Arab nations, under Sharia law, but his voice was becoming increasingly blurred and weak. After about two minutes, Hamza said, "I would now like the antidote for the viper bite. I am weakening and my memory is not functioning properly. My arm hurts terribly."

"You mentioned a contact in Tangier, Hamza. Who is it that betrayed me?"

"Give me the anti-venom shot, and I will attempt to remember," Hamza said.

"Oh, I was untruthful about the antidote, Hamza. We have none. I'm just going to sit here and watch you die, wishing that you could suffer as much as you have made so many suffer. But you will suffer in another world."

There's my lad. I was afraid you were just going to shoot him.

Hamza's eyes went wide as the betrayal pierced the fog of his brain.

"You cannot," he gasped. "I am essential to the return of the caliphate. It is not yet my time."

"It is your time, Hamza. Allah will not welcome you, mark my words. I am a *Sayyid*, a direct descendant of Mohammed. I have spoken with him in a dream, where he was mounted on a magnificent white stallion. You have perverted the word of Allah. For this you will spend eternity in the flames of retribution. Allah has sent your victims to magnify your pain with lessons in cruelty learned from you. Each will get a turn, then again."

Hamza's mouth opened twice, then finally squeaked out a "No, no." His widened eyes closed slowly and his breathing stopped.

Jerome stood and slowly shook his head.

"I like it better when they die right after I shoot them," he said. "You're a hard man, Cooch. You are increasingly an Arab." He turned and walked out the door as he muttered, "I guess that's not new news. Damn, that was ugly."

Alex took a last glance at Hamza's twisted face, then reached for the bolt cutters. After a few moments, he picked up the computer and the notebook and hurried to follow Jerome out the door. As he caught up to Jerome, he said, "Have one of the squad leaders toss that place if we have time. There may be more than one saw-scale viper nesting in there, so let them know about the sizzle. Maybe Big Daddy Sawscale just went to the Seven-Eleven for a mouse. When he figures out that we shot Mama, Daddy's going to have a nasty case of the red-ass."

Jerome grimaced. "You can bet your sweet ass that they'll be careful," he said. "I've been crawling in the bushes for twenty-five, thirty years, and I hate snakes."

"Go figure. I didn't think I'd end up single and thinking like an Arab."

Alex plucked his Kphone from its holster on the left side of his vest and nearly dropped it. He had forgotten that the hand that grabbed the phone was missing an end joint. He held it up and punched a few keys with his right.

"November Sierra, Alpha One," Alex said into his phone, then pressed his thumb over the reader when the hollow voice directed.

"This is November Sierra," Mac said. "Good job there, folks. We saw some surveillance from the Predator that popped the Hellfire out. I think you did the bad guys some serious damage. I see big contract bonus dollars in your future. Did you find anything worthwhile among the wreckage?"

"We found Hamza. He was snake bit and didn't survive. You'll get the finger. Here are a couple of photos that may interest you before we get to the wreckage," Alex said as he keyed his phone to send the images from the cave. "I think one of them is sarin in 120 millimeter mortar binary mode. The other one has warnings like it's the second coming of the plague. We don't know the lab, but Jerome says the warnings read like a hissy fit. I picked up a laptop on the way out that I'll have Emilie take a look at, then send on to you. A little paper too."

"Holy crap!" Mac said. "This is the same stuff we found on the Texas hit. Can you get those boxes out of there and back to Tangier?

Anything we can do to destroy the sarin? That stuff is too heavy to carry around."

"Last time I looked at sarin in binary mode," Alex said, "it broke down completely at fifteen hundred degrees Celsius. I have thermite and C6. Talk to the chemwar weenies in Maryland and tell me what to do. I'd really like to get out of here before the Yemeni Army notices all these bodies and damage. Jerome says he won't let me on the Hog if I'm packing nerve gas. I don't want to walk."

"Can't blame him for that," Mac said. "The head chemwar weenie is here and just stuck a note under my nose that says thermite will disable and destroy the sarin. We really want those two steel boxes. Can you get them to the Hog?"

"Yeah, it shouldn't be a problem. I'll wire the sarin with thermite and a timer. A longer delay for enough C6 to collapse the building seems right. First, we haul those boxes out of there and get them ready to go back to the Hog. If we get caught here, I'm going to confess to being an Air Force puke and hope I get traded for a Palestinian."

• • •

Later, Alex and Jerome sat in one of the pickup trucks at the bottom of the hill as smoke poured from the small house and flames licked at its roof. After a few minutes there was a thump as the C6 detonated and the house collapsed into itself.

"Cooch, my man, I think we fucked them up good on this one," Jerome said with a grin. "I love giving these guys the finger."

"Actually, they took the finger and we got one in return," Alex said. He got out of the truck and looked over the site. "Why don't you have your guys police their brass and magazines? We'll try to make this scene look more like a bar fight than the execution it was.

Let's go look at what's left of the buildings and see if anything of note survived. The cave is history."

Several men in a pickup were dispatched to push the still-smoking hulls of the AQAP trucks from the road and to take whatever arms and goods that might be used by others to easily piece together the story of their owners' demise; vultures were already dealing with the remains. At the wadi, Alex and Jerome stood by while the motorcycles were reloaded on the trucks and strapped down. The excited chatter of survival and success grew among Jerome's men. The return to Aden was uneventful.

As they approached *Ghania*, there was a buzz of activity. A Bedouin-born architect trained at Cornell University in America had designed several standard Kufdani offices that could meet the needs of various local Kufdani businesses across the Middle East. He stood atop a stack of empty pallets, watching and supervising. Walls made of a composite material that had been cast in Tangier were being put into place at the new Kufdani office site inside a newly installed cyclone fence. More loaded pallets were placed upon the dock by the Hog's cranes. Propane-powered forklifts scurried to the new pallets and carried their load back to waiting men.

Some workers connected blocks to create walls while others pushed finished walls vertical. The Rulon system walls were about 30 percent lighter than conventional walls when fitted together as marked. The task of putting together a new office building was far faster than with a conventional set of building materials. The walls were cast from concrete slurry into molds that held a complex steel reinforcement to provide unusual strength. Courses, or pre-determined routes for conduits, were already installed through the new walls to allow electrical wire to be run, as designed, to support the work of the new building's occupants. Plumbing found similar pre-cast courses.

Yemeni employees of Kufdani had learned of the demise of the large group of Al-Qaeda from the Tangier shooters as they secured their loaded trucks in containers before they reboarded the freighter. There was a new air of happiness and determination among the Yemeni; Kufdani was indeed a good place to work.

A representative of the Kufdani People Office had arrived in Aden from Tangier by air the day before. He was busy meeting with survivors of those slain in the blast. The survivors were to be given cash payments to help ease the burden of their loss and a preference in the granting of new jobs to replace the fallen. There were a few orphans from the blast. They would be placed among the Kufdani community with those who were childless or those with families. Many were eager to take them for the extra income that would be provided and to be on record as good citizens of Kufdani Industries. The orphans would be provided with unlimited training by Emilie and her human Internet-connected training support staff to allow them to better compete for college scholarships from Kufdani when they were eligible. A select few would be sent off to boarding school at age thirteen.

On board *Ghania*, Jerome was organizing a debriefing for the operation just completed. "Lessons learned" was a key component in the training of any effective combat force. Jerome had been a guest instructor at some sessions at the Marine Corps Lessons Learned operation at Quantico, Virginia. He knew the value of immediate collection of combat experiences for tracking, dissemination, and most importantly, for Emilie's data-mining genius. His SAS-trained squad leaders were in full agreement.

The Kufdani shooters, of course, had wives, sweethearts, and families back in Tangier. This had been their first combat experience and the first validation of the effort they had devoted to preparation under Jerome's stern eye. They would brag and discuss, as soldiers do, and boast about their bonuses. They would exaggerate. Jerome wanted to make sure that the message that entered the Tangier and broader Kufdani gossip circles was the one he and Alex wanted. Jerome wanted more motivated volunteers. Both he and Alex wanted the mystique of Kufdani to spread, for many to discuss the attraction of a better and safer way to do things. Killing with suicide bombs was easy. Kufdani did it without friendly casualties and from a distance when threatened. The value of training had been shown. The value of education should consequently be at least as valuable over time. Perhaps there really was a better way to live, particularly if one was affiliated with Kufdani.

Tangier

Several weeks later, Alex was once again on his balcony in his chair, gazing at the busy harbor. There had been a waiting package for him upon his return from Aden. It contained seven elegant ceramic teapots and a handwritten note. *Hearing of your efforts at vengeance for deaths in Aden made me think of you. You have done well.* The note was unsigned. The teapots were arranged on a table beside him; four were large, two were medium and one was small. Alex had a bandage on his healing finger stump and a glass of wine in his hand. Attitude changes were progressing. The gun had joined the kind word and apparently provided synergy. Alex smiled at the thought of informing the president.

Inshallah.

Author's note:

Some of the early readers of Patriot told me, "I'm glad that you didn't go into a lot of detail about some scenes from your first novel, Cooch, given as background, because I already read Cooch. But I'm not sure I'd feel that way if Patriot was the first of your books I read."

I don't have it in me to write a series that keeps everyone caught up on everything, so I decided to provide a path, via footnotes, for those who are curious. There is a .pdf of Cooch, my first novel, on my website with pointers to appropriate sections at www.robert-cooknovels.com/footnotesPatriot I'll put up a better .pdf soon.

I may ask for an email address from those who come to my website for something. We've had some evildoers mucking about. I promise not to share sell or share your email address. I will email you from bob@robertcooknovels.com when something of note happens, with an email title of "More on Cooch" if you want to block it. It shouldn't be more than two or three times a year.

For those who want to communicate with me, please e-mail bob@robertcooknovels.com

I'll also be blogging a bit from my website. There's a link on my website.

An excerpt from the next in the Cooch series of national security thrillers, *Pulse:*
  Release date summer, 2013

The Islamic Republic of Iran

THE HOLY CITY OF QOM

PRESS RELEASE: SUBJECT: ANNIHILATION OF ISRAEL INFRASTRUCTURE

WEDNESDAY, 31 DECEMBER, 2330 HOURS, GMT

THREE IRANIAN PATRIOTS WERE MARTYRED TODAY IN AN ACT OF WAR BY THE ISLAMIC REPUBLIC OF IRAN UPON THE ILLEGAL JEWISH STATE. AS A RESULT OF A SMALL NUCLEAR EXPLOSION CREATED BY THE EFFORTS OF YOUNG SCIENTISTS OF ISLAM, THE STATE OF ISRAEL HAS LOST ITS ENTIRE ELECTRICAL SYSTEM. FEW, IF ANY, OF THE JEWS LOST THEIR LIVES, BUT THE ZIONISTS HAVE TODAY LOST THEIR ABILITY TO THREATEN ISLAM. THE ELECTROMAGNETIC PULSE ASSOCIATED WITH THE IRAN'S FIRST DEPLOYMENT OF ITS NUCLEAR WEAPONS HAS DESTROYED ALL EXPOSED ELECTRONICS IN THE JEWISH STATE.

THE LONG-OPPRESSED FORCES OF IRAN'S ALLIES, HEZBOLLAH, HAMAS AND THE ISLAMIC JIHAD HAVE TONIGHT ATTACKED THE ZIONISTS ACROSS THEIR ILLEGAL BORDERS IN ORDER TO FINALLY RECLAIM THEIR

HOMELAND. OTHER THAN GOVERNMENT OFFICIALS AND MILITARY PLANNERS, THERE HAVE NOT BEEN AND WILL NOT BE WIDESPREAD EXECUTION OF THE JEWS. MOST SURVIVORS WILL BE GIVEN OPPORTUNITIES TO SERVE THE SHIITE VICTORS AND TO ATONE FOR THE SINS OF THEIR FATHERS

THE ISLAMIC STATE OF IRAN HAS TWO ADDITIONAL COMPLETED NUCLEAR WEAPONS AND SEVERAL NEARING COMPLETION. ONE OF THE COMPLETED WEAPONS HAS BEEN DEPLOYED TO EUROPE AND THE OTHER TO THE GULF OF MEXICO. ANY ATTACKS BY INFIDELS ON IRAN OR ITS PEOPLE WILL CAUSE ONE OR BOTH OF THOSE WEAPONS TO BE DETONATED AND THE INFIDELS THERE WILL JOIN THE ZIONISTS IN LIVING WITHOUT MODERNITY AS THEY SO RICHLY DESERVE.

ALLAHU AKBAR.

GO TO WWW.ROBERTCOOKNOVELS.COM TO TRACK PROGRESS OF PULSE.